PLAYING GOD

Katherine Russell Becker

For Paul,
always there,
before, during and after

PART I

EARLY DAYS

CHAPTER ONE

September 2003

PHILLIP

Out of nowhere, blurred vision and pain that throbbed with every heartbeat forced him to his knees on the coffee-stained carpet in the editing room. He fought to keep the nausea in his belly from erupting and lay on the floor even after the newscast had gone off the air. Standing over him, the nerdy meteorologist who for a brief moment had toyed with the idea of going to medical school, pronounced his diagnosis. Thinking back on it now, Phillip was certain that his first migraine headache had appeared just as he'd begun to suspect that he no longer had the heart for any of it.

Recovery was slow. In the days that followed, sitting at his desk in a robotic trance in the middle of an ordinary week, he stacked folders into neat piles and spent several minutes re-arranging paperweights on top. Beside the familiar chipped mug filled with sharpened pencils, he placed a photograph mounted in a ceramic frame his daughter had made in art class. Leaning back in his chair, he closed his eyes and concentrated on rhythmically breathing in and out. The flashing button on his desk phone announced messages he hadn't bothered to pick up. He tried to remember the last time there hadn't been any messages and wondered if anyone ever got to the end of the queue.

Can't do it, he sighed. *Not today.*

Summoning energy he didn't feel, he pushed his chair away from his desk and swiveled 180 degrees to take in the bustling newsroom. He hoisted himself up and made his way over to the window, where for at least ten minutes he stood and witnessed the trees beginning to shed their autumn leaves.

Phillip Lynch could think of little before him that he looked forward to and nothing behind him worth remembering, and it was in that moment that he started to imagine an assortment of scenarios. After that, the juggling of different possibilities became an addictive mental pastime, one that he couldn't seem to stop. Trapped in editorial meetings about what was and wasn't newsworthy, or at Gracie's piano recital where girls in ruffled dresses plodded through tunes from *The Little Mermaid*, or feigning interest as Susan recounted her sister's latest calamity, Phillip began to make a plan.

Eight years after he had started working at the TV station, the board of directors rewrote its original mission statement, and a new program director arrived on the scene to remap the entire broadcast direction. Phillip had been working on several projects, and every one of them, in various stages of development, was now unsuited to the station's new direction. Management encouraged him to come up with fresh ideas on the double, or to start pounding the pavement with his resume in hand.

On the home front, his fourteen-year-old son had just begun a college prep high school with a price tag that exceeded what they could afford, and his eight-year-old daughter was midway through years of shiny metal braces guaranteed to produce a picture-perfect smile. As if that weren't enough to make a man sprout a sudden explosion of gray amid his thick dark curls, his in-laws had been hinting about a visit. Phillip sighed and rolled his tongue over a sore gum that probably meant he'd been grinding his teeth again. Lately he hadn't been sleeping well. He'd rubbed his eyes at breakfast nearly every morning that week and had to ask his wife to repeat whatever it was she had just said. By then, Susan had given up trying to remind him to pick up a gallon of milk or a loaf of bread on his way home. At the office, he had been observed at his desk staring into space, sometimes pausing at length in mid-sentence as the cursor flashed on and off. His boss, commenting that some recent submissions had been less than compelling, chalked up his lackluster performance to the general malaise everyone was feeling.

"Creative types all go through dry spells," the boss had said with a shrug. "Nothing to think twice about."

God only knows how long he'd been moving through the days on autopilot, not feeling bad, but not feeling good either. Phillip knew he'd been going through the motions, and he had to imagine that everyone else knew it, too. After a particularly rough week at work - a week in which two of his pieces had been rejected for inadequately verified sources and a third had been judged *lacking in sufficient audience interest* - it seemed to him that there was only one thing to do. All weekend as he mowed the lawn and took out the trash and sleep-walked through a hundred other ordinary chores, he deliberated, going back and forth over the idea, looking at it from every angle. By Sunday afternoon when he drizzled lighter fluid onto the black briquets and struck a match, he had made up his mind, and he knew there would be no turning back.

On Tuesday morning, in the tidy split-level home nestled on a tree-lined suburban street just south of the fog line, Phillip forced himself to swallow a spoonful of the sticky oatmeal his wife had placed in front of him. He buried his face in the morning paper to avoid being drawn into the kids' rehashing of *Survivor*, fixing his eyes studiously on the *Chronicle's Sporting Green*. Susan handed all three their lunches and sent them off for a good day, just like always.

"Let's go, everybody! Time to get in the car. Gracie, don't forget your new glasses. You left your cleats on the front porch, Andrew, and they're full of mud," she called out as she wiped a speck of oatmeal from the corner of her husband's mouth.

Gracie remembered she'd left her homework upstairs. Andrew grumbled they'd be late again as he grabbed his cleats and headed out to the Volvo in the driveway. Susan handed Phillip the car keys. His gut rumbled as he backed the boxy ten-year-old sedan out of the driveway and tried not to look back at his wife in her pink terrycloth bathrobe, waving cheerfully from the open doorway.

He dropped the kids off at their respective schools, kissing his daughter on the cheek and patting his son's back, not allowing his gaze to linger on either of them. A brightly colored banner caught the corner of his eye: Parents Back to School Night - Save the Date!

4

Keep moving, he whispered under his breath. *Don't think.*

He stopped at the dry cleaners to drop off his navy-blue suit. As the clerk turned away to print out a receipt, Phillip quietly tucked his wallet into the back pocket of the trousers. "Be back Saturday," he called over his shoulder before hurriedly climbing into the car. He turned the Volvo toward the freeway entrance and gunned the engine as he approached the on-ramp. He'd chosen the southern direction because the weather in San Francisco was beginning to grow chilly, and anywhere south would be warmer. The air felt crisp and cool, and he'd seen a hint of frost on the windshield as he'd started the car. Phillip settled back and turned the radio dial to a jazz station before driving over a hundred miles with no particular destination in mind, stopping only to get gas and stretch his legs.

By then the morning mist had cleared to reveal a cloudless September day, and as he filled the tank, it struck him that he was completely out of anyone's reach. Although just last winter he had been given a cell phone to use for work, he deliberately left it charging on his desk. His wife of fourteen years, his bosses and colleagues, his parents, the accountant who prepared his taxes every year, and even his tennis partners - guys he'd played doubles with nearly every weekend - all of them would wonder where he was and what possibly could have caused him to vanish so suddenly. If asked, they would say that he was an agreeable fellow, easy to get along with. They would declare with certainty that he had never seemed temperamental or unstable in any way. His friends and coworkers would insist they had never seen him fly off the handle, slam a door, or storm out of a meeting. If he'd been down in the dumps lately, they couldn't say they'd particularly noticed. In the days ahead when the news surfaced, they would all be asking themselves whether they'd ever really known Phillip Lynch at all.

As he continued on his southern journey, the uncomfortable rumbling that had plagued his gut since breakfast began to subside, and a calm nothingness took up residence. He opened the window, taking a deep, cleansing breath, feeling neither happy nor unhappy. If he felt anything at all, it was an emptiness in the core of his being in the place where disappointments and secrets harbored over too many years had festered. Too late he had begun to see that keeping those secrets might have granted them far more power than they should ever have had. A few mellow notes from Miles Davis on the radio helped to soothe any remaining discomfort, and Phillip knew that what he was about to do was right.

He knew it was his lifetime habit of accommodating everyone around him that had squeezed and molded him as easily as a block of clay, both that and the relentless expectations of those who professed to love him. When he'd wondered whether there was still time enough to start over and do it all differently, he'd discovered that he had no desire to come up with a solution close to home. The ties that bound him there seemed like cheese that had been stretched to the breaking point, stringy cheese full of holes. More than he'd wanted anything for a long time, Phillip ached to break loose, to walk away from everything he'd known before this moment. Every nerve in his body pulsed with a greedy hunger, and he knew it was the only way he would ever grab the reins and own his own life.

With sweaty hands gripping the wheel, he headed further and further south. The sun beat down on the dirty windshield, and surprised he hadn't thought of doing so earlier, he loosened his tie and rolled up the sleeves of his shirt. Hungrily, he reached inside the brown bag on the seat beside him. By the time he had polished off the cookies Susan had tucked into his lunch, the muscles in his back had lost their tension, his shoulders had dropped at least an inch, and he'd begun to register equal parts exhilaration and panic.

CHAPTER TWO

September 2003

BRADY

"It's just for a little while, Dad," Tony Brady's son had assured him when he'd asked to camp out in his father's one-bedroom flat in the Outer Mission. "Seriously, as soon as I get a job lined up, I'll be gone. You won't even notice me." Looking his dad in the eye, he'd added, "and you know I'm totally clean now."

Brady had replied that of course Shane could stay with him, declaring that he was more than willing to help out, and it was the God's honest truth. He'd started to give his son's narrow shoulders a squeeze but pulled back, afraid that a twenty-eight-year-old might be embarrassed by an overdose of affection. Despite the brave face Shane showed the rest of the world, his father knew how fragile the kid was. He'd been that way ever since his life had cratered at the tender age of twelve.

What else could any parent do? the young man's dad had asked himself.

Shane had just been released again from rehab, a six month stay this time for the cocaine addiction that, coupled with his preference for a daily regimen of marijuana and beer, had once again derailed him. Every member of the family had spent half their lives trying to help the guy get back on his feet, but sooner or later something or someone always dragged Shane back into the darkness. For years the kid had hovered on the razor edge of disaster at any given moment, and Brady knew why.

Of course he could move in, he told Shane.

It wasn't until several weeks later when he opened the front door of the cramped apartment and came upon the unmade sofa bed in the parlor and the oil-stained pizza box on the kitchen table that Brady wondered if he'd been too hasty. He held the one remaining slice of pepperoni up for inspection and sniffed the aroma permeating his home. Recognizing the smell of dirty socks and sweaty sheets and not the acrid scent of marijuana, he stuffed the pizza box into the trash and began opening windows.

When he'd unpacked the bag of groceries he'd left on the counter, he poured himself a beer and sifted through a pile of mail. A couple of bills, a membership coupon for the local gym, a postcard from his youngest featuring a picture of her college campus, and a letter from a client. He hoped the envelope would contain a check.

Helping himself to a long swallow of beer, he flipped over Bridget's postcard and chuckled at the endearing X's and O's at the bottom of her message. He slid the card between the salt and pepper shakers to show to Shane and carefully opened the client's letter. A personal check fell from the envelope as he unfolded the hand-written letter inside.

Dear Tony,

I can't thank you enough for the way you conducted the search for Norbert's grandson. It means so much to him to have found a family member who will help him put his affairs in order. Since Norb's illness has progressed so rapidly, he probably doesn't have much time left. Reuniting with his grandson was his dying wish, and I will always be grateful for your persistence in finding him. Please do not hesitate to use me as a reference so I can recommend you to other clients.

Brady smiled, recalling how easy it had been to locate the old man's grandson, almost effortless. He wondered what the next case to cross his threshold would be and hoped for something more challenging. He was hungry for the kind of complicated case that would make him roll up his sleeves, something puzzling that would put all his skills and expertise to good use. Doing difficult investigative work was what he lived for, and a thank-you letter full of praise like this one confirmed he'd made the right decision thirteen years ago.

He heard Shane's key turn in the lock and craned his head toward the door.

"Hey, Dad," his son muttered, letting his dirty backpack fall against the kitchen door as he plopped down heavily at the table.

Brady thought twice about inquiring how the job search was going. "You hungry?" he asked instead. "I was just about to fry up some franks. Maybe heat up some beans, too. Think you could go for some of that?"

Shane shrugged. "I could eat." He glanced at his father's beer. "Okay if I have one of those?"

"Sure, help yourself." Brady opened a cupboard to rummage for a frying pan and hoped the kid wasn't slipping into old habits. "Hey, clear off the table, would you? And grab us a couple of plates while I get things going here, okay?"

He tore open a package of frankfurters and slid them into a pan. As they began to sizzle, he rifled through the fridge for mustard and turned up an old jar of relish and half a package of buns. He knew Shane would talk when he was ready and didn't want to pressure him, imagining it couldn't be easy finding any kind of employment with his spotty resume. Within minutes, a sweet aroma wafted through the quiet kitchen, and Brady reached up on the windowsill to tune the radio to the station they both liked. Maybe the music would cheer things up.

They were both hungry, and they polished off the simple meal, mopping up the baked beans with the ends of the buns. Between bites, he kept up a friendly chatter. He slid Bridget's post-card across the table to Shane, pointing out her girlish signature, and went on to describe the letter he'd received about the case he'd just wrapped up.

His son didn't say much until after his second beer when he blurted out, "I don't know if I'm ever going to find a job, Dad. It's useless. No one wants to hire a guy like me."

"Come on now, I'm sure that's not true." Brady tried to muster a confidence he wasn't sure he felt. "At some point, someone is going to be willing to take a chance on you, don't you think?"

"I don't know. It's been almost a month already, and nothing. Not even a bowling alley or a gas station. I've filled out about a million applications so far, and I haven't gotten a single call. Not one."

"That's tough," Brady agreed, leaning forward. "Listen, I was thinking earlier, maybe what you should do is reach out to people we know, like friends of the family. What's that old saying? It's not what you know, it's who you know that gets you hired. Isn't that what everybody says now?"

Shane lowered his eyes. "I don't know, Dad. I feel like such a loser. I know I've let you down. The girls have already figured out how to move on. Look how great they're doing, and Anthony." His voice had dropped so low that his father could barely hear him. "I'm the only who can't seem to get past it."

The ring of the telephone startled them both, and Tony jumped up to grab it, grateful for the interruption.

"Tony Brady here," he answered. A smile stretched across his face as soon as he heard the caller's voice. "Anthony, speak of the Devil! We were just talking about you. Hey, how's my grandbaby doing? Tell Grandpa what amazing thing my little sweetheart did today!"

"Hey Dad, she's doing great. I just called to check up on you guys. How's it going? The kid okay?"

Brady glanced at Shane's cheerless face. "Not so good. He's discouraged about the job situation."

"Still no offers?"

"None yet. Got any bright ideas for your brother?"

"You know, I just might. I ran into an old buddy downtown today. He's got a vet practice over in Potrero Hill. He was saying the guy who was helping out just up and quit on him without any notice. Maybe he could use someone like Shane."

"No kidding? But don't you need some kind of license for that kind of work?"

"I don't think so, it's pretty basic, I think. You know, cleaning the cages and stuff like that. I can ask him, anyway, if Shane wants. Is he there? Put him on."

"Hold on a second." Brady covered the mouthpiece.

"Hey, buddy, cheer up. Your brother wants to talk to you. Says he might have a lead on something."

Shane took the phone into the next room. "Hey, what's up, Anthony?"

Brady began to wash up. When he'd put everything back into the cupboards and wiped down the table, he cocked an ear. Hearing nothing but silence, he filled a trash bag with the remnants of their supper, walking down the narrow hallway to the garbage chute. When he returned, he found Shane pacing back and forth in the apartment's tiny living room.

"Well? What did your brother have to say?"

Shane stopped pacing just long enough to blurt out his nervous reply. "He said he'd call his friend and ask the guy if he could use me. Maybe he can try me out. I don't know how I can start working unless somebody gives me a chance, Dad. He's an old friend from high school and Anthony says he's a real good guy."

Brady beamed. "That sounds good, buddy. Let's see what happens." He hesitated. "Listen, I've been thinking about what you were saying earlier. You know, about being a disappointment. You shouldn't feel like that, Shane. Your mom and I know how tough things have been for you. It's not that we're disappointed in you, we just feel bad for you. We wish after all this time you could give yourself a break. Let yourself off the hook a little."

Shane resumed his anxious pacing. "I can't, Dad, I can't give myself a break. I can't ever forgive myself. That's just the way it is." His voice thickened, his words erupting in a rush. "Maybe nothing would have happened if I'd have been there, but I wasn't. I didn't go with him, and I'll never be able to let myself off the hook for that."

"But it wasn't your fault, son! Didn't they get you some counseling when you were at the rehab center? You know, like tell you how important forgiveness is?"

Brady reached out and clamped his hand on his son's forearm to stop his frantic pacing. "Listen, bottom line is we all need to forgive ourselves in order to move on. To tell you the truth, it might be the only really useful thing I ever got from the Catholic Church, learning how to forgive others, learning how to forgive myself."

Shane stared at his father, looking desolate. "None of that Catholic mumbo-jumbo works for me. What kind of God would let something like that happen? I don't believe in God, Dad, and I don't know about forgiveness, or anything like that. That's just not the way things work for me." He turned away and picked up the TV remote, clicking through channels to look for the Giants game.

Brady was in the kitchen brewing fresh coffee when the ring of the phone again made them both jump. This time Shane got to it first.

"No way! Really? What's his number? Wait, let me grab a pen."

A crumpled receipt and a pen emerged from deep in the pocket of Shane's jeans.

"I'll call him first thing tomorrow. This is great stuff, Bro. Thanks a million."

Brady watched as tension drained from his son's face.

"I can't believe it! He says I need to give him a call tomorrow, but basically, the guy went for it. He's willing to try me out. If it works out, he might hire me," Shane exhaled with relief. "Maybe I can even start, like right away!"

"That's terrific! Listen, you'll be on your feet again in no time, son," Brady grinned. "Hey, you know what, though? It's been kind of nice having you bunk here with me for a little while." He cuffed his son's shoulder affectionately. "Who's going to watch the Giants games with me once you move on?"

Nearly giddy, Shane laughed out loud. "See, I told you it was going to be temporary, Dad!"

Minutes later, the fresh pot of coffee was only half gone when a news bulletin flashed across the screen, interrupting the Giants game with the announcement that a Bay Area TV reporter had been reported missing. A familiar face from a local channel, the missing man's colleagues were puzzled at his sudden disappearance, and his family was frantic with worry.

Before Brady even had the chance to get a good look at the guy in the news bulletin, the telephone rang for a third time.

"Anthony Brady, Investigative Services. How can I help you?"

CHAPTER THREE

September 2003
PHILLIP

The day before he left, Phillip stuffed a nearly full box of Andrew's power bars from the last Costco run into his briefcase. Next, he visited the credit union on the first floor of the building where he worked and withdrew the $31,000 and change he had squirreled away over the years. Carefully separating the bills into three large envelopes and sealing them with masking tape, he tucked the bulging envelopes into the zipper section in the center of the battered old briefcase. Then he slipped the remaining stack of twenty dollar bills into a fourth envelope, one that he could easily reach into for immediate access, although he hoped not to burn through the bills too quickly.

Certainly it was a lot of cash, but Phillip reminded himself it wasn't money that anyone would miss. Susan didn't even know about the account, opened his first year at the station when he'd begun to salt away a few hundred a month. As a boy, he'd been taught to save part of his allowance for a rainy day, and as a working-man, Phillip delighted in the idea of stacking up *fun* money.

He liked to visualize it compounding every day, even if he'd never really given any thought to what he was saving for, and he knew that if he'd breathed a word about it to Susan, the money would be spent in a heartbeat to replace perfectly good appliances or to fill the yard with overpriced patio furniture.

It wasn't that Susan was a spendthrift. It was just that the two of them didn't seem to be on the same page about anything anymore and hadn't been for years. Certainly not since Gracie had come along, and probably even before that, Phillip admitted when he was honest with himself. The two of them simply hadn't been in sync.

They probably should never have gotten married in the first place.

They had barely known each other, and somehow almost immediately, Susan had wound up pregnant. The months that followed that surprising discovery were like a blur. At twenty-two he'd barely completed his final semester of college in time to find himself a husband and a father, and his disappointed parents had insisted at once that he square his shoulders and buckle down to support his new little family. Truthfully, at the time he wasn't completely unhappy about it, and he believed himself up to the task. His young wife was pretty, the new baby undeniably cute, and it was kind of fun coming home to a wife and a child at the end of a busy day. They laughed about calling their first few months of married life *the peanut butter and jelly years*, years when they rarely had enough money for a pizza or a night out of any kind. It had been like playing house, pushing the second-hand stroller around their Outer Sunset neighborhood and splurging on a Sunday rowboat ride on the lake in Golden Gate Park. They were newlyweds and had their whole lives in front of them, and later, there would be another baby or two to make, and he looked forward to it all.

When had everything changed? Phillip had asked himself too many times to count. *Was it his fault? Was it hers?*

Maybe it wasn't anyone's fault when the hopefulness of those early years turned into disappointment and they each began to obsess over what was and what wasn't going to be possible for them. She tried to deny the frustration of failure every month when, after surprising speed conceiving Andrew, they just couldn't get pregnant, and he tried to roll with the punches as they began to realize that life might not hold the future they had never doubted would be theirs. Every song he heard on the radio knocked the wind out of him. *You can't always get what you want*, the Rolling Stones sang in an upbeat major key. *You've got to know when to fold 'em*, crooned Kenny Rogers.

He couldn't blame Susan for what happened, and he certainly didn't want to blame himself. *No,* he knew with certainty, *it wasn't anyone's fault,* and he figured it may even have been predictable when the marriage began to crumble. Whatever carefree joy had once been theirs evaporated as sadness and shame took the place of passion and pleasure and they struggled under the strain of the secrets they'd promised to conceal. While leafing through a self-help book at the library, he read that most people's unhappiness comes from the gap between their expectations and reality, and reasoning that he couldn't do much about reality, Phillip determined that it might be best for him to abandon the expectations he had.

Nothing stays the same. Holding onto the way things are is like trying to grab a rope as it's yanked through your hands, he thought to himself. *You're left with a nasty burn.*

Unfortunately, Phillip was a young man when he arrived at this sober conclusion, a young man with his whole life in front of him, and immediately, the colors of the universe around him began to dim. After that critical moment, he found it was harder to feel much pleasure, or love, or hope. After that moment, it was harder to feel anything at all.

The radio station he'd tuned to was broken up by static, and he turned it off. After five hours of driving, he pulled off the highway into a shopping plaza on the outskirts of a town called Lancaster and parked beside a big box store.

Phillip had never set foot inside a Walmart before and wasn't sure there even was one back home. With surprise, he discovered that he could buy pretty much anything there: a sleeping bag and a backpack and clothes and all kinds of sundry items he could stuff inside. He debated for a while before deciding against the sleeping bag, unable to picture himself sleeping anywhere but in a warm bed. He chose a warm black hooded sweatshirt, jeans and a pair of sneakers, along with underwear and a couple of lightweight polo shirts and jogging shorts. His stomach rumbling, he headed to the McDonalds counter at the front of the store where he wolfed down a couple of burgers. In the men's room, he scrubbed his face and changed into the more comfortable sneakers and jeans. Stuffing his dress shirt and tie into the trash receptacle, at once Phillip felt lighter. He ran a hand through his curls and studied himself in the cracked mirror, rubbing the slight stubble on his chin and wondering if perhaps he'd grow a beard, or maybe a moustache.

It was mid-afternoon by then, and as the burgers and fries settled heavily in his stomach, he forced himself to admit that he didn't know where he was going to spend the night. At work whenever he found himself stuck at an impasse, a short nap had always provided him with fresh ideas, and sleepy from the long drive, he decided to take advantage of the inviting recliner on display in the Walmart patio department. Stretching out on a chaise lounge with cheerful yellow cushions, Phillip yawned and closed his eyes, quickly surrendering to a lull that reminded him of slipping into soothing anesthesia.

Twenty-five minutes later, he was shaken back to consciousness by a burly six-foot guard sporting a crisp khaki uniform. The dream he'd been having was the sort that a long nap can produce, at once both pleasant and anxious, and woefully familiar: a broadcast deadline loomed while he and his editor tried to squeeze a complicated story into a ninety second time slot. Deciding what to leave on the cutting room floor had always been his least favorite part of the job, and when Phillip returned to consciousness, he found himself dripping in sweat.

Thank God I'm done with all that, he muttered under his breath.

With burly arms folded over his broad chest, the security guard cocked an eye at the fellow he'd caught napping on the patio furniture and asked, "Is there some reason you're sleeping here, Sir?"

"No. I mean, yes. The thing is, I'm a bit down on my luck," Phillip stammered. He grinned sheepishly as he explained. "This was the only place I could think of. I just meant to lie down for a minute."

Phillip was lucky; strangers seemed to trust him. He was the kind of person that others warmed up to easily, and he knew it, and he set to work projecting the unthreatening manner he'd developed as a reporter. He hoped the Walmart security guard looking him over would see that the fellow who had stolen a nap on the lounge furniture was probably not harmful and certainly not dangerous. When he'd surmised that the guard wasn't angry, he asked if he could suggest a place to spend the night, ideally, a place that was free of charge.

"You can't sleep in the store, but I could recommend a shelter not far from here," the guard proposed, relaxing his stance with a sigh. "I can show you how to get there."

Phillip offered the guard a broad, friendly smile. "Really? You'd do that?"

"Sure, no problem." The guard consulted his watch. "You'd have to wait 'til my shift ends at five. The one I'm thinking of, it's out in Antelope Valley, I could drop you at the bus stop so you could pick up their shuttle." He glanced at the patio tables and chairs surrounding them. "You'll have to leave this area, though. You can't stay here."

Phillip scrambled off the chaise lounge and returned to the family car in the parking lot. He stuffed everything he thought he might need into his new backpack and moved all the contents of his briefcase to the new bag, including the neatly divided envelopes of cash. He pulled the insurance documents out of the Volvo's glove compartment, tore them into pieces and drove to the farthest corner of the Walmart parking lot. With one last look at the familiar keychain with the silver P on it, the one the kids had given him on Father's Day, he heaved the briefcase into the large blue dumpster behind the store.

No turning back now, he told himself. *Don't think. Keep moving forward.*

He wondered if Andrew and Gracie were home from school by now. Possibly, Susan and the kids hadn't yet realized that he was gone. He hoped they wouldn't get the police or his parents or his boss involved, but he suspected they would. As he stood beside the pungent dumpster, he allowed himself to imagine the scene that was probably about to unfold inside his family's home. For the hundredth time that day, Phillip stopped to ask himself if he were certain it was worth it, knowing that the cost of the odyssey he had embarked on was going to be very, very steep.

A string of regrets and disappointments accumulated over time had brought him to this moment, but it wasn't as if there had been one unforgivable transgression. No specific breaking point had suddenly been reached. Second chances often require nerves of steel, and he clung to the fervent hope that starting over would give him the second chance he longed for. Turning away from everything that had mattered to him until now, Phillip asked himself again if the path he had chosen was worth it, and at once he knew that it was.

The remorse he felt for his family was accompanied by a certainty he couldn't explain. His decision was very likely the first important one he'd ever made without consulting anyone else, and it had been a long time coming. A voice that had been quiet far too long had finally spoken, and he knew he had to act now if he was ever to restore the vibrant color that had been missing from his life.

The tantalizing chance to start over stirred in Phillip's heart, propelling him forward with an energy that felt like rocket fuel. He turned away from the blue dumpster and restlessly began jogging the six blocks behind the Walmart parking lot. Just before five o'clock, his face flushed from exertion, Phillip strode into the brightly lit store to wait for the security guard near the front door, his heart pounding with a ripple of anticipation for the next leg of his journey.

CHAPTER FOUR

September 2003

BRADY

The phone call was long distance, from three thousand miles away. In McLean, Virginia, the ex-military man introduced himself crisply even as he stuffed his shaving kit and favorite slippers into a well-travelled suitcase. Brady thought he recognized the familiar squeak of a medicine cabinet door while Phillip's father hurriedly explained the reason for his call.

"Susan may not want us underfoot, but my wife and I are heading out to the coast in the morning. Something has happened to Phillip, we don't know what, but there has to be some logical explanation. Alice will be a big help with the grandkids, and she'll see to it that we all get fed. But you and I both know this kind of thing needs a man to take charge, you know, someone to make the police buckle down and do their jobs. An attorney I know from the Pentagon gave me your number. Says you helped him out on a case once. Listen, Mr. Brady, we need a private investigator, and if you think you can help us find our boy, I'm prepared to post a substantial reward. I'll be damned if I just sit back and wait, no siree. That's never been my style."

Brady heard the metallic snap of a suitcase lock as the commanding voice continued.

"I've been around long enough to know you've got to put some pressure on the authorities or they won't do a damn thing. If you don't keep the pressure on, you won't get any results."

"I certainly see your point." Brady had been scribbling notes on a nearby pad. "When will you and Mrs. Lynch be arriving in San Francisco?"

"Tomorrow, and believe me, we'll find him. One way or another, we're going to find our boy. Look. Someone knows what happened. Someone knows where he is. We just have to approach the problem logically," Phillip's father concluded, sounding a good deal more upbeat and confident than Brady guessed the retired Army officer felt at that moment.

He explained the terms of his contract, and just before they signed off, Lieutenant Colonel Roger Lynch rattled off a list of people he urged Brady to get in touch with right away. At the top of the list was Susan, the missing man's wife. The investigator entered the date and time on a fresh page in his notebook and dialed the number. Susan picked up on the first ring, explaining that she was keeping her voice low so the kids wouldn't overhear her.

Despite the barely discernable undertone, he sensed her panic. He introduced himself soothingly. "Please tell me what's happened, Mrs. Lynch, and I'll do whatever I can to help."

In a halting voice, Susan described how she had first called Phillip's cell phone over and over, leaving a bevy of urgent messages, at first simply asking, but then pleading, for her husband to call home, wherever he was.

Brady heard something being poured into a glass, and then a short pause.

"I needed that," she confessed.

"Let's start with the morning. Did your husband go to work as usual?" he asked gently.

"Yes, but the station said he never showed up and he didn't call in. He dropped the kids off at school as usual, he does the morning and I do pickups. The kids said there was nothing out of the ordinary about the ride to school. The police said it's too early to be concerned, not even 48 hours, but the thing is, Mr. Brady, nothing like this has ever happened before. It's just not like Phillip to disappear."

"Have you given the police a description of the car?"

"Yes, I told them it's an old white Volvo sedan, and they said they'd try tracking it down. The insurance company had the license plate number, I couldn't remember what it was. Oh, and the police said they'd check to see if Phillip's credit cards were used anywhere."

Brady drew a line beneath *white Volvo sedan* on his notepad. "Has anything unusual been going on in the family lately? Any particular stress at home?" he probed, his voice measured.

Susan groaned. "No, Mr. Brady. We weren't fighting, if that's what you mean."

"What about activities in the neighborhood? Has there been any recent crime you're aware of?"

"No! This is a nice, safe family block. The kids ride their bikes to the park. And our street always seemed like a sleepy little slice of suburbia." Her voice had begun to rise. "What on earth could have happened, Mr. Brady? What am I supposed to tell the kids?"

Susan's voice had become loud enough that Brady thought perhaps the children, if they were nearby, could hear her and thought it best to keep the call short. "Tell you what, why don't you try and get some sleep now, and let's talk again in the morning, Mrs. Lynch. Meantime, perhaps you could put me in touch with one or two of your husband's colleagues?"

She suggested a fellow reporter named Sam might be found at a local pub and gave him the address, explaining that the news team liked to gather and blow off steam there after the evening broadcast. Suddenly not the least bit tired, he ran a comb through his hair and grabbed his jacket. The prospect of doing useful, important work again filled him with renewed energy, and with a nod to Shane, sprawled out on the couch with a bag of chips in front of the Giants game, Brady headed out.

Even in the dim light in Jake's Place, the reporter was easy to spot, holding court at center stage. Nice-looking, with an animated way of speaking with his hands, Sam Morgan held the attention of a small circle gathered around him. Office workers who'd been cooped up all day had crowded into the neighborhood pub and wriggled out of their jackets as they'd settled on the soft vinyl barstools. Brady stood at the far end of the bar near Sam's circle and waited for a chance to introduce himself. When he did, Phillip's colleague pumped his hand warmly and called out to the bartender to bring them a couple of beers. Sam gestured to the handful of Phillip's colleagues already enjoying a round.

"The guys and I, we came down tonight for a few drinks after work like always. See, we wanted to hand out these flyers the art department printed up. All the regulars here know Phillip, and we're thinking maybe we can get this whole stack spread out around town."

The reporter pointed to a cardboard box of flyers on the counter, and Brady held one up. A photograph of Phillip's face and the phone number of the TV station's help line stared back at him.

"Nice work. How long have you and he worked together?"

"Not long. We've been sharing a cubicle for a few months while they've been renovating. Phillip and I, we get along fine. We don't get on each other's nerves like some guys. Like if one of us has a personal call to make, we always use the conference room. You know, for privacy. Anyway, reporters don't hang out at our desks much. One of us is usually out doing an interview or in the edit room putting a story together."

"Anything out of the ordinary going on at work lately?"

Sam shrugged. "Work's been kinda stressful, to tell you the truth. I mean, we're used to having deadlines and stuff, but it's been different lately. Thing is, we got this new program director, and everybody pretty much hates the guy. Ever since he got here, he's been pushing us to do more educational stuff, not so much news and features. See, he got this grant for us to do what they call K-12 programming, you know, educational type stuff the teachers can use in classrooms." Sam's grimace made it clear what he thought of the suggestion.

Brady looked up from his notepad. "So, was that a serious problem? For Phillip, I mean?"

"Well, it's not a life-or-death thing, if that's what you mean, but none of us are too excited about making these changes." He pointed to the noisy gang draped around the bar. "We all hate it, you can ask anyone here. But, no, I wouldn't say Phillip seemed all that upset. He's a roll-with-the-punches kind of guy." Clearly puzzled, Sam frowned. "Thing is, he's not the kind of guy who just doesn't show up for work one day. He's reliable, a good reporter, always prepared. The kind of guy you can count on." He pursed his lips thoughtfully, and Brady waited in silence, watching him carefully. "But you know, even if he was getting bugged at work, hey, it's just a job, you know? Work isn't everything, is it? I mean, like, it's not your whole life. And things at home? Let's face it, we all have stuff going on sometimes, but I never heard him grumble about any problems at home."

"Did the two of you usually discuss that kind of thing, you know, talk about what was going on in your personal lives?"

"Not really," Sam admitted. "But if things at home were dicey for some reason, for sure he would have mentioned it. You know, complained about it. Wouldn't he? Doncha think?"

"You'd certainly think so." Brady reached into his wallet and dug out a business card. "Listen, Sam, if anything new occurs to you or your colleagues, I'd love to hear from you."

Sam finished off his beer and wiped his mouth. "Sure thing. I hope there's some simple explanation and Phillip turns up soon, and I hope he's ok, wherever he is." He pocketed the card without stopping to read it and shook Brady's hand again.

"Yeah, me too," he agreed, heading for the exit. "Thanks for your help, Sam. Let's stay in touch."

In the back of Brady's mind, he was beginning to form a picture of the missing man, but the picture was sketchy at best. He decided the best thing to do was to visit the man's home as soon as he could and get to know each member of the family. He'd check out the neighbors, too, and the area around the TV station. Then, when Phillip's parents arrived tomorrow, he hoped to fill in some blanks about who exactly he was looking for.

It was close to midnight when he put his key in the door. The tiny apartment was quiet, the only sound the wind rattling the blinds on the kitchen window Shane had left open. A hastily scribbled note on the table grabbed his attention.

Hey Dad, some lady called for you 2 times! From Australia!! She says call her back right away. Sorry I didn't wait up.

There was a long string of numbers scribbled underneath, and Brady wondered who had been trying to reach him this late. Padding to the bedroom after what had been a long day, he changed into pajamas and stood at the bathroom sink brushing his teeth, telling himself he'd return the call in the morning. His plans were thwarted when the phone rang for what seemed like the hundredth time that day, and a long distance operator connected a call from Sydney, where it was the middle of the following day.

"Oh, finally!" a woman's exasperated voice on the other end of the line exclaimed. "Elizabeth Lynch here. I'm Phillip's sister, Beth. For heaven's sake, here I am on my first real business trip, and my parents track me down halfway across the world to tell me my little brother is nowhere to be found," she fumed, adding that in her opinion, he had always taken too much of their mother's attention.

"You have to understand, Mr. Brady. My mother is something of an alarmist when it comes to Phillip. I had to remind her she'd told me they'd just had a conversation the other day."

"Oh? When exactly was that?"

"Well, let me see. It was on Saturday. Mom said he'd called after his tennis game, sounding chipper, bragging he'd won the game. Now she's saying that since he was perfectly fine then, something horrible must have happened to him."

"It's much too soon to speculate on what's happened just yet, Miss Lynch."

"Right? I know it is! That's exactly what I told her! I said, Mom, you're just jumping to conclusions like you always do." Brady sensed Beth's frustration. "But I had to remind myself it was probably not the best time to bring that up. I had to bite my lip."

"Probably a wise choice," he said soothingly.

"But you know how mothers are," Beth went on, imitated her mother's lilting voice. "Never you mind," she said. "These things are a mother's intuition. No matter how old you two are, you're still my children, and I just know if something's not right," she scoffed. "Then, get a load of this, she went on to say she was praying for Phillip, and I should, too."

"Well, if it helps, there's nothing wrong with a little prayer," he chuckled.

"Oh, I gave up all those useless childhood rituals a long time ago, Mr. Brady." He could almost see her rolling her eyes. "But I know better than to argue with my parents about religion."

Brady rubbed his tired eyes and tried to steer the conversation back on track. "When did you last talk to your brother?"

Beth hesitated. "Phillip and I hadn't actually connected for a while, but then you know, he and I were never exactly close. Not exactly two peas in a pod."

"Is that right? What about Susan, his wife? Do you stay in touch with her at all?"

"A little. See, I'm godmother to their son. Andrew's a great kid, actually. He likes me to send postcards, you know, when I travel. The kids' school pictures are up on my fridge. You know those cute little photos they take at school?" She paused, and Brady waited for her to go on. "It's funny, the kids don't look at all like Phillip. They're both blonde, like Susan. The little one, Gracie, she's the spitting image of her mother."

The young businesswoman confided that the next few days were tightly scheduled with meetings and breakout sessions. She said she was excited and a little nervous about co-hosting the conference with her boss tomorrow. "But do you think I should change my plans, Mr. Brady? Should I drop everything and rush back to the States?"

Brady guessed that it was hard to imagine how she could possibly be needed at this moment, and his reassurance seemed to comfort her.

Beth exhaled with obvious relief. "Good. Sometimes it can seem like I'm awfully selfish, but the truth is, I really need to focus on work."

He promised to keep her up to date.

"Thanks, Mr. Brady. Where do you think my brother could possibly be? What could have happened to him?" Her voice faltered slightly for the first time. "I don't know, maybe a little prayer would be a good idea." During the pause that followed, Brady could have sworn he thought Beth was crossing herself. "You think maybe I should ask God if he could just keep Phillip safe, wherever he is? You know, in case He's listening?"

CHAPTER FIVE

September 2003

PHILLIP

The name stitched onto the crisp khaki shirt read *Steve* in bright red script.

"No problem at all," the guard assured Phillip. "It's only a small detour for me. I always take Palmdale Boulevard on my way home anyway, go right past where the shuttle stops." As they reached the intersection, he pointed out the corner where a van from the homeless men's shelter was due to arrive, a long white van that would ferry all the men waiting to nearby Antelope Valley.

Phillip slung his new backpack onto his shoulder and climbed down from the pickup truck. "Thanks, man, really appreciate it," he waved as the guard shifted into gear and took off down the road.

He surveyed the two men waiting at the bus stop, an older man leaning on a cane and a young blonde fellow with a pony-tail. Brightly painted tattoos ran up and down the younger man's long arms.

"This where the bus picks up for the shelter?" Phillip asked as he joined them.

The tattoo bearer looked at him through half-shut eyes and slowly made a thumbs-up sign. "Yup. You a new guy?"

Maybe this new shirt and jeans wasn't the best idea, Phillip wondered, seeing himself from the young fellow's point of view. He did his best to mimic the man's slouch and immediately slipped into his easy lingo. "Guess it's pretty obvious, huh? How's it work, anyway? Is it hard to get in?"

The older man pointed his cane at him. "Might not be an open bed."

"Got it," he nodded. "So if I'm lucky, how long would they let me stay?"

The pony-tailed man stepped off the curb and leaned into the street, squinting at the traffic barreling towards them. He jerked his head toward the boulevard. "Bus coming," he announced as he flagged down the van. "If they've got one, the most they let you crash is six weeks."

Phillip's eyebrows arched in surprise. "No kidding, six weeks? Wow, that's a lot longer than I thought."

"Yeah, it's a pretty good deal. No charge." The van's accordion doors opened, and the tattooed man tossed his cigarette to the ground.

The older man used his cane to inch toward the curb. "But they got their rules, and you got to follow 'em."

The van headed down Palmdale Boulevard as soon as they'd climbed on board. Phillip settled back in the spongy seat, glad for the chance to gaze out the window at the town going by. Pausing twice more to collect passengers before turning east, the shuttle pulled to a stop in front of a large warehouse-like structure at the end of a nearly abandoned street.

He looked as far as he could to his left and then to his right. Down the road, he made out a filling station with a convenience store attached, but no houses or apartments, no restaurants and no shops. Miles of sparse scrub brush dotted the lonely horizon, broken only by the cracked ground baked dry in the desert heat. In front of Phillip, the only sign of life in the desolate landscape was the broad cinder block shelter.

Could be my new home, he shrugged, mulling over what the men on the bus had told him. *Six weeks free?*

Up until that moment, it hadn't even occurred to Phillip what the duration of his stay was likely to be, but surely six weeks would be sufficient. In fact, as he followed the others inside, he thought to himself that nearly two months might as well be a lifetime.

Don't get ahead of yourself. Wait and see, he cautioned inwardly.

At the reception desk, he was relieved to find out that space was indeed available. Peering past the counter into the lodging area at a dozen unoccupied cots, he guessed that arriving on a Tuesday evening was a lucky accident.

"Write your name in the register," the harried attendant barely out of his teens instructed, pointing to an empty slot in a ledger. "Then sign the rules agreement for new arrivals." He pulled a printed form out of a manila folder.

Phillip hesitated, chewing on his lip.

What name do I write in the register?

The answer came to him straight out of the blue, and he smiled, thinking it was just clever enough to avoid drawing notice. Awkwardly, using his left hand instead of his usual right, he scrawled *Steve*, thinking fondly of the Walmart security guard, and next to it, *Phillips*.

Squinting at it, he saw that his penmanship bore a strong resemblance to chicken scratch.

The distracted staff at the front desk did not ask for any identification. A large cardboard sign on the wall announced the shelter's inviolate rule that residents vacate the facilities each day at 7:00 a.m. sharp, and Phillip was advised that a van would be available at that time every day to ferry residents back into town, where they were expected to pass their daytime hours.

"Welcome," the attendant added, almost as an afterthought. "Remember to be on time for the morning van." He handed Phillip a copy of the shelter's *Do's and Don'ts,* sitting in a wire basket on the desk. "They won't wait, and it's a long walk."

"Got it. Is there somewhere I can wash up?"

The attendant pointed out the washroom tucked away in a far corner of the cavernous dormitory where the coughs of old men bounced off unpainted sheetrock walls. Phillip quickly located the bed assigned to him, a lower-level bunk with a thin blanket, and began to settle in for his first night away from home. Although still early in the evening, he stretched out gratefully on a slender cot four feet from another just like it, in a row of many others, all neatly arranged in the high-ceilinged room that he guessed might once have been some kind of warehouse. He glanced around the oversized room to take in his surroundings and saw nothing the least bit familiar, no bookcases stacked with books, no overstuffed easy chairs to lounge in, no cozy fireplace, no computer workstation, no television set, not even a coffee pot. There was nothing in his new environment that could possibly remind him of home, and the buzzing fluorescent lights overhead flickered. He reached down for the Walmart backpack tucked under his cot, taking it with him on his way to the washroom. He knew he couldn't afford to let anyone get their hands on those sealed envelopes.

As night-time drew near, Phillip stretched out with his eyes closed and picked out the sounds in the unfamiliar shelter. The cavernous bunkroom was quieter than he'd imagined it would be, as nearly a hundred men removed shoes and draped trousers over bedrails and plumped up well-worn pillows. Unexpectedly, fatigue began to wash over him, and he breathed deeply, welcoming the soothing escape that exhaustion promised. Although not an especially tall man, he rolled over on his side, bending his knees to fit on the strange new bed.

It had always been his bedtime habit to review his day as he succumbed to sleep, but he forced his conscious thoughts away from what he'd left behind, focusing instead on counting his breaths in and out. *You had to do it,* he told himself. For as long as he could remember, Phillip had followed a script that seemed to have been written before he was even born. He'd gone to college as expected and done well enough there, while working part-time to help cover the cost of tuition. After graduation, he'd settled down to earn a living and provide for his new family. His aim had always been to make those around him happy, often at the expense of his own pleasure, and most of the time, he wouldn't have known what else to do. He was proud to say that he'd never intentionally hurt anyone before. And yet Phillip was aware that what he had done today had not been according to any script. What he had done today would have been considered strange by any measure, and he knew that it was not, as a rule, how good husbands and fathers were supposed to behave. By any measure, he knew that what he had done simply wasn't normal.

He sighed, wondering what *normal* even meant, when even as a child he had often felt out of sync with his family. Mom and Dad's tendency to compare his meager accomplishments with those of his older sister had only made his discomfort more acute, like when he'd tried to follow Beth's footsteps, memorizing four-syllable words to compete in gut-wrenching spelling bees. He had always been knocked out early on some entry-level word, while Beth had brought home a pile of shiny blue ribbons. He'd been following the script even as a gawky teenager, when, all because Dad had played ball in college, he'd stuck it out on the baseball team, nearly always striking out at the plate and fighting the urge to drop his head in dejection on the slow walk back to the dugout. In high school, he'd signed up for AP classes to make his parents proud. But the heavy workload was a struggle, and he'd had to abandon the honors track by the end of his sophomore year. Beth, meanwhile, was awarded the school's coveted valedictorian prize at graduation.

Mom and Dad had been over the moon.

He rolled over onto his side in search of a more comfortable position and reminded himself that everyone's parents were different in those days, so much stricter than they are now. Still, even then Dad had been tougher than his friends' dads, a disciplinarian and taskmaster who expected *Yes, Sir* and *No, Sir* even within the confines of his own home. A graduate of West Point and an imposing Lieutenant Colonel at the Pentagon, his father had donned a crisply starched uniform every day to head to his office in the nation's capital.

Did any parents ever love their sons and daughters without any conditions at all? Phillip wondered sleepily. *Aren't all relationships basically transactional?*

He could almost feel the soothing touch of Mom's cool fingers as she'd smoothed lotion on his fevered skin that time he had the chicken pox. *I always knew Mom loved me, though.* And the way she always tucked a little note into his Star Trek lunchbox, knowing he would find it alongside a gooey Hostess Cupcake or a HoHo for dessert.

Still, Dad was a different story, always somehow unreachable, and Phillip wasn't sure why. Looking back now, he could say with certainty that he'd always tried to do what was expected, but he honestly couldn't recall ever doing anything that had made Dad say he was proud of him.

Never, not even once, had Phillip heard his father say that he loved him.

No point hashing over all that again, he sighed. *What's past is past. No looking back,* he told himself.

Don't think about it. Keep moving forward.

The day had been long. His feet had slipped off the end of the cot, and he shifted his weight again. He had arrived at this moment after thirty-six years of sticking to the script, of not breaking the rules, of not making waves, and Phillip was tired.

Bound to happen sometime, I guess. Might say it was fate, in a funny way. An almost ironic half-smile flitted across his lips, and Phillip yawned, finally succumbing to slumber.

Hundreds of miles to the north, those at home were trying to make sense of what had happened, and none of them would find anything about his disappearance to smile about.

CHAPTER SIX

September 2003

BRADY

Cheery perennials in the flower beds of the suburban split-level home greeted him as he stepped onto the porch to ring the doorbell. Brady took note of the freshly mowed front yard as he waited and peered through the window when no one came to the door. Holding the phone to her ear, a woman in a bathrobe and slippers waved him into the kitchen and pointed at the Mr. Coffee machine. He found a clean mug with *Fisherman's Wharf* inscribed on it and helped himself, leaning on the counter and listening to Susan's side of the conversation.

"I feel like I'm in a bad dream. I don't think any of us has slept a wink for days, I know I haven't. Phillip's parents have taken over the living room," she moaned into the receiver. "The house is in total chaos. I'm somewhere between numb and exhausted. I'm just so tired of telling everyone over and over again, no, we didn't have a fight, and no, I don't have any idea where the hell he could be." Susan rummaged through the kitchen drawers, a book of matches in her hand. With a sigh, she pulled a wine glass from the dishwasher. "No, no more problems than usual. And a midlife crisis? That just doesn't seem like Phillip. Everyone says there must have been an accident, or maybe he was mugged. I spent yesterday calling hospitals looking for him. The thing is, Becky, it's been three days now, and the cops don't have a clue." She examined the wine bottle on the counter and poured herself a glass. "What am I supposed to think? How can someone you live with and eat breakfast with every morning just disappear after fourteen years of marriage? The father of your children, the man you're raising your kids with!" Susan rubbed her eyes. Traces of mascara smudged the dark circles below them, and as she turned away from the sink, she seemed to notice Brady for the first time.

"Listen, Sis, that investigator Roger hired is here. I've got to go. Call me later."

She apologized for keeping him waiting. "I'm so sorry, Mr. Brady. You must think I'm nuts, going on like that. We're all going a little crazy around here."

"Oh, don't you worry about me, Mrs. Lynch. This is probably the first moment you've had to yourself."

"How'd you guess?" She took a gulp of her drink. "You met Alice and Roger when you came by the other day, and finally today Alice got Gracie to go back to school. Just about broke my heart when she asked if Daddy didn't love us anymore. Poor kid, I didn't know how to answer her." Susan covered her mouth with a hand that Brady could clearly see was shaking. "It's hard to be careful about the kids' feelings when I'm beginning to wonder the same thing," she confessed in a broken voice.

Brady knew that waiting to find out what has happened can feel like a nightmare, hours suspended in a frantic limbo of uncertainty. He tried to console her. "Believe me, I know. Has there been any news at all?"

"In a way, yeah, there has." She rifled through the kitchen drawers again, impatiently sorting through snub-nosed pencils and rubber bands. "Do you happen to have a cigarette on you Mr. Brady? I quit smoking ages ago, but now I'm just dying for one."

"No, sorry, I don't smoke. And please, call me Tony."

She abandoned her search and tossed the matchbook onto the counter.

"Tell me what this means, Tony. Yesterday Alice ran a bunch of errands for me. She picked up our stuff from the dry cleaners, and they told her Phillip's wallet was in the pocket of his trousers. Of course, they didn't know he's missing. The police say that explains why none of his credit cards have been used, but what does any of it mean? He doesn't have his wallet with him! He doesn't even have his driver's license!"

Brady's eyebrows arched. "That *is* a surprising discovery," he agreed. "So, you shared this information with a detective from the police department?"

She waved her hand dismissively. "They just keep saying they're working on it, you know, putting together some kind of profile. But, think about it, he must have known he didn't have his wallet." Her lip trembled, and her eyes filled with tears that threatened to spill over. "The cops are suggesting Phillip may have left on purpose. They said there's no evidence of kidnapping or

45

abduction, and they don't suspect foul play." She shrugged, a catch in her voice. "Say they're right, then what?" She reached into her purse to find the makeup mirror, buried beneath a vial of perfume and a dirty hairbrush. "Can I possibly not have had any clue what was going on with Phillip? She held up the tiny mirror and squinted at her reflection. Red and puffy eyes gazed back at her, and she dabbed fresh powder onto her face. "Okay, things weren't always hunky-dory with us, but still. What, did my husband have some kind of secret life?" Susan snapped the compact mirror shut with a flash of anger.

Although he had to admit that the details Susan had revealed had caught him off guard, Brady did his best to assure the distraught wife and mother that he'd dig in to find out what it all meant. He took down the names of the policemen she'd talked to, and noticing how quiet the house was, asked when he could meet with her in-laws again. Susan replied that Roger and Alice had gone on a run to Costco and said she'd let him know when they returned.

He was beginning to suspect that perhaps things in the Lynch family were more complicated than they had initially seemed. *As usual*, Brady thought to himself as he packed up his notes and set his coffee mug in the cluttered sink. *About time to find out what the cops are doing.*

His was a familiar face at the Special Victims unit south of Market Street, and the friendly security detail at the entrance greeted him with the news that Brady's old boss in Missing Persons had finally made lieutenant. With a receding hairline and a paunch, Dave O'Malley pumped Brady's hand warmly as soon as he saw who it was. He motioned the former detective into his closet-sized office, tucked away in a corner of the squad room. Brady lowered himself onto the green desk chair across from O'Malley and instantly recalled the discomfort of the creased vinyl furniture.

"What brings you downtown, Tony?" the lieutenant asked, popping a Maalox tablet into his mouth from an oversized bottle on his desk.

"I've been hired by the family to look into the Phillip Lynch case, Dave. Apparently your guys have already spoken with the wife. Anything you can tell me?"

O'Malley rose from his desk to close the office door. "The lead detective assigned to the case is Carlos Salcedo, and I'm afraid he wouldn't be especially keen on sharing info with anyone outside the force."

"I figured it'd be a long shot," he shrugged.

The lieutenant's fingers rested on a metal file cabinet near the door. Sliding it open, he pulled out a small bottle and offered Brady a drink before taking one himself.

He doesn't look too good, thought Brady. *Can't be long before retirement.*

"Listen, Tony, I can put some pressure on the guy to set aside his reservations, just this once." O'Malley returned the bottle to the cabinet. "Hang on a sec, I just saw him in the squad room. Let me see if I can grab him."

Brady's eyes followed him as his old boss stepped out of the closet that was his office and crossed into the adjoining squad room, where a row of desks lined the cinderblock walls and boxes of overflowing files sat stacked one on top of the other on the cement floor. Cops wearing street clothes bent over their computers, the only sound the clicking of fingers on keyboards. There wasn't much privacy in the communal setting, and the detective's words filtered back clearly to where Brady sat waiting.

"Geez, Lieutenant, guys like him just want to pick our brains," he heard Salcedo grumble. "They think we don't know how to do our jobs. They think they're smarter than us. Frankly, boss, it's insulting."

"Yeah, maybe so," O'Malley replied smoothly. "But this particular PI, well, he and I go way back. He's one of us."

There was a pause. "Yeah? How's that?"

"Tony was a beat cop for a lot of years. In the Richmond. Then he made detective, a damn good one. Specialized in missing persons. Retired after putting in his twenty years and then went out and got his PI license. He was good police, and he's a good investigator. He's especially good at finding missing people."

Brady saw the lieutenant shoot Salcedo a knowing look as he added, "See, Carlos, it's personal for him."

"So let me get this straight." Clearly disgruntled, Detective Salcedo cocked his head to the side. "Is this his case or our case, boss? What are you telling me?"

O'Malley threw a friendly arm around Salcedo's shoulders. "How about we try and work together on this one," his supervisor suggested with easy diplomacy. "How about we cooperate? In my experience, teamwork's always best in a situation like this."

Without waiting for the detective to reply, Lieutenant O'Malley turned on his heel and headed for the coffee in the corner of the squad room.

"Tell me something, Tony," he asked as he kicked his office door shut and thrust a stale sugar doughnut at Brady. His old boss winced as he took a sip from a chipped *San Francisco Giants* mug. "Why does this slop always taste like laundry detergent? And why do I keep drinking it?"

In deference to his superior, Salcedo grudgingly put aside his reservations and agreed to share what he knew about the missing reporter's disappearance. It wasn't much.

"Look, Brady, there's not a lot to tell you. After the wife called 911, we advised her to wait a few hours to see if he turned up. You know how it is. A lot of these cases, they have some kind of fight, the guy just needs to cool off, maybe grab a beer with a buddy or go for a drive to clear his head, and then ends up back home real soon."

"Sure, that happens a lot," Brady agreed. "But when it didn't?"

"Right. That's when we actually started working the case. The only real information we had was a description of the car he was driving, so we ran the plate. There were several sightings of white Volvo sedans between northern and southern California, and the match turned up in a remote corner of a Walmart parking lot down south in Lancaster."

"Interesting. Over three hundred and fifty miles from home," Brady made a note. "So is that where you're focusing your search?"

"Yeah, sort of. We hoped we'd pick up an identifying visual on him from the parking lot security cameras, but the one near where the vehicle was abandoned wasn't functioning. Apparently it hasn't worked for some time. In fact, it turns out their whole surveillance system is poorly maintained. The cameras inside weren't operational, either." He paused as he watched Brady scribble *Walmart cameras* on his pad. "Not as much help as we'd hoped."

"So where do you go from here?"

"Look," Salcedo bristled with annoyance, "the guy didn't carry a pager or a phone. He left the friggin' mobile phone on his desk back in the office. The folks at the TV station were great, they ran a bunch of announcements with recent photographs. Everyone there, his boss and the rest of them, everyone has been cooperating with us. Doesn't seem like they're hiding anything."

"Are you thinking of doing polygraphs on anyone?"

The detective shrugged. "So far no one has been able to give us any reason for his disappearance. Not his colleagues, not his neighbors, not his family. Everyone says Lynch was a stable, predictable guy. We'll use 'graphs if we decide it might be useful, but look, you know as well as I do, in 99 percent of these cases, someone who disappears all of a sudden like that has gone missing on purpose."

Brady tried to figure out if the cop was getting frustrated or just bored.

Salcedo continued. "It's too early to rule anything or anyone out yet, but I'm not seeing a motive for foul play here. We'll keep digging, and we'll keep the hotline going, sure. Working with the public is an important part of our procedure, and maybe we'll get some intel that way. But you know the stats," he repeated, eyeing Brady squarely. "Let's face it, the guy didn't leave any traces. We don't know that he even wants to be found."

Detective Salcedo waved his hand toward the overflowing boxes of files on the floor beneath his desk. "Statistics say that over half of all our cases never get solved. You know, Brady, at some point on these cases we just have to face the facts. This just might be one of those times."

CHAPTER SEVEN

October 2003

PHILLIP

Settling comfortably into a routine, Phillip's first weeks at the shelter passed without a hitch. Each morning he headed to the communal washroom, finding it more than adequate, and then boarded the van to Palmdale Boulevard. Springing for an economical breakfast at McDonald's, he scanned the morning paper and lingered over cups of watery coffee. Each morning as he left the shelter, he gratefully accepted the brown bag lunch the staff handed out, and this he usually enjoyed around mid-morning in the park. Inside the bag he was sure to find a baloney or salami sandwich on spongy white bread with lettuce and a slice of American cheese, celery or carrot sticks and a small package of cookies. His favorite was Chips Ahoy. It was the kind of lunch that no one of any age could object to, and the childlike simplicity of the brown bag meal pleased him. Food was not permitted in the shelter, so before he lined up for the van at day's end, hungry or not, he made sure to supplement his fast-food breakfast and bag lunch with a hearty supper. He usually opted for a helping of shepherd's pie or squares of cheesy lasagna from the hot food buffet at Whole Foods, a place he figured he was unlikely to encounter his bunkmates from the shelter.

He paid for his supper by reaching into the envelope still crammed with small bills, pleased that in nearly a month's time, he'd spent hardly any of it. He'd bought only such necessities as toothpaste and nail clippers, a nylon parka when it had rained one day, a package of athletic socks and a pair of earplugs, indispensable in his new digs. Recalling the credit card charges they'd mounted up every month for what had seemed like vital purchases, Phillip was elated to discover how little he really needed. The simplicity of his new life suited him.

He knew he couldn't afford to get sick and did his best to stay healthy, walking or jogging everywhere. He did chin-ups on the bars in playgrounds and considered picking up a second-hand bike. Exploring the town with his keen reporter's eye, he began noticing *help wanted* signs at gas stations and coffee shops and wondered what sort of employment he might find. Filling out an application for part-time work in a bookstore, he paused at the line calling for a social security number, tossing the form into the trash on his way out of the store.

I guess I'll have to find something under the table, he figured. He'd seen a posse of broad-shouldered men gathered in front of the Home Depot, hoping to be hired for manual labor. *Maybe I could join them*, he debated, examining his muscles and feeling fit.

One morning while jogging down the side streets behind the town's main artery, he swung by a theater marquee advertising classic movies for a couple of dollars on Wednesday afternoons.

Intrigued, he stopped to peer at the list of films taped to the ticket window. The old theater soon became Phillip's weekly indulgence. Inside the dusty sanctuary, he leaned back and enjoyed the chance to escape to other worlds. Once, after a night in which he'd been disturbed by someone's incessant coughing, he even managed to take a nap as Humphrey Bogart and Katharine Hepburn floated down the Nile in *The African Queen.*

In early October, Phillip made another pleasing discovery. One afternoon as it began to sprinkle, he ducked into the vestibule of a building and stumbled into the quiet oasis that was the town's library. He approached the gray-haired librarian to ask about taking out a library card.

"You'll need two forms of identification," she informed him.

"Oh, that's a shame." Phillip patted his empty pockets. "At the moment, I'm afraid I don't have any ID with me."

"You're always welcome to browse, or sit and read, if you like," she suggested. "We have a reading room just to the left of the reference desk, and we carry daily newspapers from all over." She pointed to an area behind the children's section. "The seating is comfortable and there's good lighting there. Why don't you take a look?"

In this serendipitous way, Phillip cultivated the habit of passing entire afternoons ensconced in an overstuffed armchair in the library's reading room, where sunlight shining through the windows and the warm gas fireplace made the room feel cozy. Sometimes curious children poked their heads in, but for the most part, Philip basked in long stretches of silence, delving into an array of subjects that interested him. There had never been enough time to read for pleasure, and the demands of college and then his job had transformed that simple childhood joy into the drudgery of required reading. He began to select books at random, choosing a science fiction anthology, followed by a book on the Civil War. He feasted on whatever caught his eye until it dawned on him that perhaps he should focus on subjects he had always wanted to know more about, and he began systematically to make a list.

He liked to visit the library after his lunch in the park, and sometimes as he walked through town, he treated himself to an ice cream cone. One warm autumn day, just as he dipped his chin to prevent chocolate from dripping onto his sleeve, he stepped off the curb at Main Street, recalling the books he planned to look for. Headed towards him in the crosswalk, an attractive young woman pressed her slender dark fingers into the freckled arm of her smiling boyfriend. The two laughed playfully at something he had said, and as they crossed in front of him, the girl lowered her almond eyes, eyes he saw framed by curly black lashes. As they reached the curb, the sandy-haired boy turned towards his girl, and the lovers stopped and kissed, long and deep, a kiss so long that the pedestrians behind them were forced to part. Phillip had been close enough to take in the young woman's musky perfume and to notice the length of her eyelashes, and he stirred with a familiar heat. The couple's palpable intimacy, obvious and unavoidable, left him feeling he'd seen something he shouldn't have, and he looked away, embarrassed.

An unanticipated wave of melancholy descended on Phillip, and suddenly he felt lonelier than he'd ever been. Staring at the ice cream dripping onto his fingers, he exhaled noisily and tossed the forgotten cone aside.

It's a new world now, he reminded himself flatly, using a napkin to wipe the sticky spot of chocolate on his jeans. *It's not out of the ordinary like it used to be. Times have changed.*

In fact, there had been nothing the least bit out of the ordinary about the intimacy he had just witnessed. Traffic hadn't come to a halt and alarm bells hadn't rung because a white boy had kissed a black girl on a public street in the middle of the day. Not a single bystander had eyed them with shock, or disgust. He might have been the only passerby who had even really noticed them. His hand rested reflexively on his belly thinking that was where the sadness resided, but he found he was mistaken. The tenderness had settled just above his rib cage on the left side of his body, right under his heart, and moving his hand away from his belly, Phillip remembered Chloe.

She was the first woman he'd ever loved. There was no way for him to know it at the time, but never again would he be capable of such surrender, never again would he lose himself so urgently to desire, wanting her so badly that everything else evaporated at her slightest touch.

He'd been smitten by her sculpted cheekbones the very first time he'd seen her. How perfectly their young bodies had fit together making love, every nerve in his body vibrating and humming with aliveness. Chloe's mouth slightly parted for his tongue had made his blood pulse crazily and his heart beat so loud he could almost hear it. In no time at all, he'd become completely addicted to the lure of their passion. Those first few months as a college freshman, juggling classes and a work-study job, he'd invented ways to sneak away with his lover, kissing and laughing and kissing again as they lay close together on blankets in the park during afternoon picnics that stretched into evenings in dorm rooms where socks tied to doorknobs sent a signal to roommates to come back later. The snatches of time they could be alone together were as exciting as they were terrifying, and both reveled in their infatuation with each other.

On the street where the couple had stood and kissed, a wave of remorse washed over Phillip, and as he forced himself to continue down Main Street toward the library, he tried in vain to reignite his enthusiasm for the pleasant afternoon he had planned.

Everyone has a weakness for his first love, he consoled himself, and certainly the statement was at least partly true. But it was he who had broken his lover's heart. Chloe, bewildered when the affair ended, had pleaded with him not to go. She'd thought the intoxication was as real for him as it was for her, but that was all before the world outside broke through, before that intrusion methodically shattered their fragile bond.

He knew perfectly well why everything had unraveled.

We didn't have anything in common, Phillip murmured under his breath. *We came from such different worlds, and we were so young.*

He'd started college with the vague notion of majoring in English when the idea of becoming a journalist hadn't even occurred to him yet. Chloe lived near campus with her sister and dreamt of becoming a model someday. The different worlds they came from meant they hadn't been able to talk, really talk, about any of the things he wanted to discuss. Certainly not what he'd been learning in his classes or the books he'd read. That was what he wanted to talk about, while she was captivated by the latest gossip in her movie magazines. He'd be the first to admit that Chloe was a knock-out, a real stunner, but he wasn't particularly interested in which celebrities were seen on Hollywood Boulevard last month or with whom.

He'd known from the start she wasn't a student. He'd noticed her in the dining hall where she worked when he'd pushed his tray past her station, pausing to stare at the dazzling girl behind the counter. Lingering after dinner and hoping she would notice him, he'd been elated when she'd approached his table. The girl was so unlike anyone he'd ever known, her scent and her skin so utterly unfamiliar, and he was soon drunk on desire.

He knew, of course, that they'd never had much in common. One night that winter it had grown late and she had stayed over, the two of them nestled like spoons in his narrow dorm room bed. In the morning she accompanied him to his favorite class. Led by a charismatic professor that everyone adored, the lecture that day was on *The Odyssey*. The entire class, Phillip included, had been held spellbound, but Chloe, unfamiliar with the tale, complained she'd been bored to death. Their connection was rooted in their unmistakable sexual electricity, its smoldering fire bursting into flame whenever they were together and making it possible for a long time for him to overlook any doubts.

In the spring of his freshman year, his parents came for a visit, and he introduced them to his girl. He wasn't surprised by their lack of enthusiasm for her, but the force of their disapproval made Phillip start to question everything. His father kept insisting that he was wasting his time on someone who wasn't his equal, relentlessly pointing out the differences in their education and skin color all in one breath. He wondered which bothered his father more and began to suspect that his parents' disapproval was perhaps more than he was willing to combat. He had only recently left his childhood home, living on his own for a few short months, and never before had he rebuked his parents' advice. The prospect of going against them now left Phillip feeling exhausted, and besides, in his gut he suspected that they just might be right.

He felt himself pulling away from her, spending more time with his roommates and disappearing for long, solitary jogs around campus. The affair, begun before he had turned nineteen, was over within the year, leaving him in a gloom that lingered the remainder of the term, no matter that he'd been the one to end it. He smoked grass with his buddies and drank too much beer, somehow muddling through the term without failing his classes, and after they broke up, Phillip didn't date anyone again until the fall of his senior year, when he met Susan.

He hadn't thought much about Chloe in the years that followed. Once, he came across a book that brought her to mind, and when he'd leafed through it, he had been drawn into the tumultuous story of two lovers, one black, the other white. The book had been left by a houseguest, and he'd never had time to finish reading it, but the emotions the author had given voice to had stirred him that day and made him feel nostalgic for his first love.

The intimacy he'd witnessed in broad daylight on Main Street reminded him of the loneliness he felt in the deepest part of his being, and Phillip wondered with despair if that kind of love would ever visit him again.

When he reached the library, he greeted the friendly librarian, bypassing the cluster of small children sprawled on beanbag chairs waiting for *Story Time* to begin, and he headed for the fiction section, locating an entire shelf of books by James Baldwin. Recalling the title of the story that had moved him so long ago, Phillip reached for a dog-eared copy of *Another Country* and settled into an empty armchair in the reading room, allowing himself to be transported to another place and time.

CHAPTER EIGHT

October 2003

BRADY

"Looks like it might rain." Brady fished an umbrella from the hall closet and held another out to Shane. "I'll be out for a while. You got any plans today?"

Sipping his coffee, Shane grunted. "Pickup basketball game, and maybe a jog around the park. Haven't had much time to exercise since I started working."

"How's things going with the vet?"

"It's great, Dad," his son replied with a wide grin. "Been saving my paychecks. I'll be out of your hair in a place of my own real soon."

"No hurry, buddy, take your time." Brady glanced at his watch. "Got to go. See you later."

As often as they could manage it, he and a couple of other investigators met for breakfast on Sunday mornings at Blanche's Diner down on Mission Street. Each a well-seasoned professional with a rolodex full of contacts they traded back and forth, the

PIs liked to share particulars about cases they were working on, hoping one or the other might come up with something they hadn't yet thought of. The casual Sunday morning breakfasts had proven invaluable over the years, and Brady was looking forward to catching up with his buddies.

Arriving at Blanche's a few minutes early, he opted for their usual booth facing the street where through the front window he could watch gusts of wind sweep up the autumn leaves that peppered the colorful heart of the Mission District.

"Hello again," smiled the waitress who always seemed to be there.

The slender young woman wearing a flowered apron bounced on her clean white sneakers and with practiced efficiency set three menus on the table. "Do you want to wait for your friends?"

"You got it, Cheryl," he nodded, pleased she knew his routine.

"How about a glass of orange juice while you wait?"

"Sure, sounds great."

Brady set the menu aside and glanced around the still blissfully quiet diner. The deep red vinyl booths that bordered the one he had chosen were mostly empty at this hour, and the bar stools alongside the counter remained unclaimed. Outside the window, an ATM machine across the street reminded him of the conversation he'd had that morning when one of his daughters had called from her dorm.

"You won't believe how expensive my Statistics book is, Dad. $89.95! I can sell it back at the end of the term, but right now it's wiping me out," Denise had complained. "Dad, can you help me?

I'll pay you back. I don't really have a choice, Stats is a requirement, I have to take it or else I can't graduate."

"No problem, sweetheart," he'd assured his second youngest. "I'll put $100 into your account today."

Denise was a good kid, and her father was proud of her. She'd nailed down a scholarship to help with tuition, worked part-time in the college library and was on track to graduate in June. Of all the kids, he thought Denise might turn out to be the one who'd go the farthest.

He glanced up as a noisy gang of children burst through the front door and without waiting for the hostess, claimed the circular table across the aisle from him. Dressed in formal clothes, the family looked like they'd just come from church. The harried-looking parents and their energetic brood sprawled around the large table, the kids all chattering at once. The smallest boy began twirling the round tray of condiments in the center of the table before his mother managed to restrain his pudgy fingers.

Brady let his eyes linger on the group. Unwittingly, he pursed his lips. The childrens' father helped the smallest remove their jackets as the waitress cheerfully handed out menus. Cheryl glanced over at Brady and held up a coffee pot. He shook his head, and she brought three glasses of water to his booth before retreating to the kitchen.

Stealing another glance at the noisy family, Brady reached into the back pocket of his trousers and extracted his wallet, parting the billfold to pull out a worn photo lodged behind a flap of transparent plastic. Despite his familiarity with the picture, he inspected it closely, as if he were seeing it for the first time. The photograph was one of those full color images that had been staged with studied precision, all seven subjects posed beside a Christmas tree dressed with plastic holly and surrounded by artificial snow. A younger version of himself gazed back at him, fit and confident in his crisply pressed blue policeman's uniform. Seated before him so that his hand rested loosely on her shoulder was a pretty chestnut-haired woman, reaching in vain to prevent the toddler on her lap from toppling over. He chuckled, remembering Bridget, with her thumb perpetually stuck in her mouth at that age. Another little girl, slightly older than the squirming toddler, stood at the woman's other shoulder. Cherubic-looking Denise wore a bright red sweater dotted with tiny reindeer. Brady's forefinger traced the right side of the picture where three skinny, shiny-faced boys, their hair slicked back, held themselves rigidly at attention. The two tallest stood proudly behind their mother, and the shortest, whose straw-colored curls had slipped onto his forehead, clung to Brady's elbow wearing the oversized smile of a boy still young enough to believe in the magic of Christmas. He recalled that the holiday photo had been posed just as autumn leaves were beginning to turn and later turned into a card that would be sent to friends and loved ones far and wide. *Merry Christmas from the Bradys* the card would proclaim in a cheerful holiday greeting.

He looked up from the faded photograph in his hand. The waitress had poured juice for the sprawling family and was busily jotting down orders for waffles and scrambled eggs. The youngest child ran a Hot Wheels car back and forth around the silverware. Outside on Mission Street, a familiar Buick had pulled up at the curb. Brady slid the photo back into its usual resting place in his billfold and reached into a flap in back to pull out a tiny dog-eared black and white snapshot, a school picture of the youngest of the boys in the Christmas photo, the one with the oversized smile. Again, an untamed lock of hair had fallen onto the boy's forehead, and on the back, the smudged words, *Brendan, age 8,* had been written in his own hand.

Brady touched the boy's forehead softly before tucking the picture away, raising his head as his colleagues appeared in the doorway. He slid out of the booth and stood to greet them, slipping the billfold back into the pocket of his trousers.

"Hey, what's happening, Tony? How's it going?" His buddies shook his hand and settled into the seat that faced him.

The waitress poured steaming hot coffee for all three and asked if they were ready to order.

"I'll have the deluxe pancake special," Brady told her. "Today's on me, guys," he insisted.

"Thanks, Tony. What's up?" Charlie, the older of the two friends, inquired. "You working on a new case?"

"Fill us in," the other prompted.

"Yeah, the case I'm working on is a bit unusual, I'm starting to think. My client's name is Roger Lynch. He's an Army officer, retired from the Pentagon." Brady flipped through his notes. "This was, let's see, just over a couple of weeks ago. The guy lives on the East Coast, but he has a son out here who disappeared. He and his wife flew out immediately and we've been talking nearly every day since. This fellow Lynch is a take-charge kind of guy. Not inclined to leave things to local police," he explained. "Doesn't have a very high opinion of the cops."

"Wait, the missing person is his son? We talking about a juvenile here?" Fit and trim from hours at the gym and handsome with a healthy glow on his lean cheeks, Joe was younger than his colleagues by more than a decade. He pushed the sugar bowl and creamer aside with practiced restraint.

"No, he's 36 years old. A family man, with a wife and two kids."

Joe and Charlie exchanged a look. "Hold on, so it's the guy's *adult* son who disappeared? Disappeared how?"

"Yep, that's right. The missing guy is a reporter from a local television station. Name's Phillip Lynch. Maybe you've even seen him on the air? So right away I put the word out that we're seeking information on the disappearance. We put out bulletins and public service announcements. Actually, the TV station made the PSAs and the flyers." Brady produced a sample and laid it on the table facing his friends. "His coworkers at the station posted over a hundred of these flyers all over the county."

"Looks pretty good." Joe peered closely at the description. "Any response yet?"

Brady shrugged his shoulders. "At first, a lot of calls came into the police hotline reporting sightings, but you know how that goes. Most were useless, a few were actually good leads. Police located his abandoned vehicle in a Walmart parking lot down in Lancaster. The guy's prints were all over the car, and his family's were, too, but no one else's. But after that, everything sort of came to a screeching halt."

Charlie reached for the sugar bowl, pulled out three packets and shook them. With a sigh, he returned one to the bowl. "Wife says I'm too fat," he grumbled. He peered into his cup as the granules dissolved in the hot liquid. "Came to a halt how?"

"See, turns out he didn't take his wallet or credit cards when he disappeared, so that's a dead end. And his cell phone was left at the office. His boss let me take a look at it, and I'm tracing all his recent contacts."

When he looked up, Brady saw that his friends' faces were riddled with doubt.

"Wait up, he left his wallet and his cell phone behind?" Charlie had raised his eyebrows. "This is starting to sound suspicious, Tony."

"You think so?" he cocked his head. "I'm not sure."

"Come on, don't you get it?" Joe chortled.

"Sounds like he might have planned his own getaway, don't you think?" Charlie asked.

"Possibly," Brady admitted. "I know it sounds like it. Maybe, but look, the way I see it, Roger Lynch hired me to find his missing son. Whether the guy left on his own or was kidnapped, either way, my job is to locate him, isn't it? I mean, after all, that's what we're hired to do, right? Investigate what happened, and take that information back to the client." He leaned forward, repeating, "No matter what, it's my job to find out what happened."

Brady tried not to notice the hint of a smirk that had appeared on Joe's face as his friend interrupted. "Woah there, cowboy. Maybe so, but think about it. If the guy left of his own free will, what happens if you find him? What do you do then? Tell him to go home?" The younger PI shook his head with irritation. "We're investigators, Tony, not the morality police!"

"Joe's right," Charlie cut in, his quiet voice thoughtful. "We don't have that kind of authority, and even if we did, guys like us have to be careful. I mean, say the fellow had his reasons for wanting to take off. You can't tell a grown man to go home. I mean, really Tony, you're not his priest. Wouldn't that be, I don't know, a little like playing God?"

"Assuming he hasn't broken any laws, that is." Joe waved his finger in Brady's face. "Let's just say what he's done may be morally questionable, but legally he may not have violated the law. We're investigators, yes, but who are we to pass judgment on another man's decisions?"

"That's right, Tony," Charlie added. "The guy has the freedom of choice. Doesn't everyone have the right to call his own shots and live his own life however he wants?"

A nagging uneasiness in his gut made Brady pause long enough to consider. The situation he found himself in was muddy and without a clear-cut answer, and he knew it was a tricky one. Since the moment he'd been hired, he'd been wrestling with the problem, going back and forth and arguing with himself. Just recently he'd concluded that since Roger was his client, a client who incidentally paid him very good money, his professional duty was to follow through and perform the job he had been hired to do, and that job was to investigate the missing man's disappearance.

"Look," he countered with sudden intensity. "I hear what you're saying, and I'm not about to pass judgment on the guy's behavior, but I think his family deserves to know what happened." He leaned forward, his voice suddenly husky. "They deserve to know, because not knowing will drive them crazy." Brady's gaze travelled slowly from one colleague's eyes to the other's. "Listen, I feel strongly about this, because believe me, guys, I know what it is to live with the uncertainty of not knowing. I know what it feels like not to have any idea what happened when someone you love simply vanishes into thin air," he snapped his fingers, "just like that."

Charlie nodded solemnly, and Joe looked away.

"And I'm telling you," Brady went on with a heavy sadness, "you never get over it. In some ways, not knowing what happened might even be worse than whatever bad news you could possibly get."

Heaping platters of omelets and pancakes appeared at their table, and the men dug into their breakfasts. They were glad for the interruption, and Brady felt his spirits lift as he listened quietly to stories about cases his friends had solved. Dousing his hotcakes in thick maple syrup, he reminded himself that a successful resolution was always a possibility.

Sipping their coffee, their bellies full, his colleagues circled back cautiously to their earlier conversation.

"So, the police doing anything?"

"Not much. You know what they always say, *limited resources,*" he grimaced, drawing a pair of quotation marks in the air with his fingers.

His buddies grunted. "Who doesn't have limited resources?"

"Yeah, and how about *our* limited resources?"

"I know, but the cops don't want to look for people they think might be missing on purpose. Look, that's what you guys thought right off the bat, too. And the cops are always ready to give up so fast. They didn't even check out hospitals near where the car was found." Brady made no attempt to hide his disgust. "They tell me they're working on it, but I don't think they've done much since the trail went cold in that Walmart parking lot. Believe me, I know how quickly the cops pack it in, I used to be part of that squad. What is it the kids all say, *been there, done that?*"

They pushed their plates away, and Brady motioned to the waitress to bring him the check.

"Anyone down in SoCal we can get to help out?" Joe wondered out loud.

"I already called a couple of guys I know down there, and they're asking around Lancaster. Basically, the fellow just vanished one day on the way to work. It's a story we get all the time. You know it as well as I do."

"Ain't that the truth?" Charlie grumbled.

"The thing is, I don't really have a good sense of who this guy is," Brady mused. "If what you say is true and he disappeared on his own steam, there has to be a reason."

He turned to look out the diner window. Happy couples strolled arm in arm on Mission Street, and kids on skateboards crowded the sidewalk. He tried to imagine how a man could just walk away from a wife and two kids. Unless there was a very good reason, he simply couldn't make sense of it.

"Seems like the guy had a pretty ordinary life. Nice family, good job. House in the suburbs. Why would he walk away from all that on purpose?" The question hung in the air. "I don't know, fellows. It's pretty hard to understand. I feel like I need to find out more about the guy. Get into his head, try to think like he thinks."

The waitress slid their check onto the table with a smile. "Whenever you're ready, gentlemen. No rush."

"Thanks, Cheryl," he said as he reached for his wallet. "I've got to figure out what he was running towards or running away from."

"Could be something was festering in the guy, something you don't know about," Charlie suggested.

"Maybe there were secrets he was carrying around with him," Joe chimed in. "Who knows?"

"Yeah, maybe. And there's always somebody out there who knows something. We just have to get the word out 'til someone steps forward," Brady reasoned. "One more thing. The guys in SoCal said there's some new computer stuff to try, like forensic databases. Said those databases are all the rage now."

Phillip's handsome face smiled back at them from the fresh set of posters he handed each of his colleagues. "Here's a stack of flyers for you guys, if you don't mind spreading the word."

*Anyone with information regarding the disappearance of Phillip Lynch
is urged to contact Private Investigators at (415) 242-4321.*

*36-year-old Caucasian Male
Height 5'10" and Weight between 165 and 175 pounds
Wavy brown hair and Blue eyes*

*Last seen on September 16, 2003, in San Mateo County,
wearing a black North Face jacket over a light blue shirt,
tailored gray slacks and black shoes*

*A $50,000 reward is offered for any information
leading to the discovery of Phillip Lynch's whereabouts.
Call (415) 242-4321*

"For sure, Tony," Charlie responded. "Let's hope you find the guy."

"Yeah, and when you do, that it's not too late to matter," Joe added.

Brady followed them out to the street where the aroma of freshly made churros drifted into their nostrils. Leaving the diner, he paused briefly at the table where the five chattering kids and their parents had long since finished their breakfast, and where the busboy was busy setting out clean plates and silverware. He shook hands with his buddies and turned toward the Muni stop to catch his bus ride home.

I know I can find the guy, he thought to himself. *That's not the problem. The thing is, if what everyone says is true, and he wasn't kidnapped and there's no foul play, what made him take off? What was it Phillip Lynch was running away from?*

CHAPTER NINE

October 2003

STEVE PHILLIPS

As the first month slipped by, Phillip found he slept surprisingly soundly, sometimes nine or ten hours a night, and there was an easy rhythm to his days. He was optimistic that his family was probably managing just fine, too. He knew there was enough money in the bank to cover the bills, and though he imagined things might have been strange at first, he had a sense that Susan and the kids were probably okay. All he was really worried about now was what he was going to do when the shelter's six-week residency limit expired. He had to admit that the oversized bunkroom wasn't the most comfortable lodging he'd ever slept in, and if he looked carefully in the nooks and crannies, the place was none too clean, but the price was right. The staff hadn't mentioned it yet, but in the back of his mind, he knew the deadline was closing in on him, and he'd become someone who chafed at deadlines of any sort. At work he'd had to contend with plenty of looming deadlines, and he bristled now at everything they represented.

At the shelter, most of the men came and went after a handful of nights, and he had maintained his distance. The tattooed fellow Phillip had met at the bus stop that first day kept to himself, bunking down on the other side of the room. They'd crossed paths at the sink in the communal washroom once or twice while brushing their teeth and they'd nodded respectfully to each other.

"Hey, I bet you're the youngest guy in here," remarked Phillip one morning as he trimmed the gray hairs emerging from his new beard. He gestured toward the oversized dormitory. "Seriously, some of these guys are geezers, right?" *Maybe he's just between jobs and a little down on his luck*, he found himself thinking.

Although the fellow's dirty hair could have benefited from some styling, the lanky six-footer took pains to keep his baby face clean-shaven every day. He scrutinized Phillip in the steamy mirror. "Don't kid yourself, I ain't that young," he mumbled in reply. "Thirty on my next birthday. Getting older every day."

"No way! You sure don't look it, man. You look a whole lot younger than thirty. Me, I always looked older than I was." He extended his hand. "Name's Steve. Steve Phillips."

"Bobby," the younger man muttered, packing up his shaving gear. "Anyway, I ain't gonna be here much longer. Friday's it for me. I'm heading out."

Phillip's eyes sought Bobby's in the mirror. "Yeah? No kidding?"

"Tell you the truth, I'll be happy to get a good night's sleep again. Man, it's a drag listening to all these guys snoring and coughing and whatnot all night long." Bobby spit into the sink and made a face. "And the smell. Drives me crazy some nights." He turned toward the door.

"Yeah, no kidding, the smell." Phillip wrinkled his nose. "You got that right. Kind of a mix of B.O. and Pine Sol. Not the best perfume, right?" Casually following behind the younger man, he slipped into his inflection. "So, where you headed next?"

Bobby glanced over his shoulder as if to check that they were alone. "I got plans. Oh yeah, I got some plans alright."

Phillip leaned in close. "Listen," he confided, "I'm dying to get out of here myself." Assuming his most conspiratorial face, he let his gaze wander around the washroom. "So check this out, man, I got an idea." He lowered his voice. "You seen those guys hanging around outside the Home Depot, right?"

Stone-faced, Bobby nodded. "Maybe. So what?"

"Well, last week I made fifty bucks hanging with those guys."

The young man's eyes widened with a flicker of interest, and Phillip paused to let the money sink in.

"Fifty bucks, I'm talking cash money," he repeated for effect. "I'm talking money burning a hole in my pocket, right about now!"

Bobby paused in the doorway and eyed him with suspicion. "Fifty bucks cash? What'd you have to do for it?" he asked warily.

"Load a truckload of firewood and haul it across town and then stack it all up neatly in some guy's driveway. That sucker's got enough firewood to last a couple of winters now. Real work, man, and none of us guys had any gloves." Phillip opened his fists to reveal the raw blisters on his palms. "I'm telling you, my hands took a beating, but it was worth it."

Bobby peered at the blisters and backed away, shaking his head. "No way, man. I don't work like that. That's not how I roll. I got another plan. A way better one."

"Oh, for sure," Phillip countered quickly, trailing behind as Bobby stepped back into the dormitory. "I don't ever want to do it again either. But listen, man, I got the cash now, so when the bus drops us off today, how about this idea?" He saw Bobby hesitate and hurriedly continued. "Look, when we get into town, I'll buy you breakfast. We get a nice hot meal, my treat, and maybe you tell me your plan and help me figure out how I can get out of here, too."

Furtively, he patted the front of his jeans where a thick roll of bills had settled into a fat lump and waited as Bobby eyed the bulging pocket. "What do you have to lose?"

"Nothing to lose, I guess. Been a while since anyone bought me breakfast. But listen, man, I'm not promising anything. I mean, look, I don't even know you."

The van the men had come to rely on every day was waiting for them out front and soon ferried the residents downtown, dropping them off just across the street from Ann's Coffee Shop. They slid into a booth in the back, facing each other, almost as if they indulged in hot meals served by perky waitresses wearing cheerful aprons every morning of their lives. Bobby pointed to a picture on the wall featuring a steaming mug of hot chocolate topped with real whipped cream next to a stack of hotcakes and a glass of orange juice, and Phillip asked for a large coffee and a couple of sugar doughnuts. The coffee was dark and hot, and with studied casualness as he dunked a donut into it, he asked the younger fellow about his plans.

In a roundabout story recounted in bits and pieces, Bobby confided that he had stumbled on yet another rent-free home that promised to be an even better arrangement than the shelter. He said he had an aunt who ran a small motel just outside town, and the night clerk there had unexpectedly quit. In exchange for a room in the back of the motel, his aunt had offered him a job.

"Night clerk," Phillip repeated, his mouth full of sugar crumbs. "What's a night clerk do, exactly?"

"Far as I can figure, not much. Man the front desk 'til seven in the morning. Make sure folks coming in late don't get locked out, I guess."

"Sounds like a piece of cake. Easy peasy."

A river of syrup pooled on Bobby's pancakes, already slathered in melted butter. "Yeah, but see I been thinking. Staying awake all night's no prob with a couple of Red Bulls. I'm ok with that. But working every day?" He stabbed the stack of hotcakes with his fork and waved it for emphasis before taking a bite. "Might be more trouble than it's worth," he mumbled with his mouth full of buckwheat.

Phillip quickly seized the opportunity he recognized as it unfolded in front of him. "I hear you," he agreed, "even for a free place to stay."

"Yeah, see, that's what I been thinking. I don't know about tying myself down like that." Bobby wiped his mouth and left a trace of whip cream on the sleeve of his sweatshirt. "Man, that just seems like a bad idea, don't it?"

Phillip was getting the distinct impression that working was something the guy had only done when he had to, and when he came up with an appealing alternative, Bobby took the bait. Persuasive and yet purposely casual with the words he chose, he inched his proposal forward bit by bit. By the time the waitress brought them their check, he had Bobby believing it had been entirely his own idea that they split the nights on duty between them and bunk down together in the motel's free guest room.

"Anything else, gentlemen?" the waitress asked, snapping her gum.

Phillip asked for the check, wondering if she even noticed what an odd couple the pair made. Listening with only half an ear by then, he reflected that he and Bobby knew practically nothing about each other. Neither had divulged how they had come to be living at the shelter, where they'd come from or where they hoped to go. Neither had shared whatever fears may have haunted them or what wounds they may have carried on the inside. Without ever revealing anything intimate or important, they'd effortlessly slipped into a casual chumminess, speculating on the upcoming Forty-Niners' game and the star quarterback's health. They devoured every bite of their breakfast, and eventually the conversation drifted to plans to move out of the shelter. Phillip tried not to appear too eager, despite the fact that inwardly every fiber of his being was pulsing with excitement. He thought the plan was near-perfect, one that far exceeded his expectations, and watching his future roommate mop up a trail of pancake syrup with a dirty finger, Phillip marveled at his good fortune.

It sure helps to have a little luck in life, he mused, concealing a silent chuckle behind a paper napkin.

A chance encounter with a Walmart security guard had landed him at a free shelter and a place to rest his head for six weeks, and he had just lucked into a free motel room in exchange for an astonishingly easy job that Bobby insisted did not require any identification or put him on anyone's payroll. Phillip knew enough to appreciate that as much as anything, luck really matters, and sometimes it matters more than anything else. He licked the sugar crumbs from his fingers and nodded as Bobby droned on about the amazing features of a Harley Davidson he once had owned, reflecting that unexpected strokes of fortune make all the difference in whether what's yet to come is a limitless horizon of hope or a future rife with despair.

He dug into his pocket for a roll of bills and left a generous tip for the cheerful waitress. Feeling as though he were walking on air, he gallantly held the door open for his new partner, and they headed out of the coffee shop into the bright fall day.

"So, tell me, Bobby," he asked with calculated coolness, "where exactly is this motel, anyway?"

CHAPTER TEN

October 2003

BRADY

Roger Lynch paced back and forth on the worn carpet in front of the living room window, his gaze fixed on a neighbor raking scattered red and brown leaves into a pile.

"Alice and I have been here for a while now, and frankly, we're more confused than when we arrived. It's like we're in a nightmare. We haven't got the foggiest idea what might have happened to Phillip. If he was abducted or mugged or whatever, why haven't the authorities come up with any ideas by now?"

From his perch on the sofa, Brady piped up softly, "The police have suggested pretty strongly that they don't believe there was foul play."

"Yeah, well, I'm just dumbfounded by that," Roger snapped, turning to face him. "The cops don't know who they're dealing with. Phillip just isn't the kind of guy they're implying. My son has always, always done the right thing," he insisted with barely disguised annoyance. "That's how he was brought up."

"Let's be patient a little longer, Roger. The reward notice has just started to bring in some tips." Brady wasn't sure whether he was trying to convince his client or himself. "Someone has to have seen something. A guy doesn't just disappear."

"That's what I think, too," Phillip's father agreed. "Someone's more likely to come forward if there's money involved. That's why I put up so much. But I'm telling you, the cops never have a clue when it comes to missing persons. They say they're working on it, but look at how slow they were to organize a search in the first place."

When Roger had offered to put up the reward money, Susan confessed to Brady she knew she should be grateful for her in-laws' help, even if the house was reeling in chaos since they'd taken over. She wasn't exactly sure how much money was in the bank, and he had the distinct impression that Phillip had handled the family finances.

Gracie drifted into the living room, clutching a small pink notebook with a metal latch she had snapped shut. She knelt in front of the sofa where Brady's legs were crossed at the ankle and set a Smurf pencil box down on the glass coffee table. He leaned over to give the top of her small blonde head a friendly pat, wondering what was going through the little girl's mind.

"Hello, Honey, what have you got there?"

He saw a flash of silver braces as she parted her small pink mouth.

Her chin quivered. "My Daddy's not home," she pouted.

Her glasses had slipped down the bridge of her nose, and with a dirty finger, she pushed the pink plastic frames back up. As she opened her diary, he saw that her fingernails had been chewed down to the quick. Peering over her shoulder, he read what was in the little girl's tender heart.

"Maybe I shouldn't have asked Daddy to build me a dollhouse like Jenny's Daddy did. Maybe it made him mad so he went away. I didn't really need a dollhouse. I could have just played with Jennys. It's all my fault," Gracie had written.

Bearing down with such force that the point on her pencil had snapped, Gracie pulled another from her pencil box and looked up at her grandfather in front of the window. She set the pencil down and went to him, slipping her small hand into his.

"Grandpa, when Daddy comes back, I'll be good. I won't bother him when he's reading the paper. And I'll be good at school. I promise. You'll see."

"Of course you will." Roger squeezed the child's fingers absently and sighed.

Her nose began to run. "I want my Daddy to come home," she whimpered tearfully.

"We all do, Honey." Brady reached into his pocket for a handkerchief and held it out to her.

She looked at it blankly and wiped her nose with the sleeve of her jersey.

"What smells so good?" She turned her head toward the kitchen. "Is Grandma making cookies?"

"Could very well be," her grandfather replied, beginning to pace again. "If you ask nicely, she might let you have one."

Brady heaved himself up from the sofa. "Come on, let's you and me go see. I could use a snack!"

In the kitchen, Susan and Alice stood at the counter in silence sharing a pot of tea. Alice poured a glass of milk for her grand-daughter, and with a smile, pointed at a tray of chocolate chip cookies fresh from the oven.

"For me?" Gracie asked. She burrowed under her mother's arm and clung to Susan's side, wrapping herself around her waist.

Alice's worried eyes search her daughter-in-law's face. Their mutual exhaustion was palpable. "If you wash your hands first, you can try one," she offered, arranging a small dish. Despair hung in the warm kitchen air, as pungent as the comforting aroma of the freshly baked cookies. "I'll just take a few of these up to Andrew's room and find out how he's coming on his homework," Alice murmured as she slipped out of the room.

Brady tried to adopt a cheerful tone of voice. "Mmm, those smell wonderful," he continued, following close behind her on the stairs. "Okay if I tag along?"

They found the teenage boy on the floor of his bedroom, positioning items with care on a large trifold piece of cardboard. An orange and black sports bag hung on the back of a chair. Alice set the dish of cookies next to a baseball mitt on the dresser and asked what Andrew was working on.

"It's my Science Fair project," he told them. "It's due tomorrow. Mr. Davidson said I could have 'til Friday, but it's not fair if I get more time than everyone else."

"Good for you." His grandmother leaned over and pushed a lock of curly blonde hair out of his eyes.

Brady peered over the boy's shoulder. "What's your project about?"

"It's about memory, how some people remember things better than other people, and why that is. I wanted to see if it's easier to remember stuff with music on or when it's quiet and there's nothing to distract you," Andrew explained. "Mom always tells me I should turn the music off when I do my homework, but honestly, music helps me study." He pointed to the center of the poster at big block letters. "That's what my hypothesis states."

Brady nodded as he read. "So, how did you go about testing your hypothesis?"

Andrew stood and reached for a cookie. "First, I organized two groups, an A and a B, and I showed them a tray of objects. You know, like a flashlight, and a toothbrush, ordinary everyday stuff. The A group had to memorize the tray while I played loud music, and the B group had silence. Both groups had the same amount of time to memorize the tray, and then they had to write down every single object they could think of." He showed them a stopwatch. "I used this to time them."

"What an original idea," Alice beamed, clearly proud of her grandson. "That's just fascinating, Andrew." The laugh lines in the corners of her soft blue eyes crinkled, and Brady could even see hints of dimples in her cheeks.

She's a pretty woman, he thought to himself.

"So, what were your results?" he asked.

"I was surprised. I thought having music on might be a distraction, you know like Mom said, but actually that group remembered more stuff than the other one. The results came out completely the opposite of my hypothesis. Turns out studying with music on is a great idea!" Andrew laughed with satisfaction. "Mom was 100% wrong."

"Yes, and you really learned something!" Alice had to stand on tiptoe as she hugged him. "You did a good job, Andrew. Maybe you'll be a scientist one day!"

He shrugged. "Lots of other kids are doing experiments with electricity and magnets and things like that. One kid is doing something kind of cool with plants and sunlight. I didn't want my project to be about chemistry or physics, I'm not really into that stuff. Mine's about how people's brains work. My teacher says that's called *Behavioral Science*, and we need to study that, too."

"I think it's a very good project, Sweetheart, and very scientific." She planted a kiss on her grandson's cheek. "Think you can take a break soon? We're all going to Fresh Choice for dinner."

He shook his head and knelt on the floor to continue working on the poster. "I better not, I gotta finish this. Maybe bring me back a couple slices of pizza."

"Mind if I hang around and keep you company?"

Brady pushed a damp towel out of the way and sat down on the boy's unmade bed.

"No problem." Andrew lay down a strip of Elmer's glue and carefully began to attach a colorful pie chart to the display.

Brady scanned the room, taking in the Giants pennant mounted over the bed and the row of trophies decorating a shelf.

"Are you a baseball player?"

"Yep, third base. You a fan?"

"Giants fan, you bet I am," Brady grinned. "What a season, right?"

"Baseball's such a great game. I love it." The boy looked up briefly from the poster. "Dad comes to all my games. He told me about this one time when he was a kid, he was in Little League, and he caught a really deep fly ball in centerfield and pretty much saved his team from last place in their division."

"No kidding," Brady chuckled. "I played Little League, too. But nothing like that ever happened to me."

Andrew turned back to the board and set two photographs side by side.

"I couldn't believe I made JV. I'm not really that good, lots of guys are way better, but Dad told me he wasn't very good at my age either."

Brady sensed an opening and pressed forward.

"How are you holding up with your dad not being around?"

"I don't know." The boy kept his eyes glued to the photographs. "Nothing makes sense, Mr. Brady. Whenever Dad went on a business trip, he always made it back in time for a game. He's missed two games already."

"Is that so?"

"Yeah, and Mom cries all the time." He frowned, as if trying to remember something. "I don't think we ever saw Mom cry before. Gracie, too. They both cry." His shoulders dropped as he turned to look at Brady. "To tell you the truth, everything's kind of a mess."

"What do you think might have happened?" the investigator asked quietly.

When Andrew hesitated, Brady suspected that nameless fears had taken up residency in the back of his mind. The boy lowered his voice until it was nearly a whisper.

"At first, I thought something happened to him, like maybe he got mugged or something. Maybe he's lying in a ditch somewhere, unable to move or speak. Or he could have had a heart attack on the way to work. Or what if he got kidnapped or something." Apprehension spilled out of him in a rising panic. "But lately I've been thinking. Maybe Dad had a whole other family, you know, hidden away somewhere. Maybe he was living a double life, you know, like in the movies?" He looked up to see if Brady thought the idea was crazy.

"Does that sound like something your dad would do?"

Andrew shrugged. "I guess not. Grandma says not to let my imagination run wild."

He leaned the trifold board against the bedroom wall and stepped back to examine it. His voice caught. "Sometimes I feel like I'm going nuts not knowing where he is or what happened."

Brady rose from the unmade bed and came closer to admire the display. "Hey, looks really great, doesn't it?" He threw an arm around the boy's shoulders. "Listen, they'll be at Fresh Choice for a while. How about we step out on the driveway and shoot a few hoops?"

Breaking into a grin with what looked to Brady like relief, Andrew bent down and reached for the basketball tucked under his desk. "Been a while." He bounced the ball twice with pent-up youthful energy. "Dad and I like to play Horse. You know how to play?"

"Sure, I do. Played it all the time with my boys. Let's go!"

The sun had already started to go down. *Better hurry*, thought Brady, following Andrew down the stairs. *Soon it'll be too dark to even see the ball.*

PART II

AFTERMATH

CHAPTER ELEVEN

Late Fall 2003

BRADY

Brady fished a box of lasagna out of the freezer, squinting at the small print on the container before he slid his rock-hard dinner into the microwave. His stomach growled, and he grabbed a handful of peanuts and popped the tab on a can of cold beer. Standing in front of the fridge, he took a couple of long pulls from his beer. A familiar photo peeped out at him from under a refrigerator magnet, and he smiled at the wrinkled face of his first grandchild, courtesy of Anthony, wearing the surprised expression of a new arrival in an overly busy world.

A blinking light on the answering machine announced the calls he'd missed. Brady set his drink down and reached for his notepad. A message from Shane saying he was on his way to check out a rental on Craigslist, another from Rite-Aid about a prescription that was ready, and a short message from the precinct. He gulped down another swallow and dialed Salcedo's number.

"Anthony Brady returning your call, Detective. You tried to reach me?"

"That's right. About the Lynch case. The lieutenant wanted me to bring you up to date."

Brady heard a rustling sound as Salcedo rifled through papers.

"One of my guys has been digging into his contacts, and a couple of interesting things popped up."

"That right?"

"You remember the guy who works next to him in the office, name of Sam Morgan? Well, we went ahead and administered a polygraph to the guy."

Brady wasn't surprised. "Morgan may well have been the last person to have seen our man."

"Exactly, that's why we did it, but we didn't get much. Hang on a sec, would you?"

He heard a muffled conversation on the other end of the line. "We asked Morgan if Lynch was maybe having an affair. You know, extramarital stuff. He acted like he was shocked, so if the guy was playing around on the side, Morgan sure didn't know about it. We don't think he's hiding anything."

Brady thanked the detective for keeping him in the loop. "Anything else turn up meanwhile?"

"Could be. The boss pulled Lynch's personnel file for us. Seems like a few years ago, he used their company insurance for what looks like some kind of counseling services. It's hard to say what it was exactly, but maybe the guy was seeing a shrink or something."

"Oh, well, seeing a therapist, that's nothing too unusual," Brady shrugged. "Happens to the best of us. Marriage isn't always a bed of roses. Maybe he and his wife were working through something." He tipped the can up and drained what was left of his beer.

"Lord knows that's true, and you're right, might not mean a thing, but could be something we ought to look into. Maybe Lynch was depressed. Unstable, like. Who knows where his head was at?"

"Sure, but no therapist is going to tell us a damn thing. That's doctor-patient privileged information."

"Fine," Salcedo acknowledged, "but there's got to be some way we can find out what was going on between him and his wife."

"You thinking you want to polygraph the wife?" Brady wasn't sure how Susan would react to the suggestion, and he wouldn't have recommended the idea. The last time he'd seen her, Susan's spirits had been pretty low.

But Salcedo didn't want to polygraph her, at least not just yet, and explained that he had a better idea. "Seems like the wife is pretty comfortable talking to you, Tony. What if you pay her a visit and say something like, you know, we're all doing everything we can to find her husband, tell her you know how hard this must be for her and the kids, that kind of thing." The detective appeared to be picking up steam as he continued in a conspiratorial tone. "I'm telling you, a little sympathy goes a long way toward getting people to open up. Give them a shoulder to cry on, and out come their deepest secrets."

"I don't know," Brady replied without enthusiasm. "I guess I could give it a try."

"Truth is, I don't have too many other bright ideas right now," Salcedo confessed. "That was a pretty sizeable reward the family put up, and I thought it might do the trick, but so far none of the leads have turned out to be useful."

Brady snapped his notepad shut and jumped up to rescue his dinner. "I appreciate your keeping me informed, Carlos. Thanks for the call. I'm sure we're bound to be more successful if we keep working together."

He peeled back a corner of the cellophane as a whiff of pungent steam escaped. The real difference between the police and himself, he thought as he sprinkled stale parmesan flakes onto his dinner, was not their diligence chasing down every possible lead. The detective had done decent work, but how long would his supervisors be willing to commit department resources to the mission? Brady was familiar with police protocol and knew it was only a matter of time until Salcedo would be given another assignment and his focus redirected elsewhere. First-hand experience had taught him that even in the most careful police-led effort, eventually the case would be allowed to grow cold. He'd learned that painful lesson when after nearly two decades as a beat cop, he'd become a detective himself. He'd worked missing persons for three years, years spent jockeying for resources, keeping cases alive by sheer will. Eventually, frustrated by his squad's dismal success record, Brady had accepted the department's standard retirement package and opted out altogether. He'd had enough.

That had been thirteen years ago, when so much of his life was already in total upheaval. His marriage unraveling, the kids with their daily dramas, all of it had driven him to make a change.

Pulling himself together, he'd bought a book and studied for the state test, earning his PI license in record time. He was eager to hang out a shingle and advertise his services, but on a shoestring budget, he'd quickly had to pivot. Attorneys were offering top dollar for surveillance on the cheating spouses of wealthy clients, and divorce cases soon became his bread and butter. The work left an unpleasant taste in his mouth, but he told himself he had to start somewhere. With a lot of effort and a little luck, business picked up and his caseload doubled, then tripled. When at last he transitioned back to investigating missing persons, he was quickly able to build a solid professional reputation, and a bevy of satisfied clients was all the advertising he'd needed.

It turned out that Private Investigator Brady was very good at finding people who had gone missing. The knowledge that no supervisor could assign him elsewhere or redirect his attention made all the difference, and his dogged perseverance paid off. After thirteen years as a PI, he could boast a nearly unblemished record, although he'd be the first to admit that the missing people he did find were not always still alive. Wondering if the Phillip Lynch case was going to be like one of those, Brady began to review his current options.

Uneaten traces of cheesy lasagna clung to his dinner plate, but he couldn't manage another bite. He rummaged in the cupboards for a plastic container and ladled tomorrow's lunch into it. Squirting a stream of dish soap onto a sponge, he considered what he'd learned so far. He'd visited the TV station and retrieved the mobile phone that Lynch had left behind. For several hours, he'd been kept busy reaching out to people the reporter had recently contacted. It had been almost too easy to chart his activities, and everything had seemed to be above board. Brady did not find a single unexplained event leading up to the moment when the missing man's frantic wife had notified law enforcement, but something he couldn't pinpoint nagged at him.

Something about it simply didn't add up.

Who is this fellow? he asked himself. *Seems like such a regular guy. What am I missing? Do I go with Salcedo's idea and get chummy with the wife?* Brady wondered who besides his wife really knew him well and decided to put in a call to the man's parents. Thinking that Susan would be out of the house and picking up the kids just before school let out, he suggested a meeting for the following afternoon.

Alice met him at the front door at 2:30 sharp, her hair a brighter shade of auburn than he remembered. He guessed she'd been to the beauty parlor and offered his compliments.

She smiled graciously, inviting him in. "We're just having a bite to eat in the kitchen."

Brady sipped the freshly brewed coffee she poured for him, and they chatted briefly until at last she asked exactly why he'd wanted to talk.

"I'm hoping you and Roger would tell me what your son was like growing up," he began, his voice warm and friendly. "I'd like to know more about him."

The visit to the salon seemed to have buoyed Alice's spirits, and the light that swept her face seemed genuine. "Oh, we're always happy to talk about Phillip! You know, he was always such a good boy. Friendly, polite, always well-behaved."

Seated beside them at the kitchen table, Roger did not look up from the stack of papers he'd been highlighting with a yellow marker. An unlit pipe dangled from the corner of his clenched lips.

How did he manage to get hold of what looks like copies of police reports? Brady asked himself, puzzled.

Alice fiddled with the belt on the faded flowered apron around her waist and continued. "He was a Boy Scout, and he liked to play baseball. Isn't that so, Roger?" She leaned forward to touch her husband's arm with gentle pressure.

He removed the pipe from his mouth without glancing up. "I guess so." Roger set the unlit pipe down in an ashtray and folded his arms over his chest as if to see where this was going.

Brady adopted a casual tone and went on. "I'm a parent myself, five kids," he grinned. "We all know, raising kids can be crazy at times, but wonderful, too, right?"

Roger gave a nearly imperceptible nod, and encouraged, Brady continued. "You have two, right? Both a son and a daughter, isn't that correct?"

"That's right," Alice chortled happily. "Two great kids. And two great grandkids, too."

Roger cleared his throat but did not reply. His eyes drifted to the pile of documents as if he were eager to get back to them.

"Tell me, how did Phillip do in school?" Brady looked from one to the other. "Some of my kids loved school, some of them not so much. Every child is unique. You can't compare them, can you? They're all so different."

Roger's delivery was clipped as he answered in a tight voice. "I'd say our two were very different."

Alice nodded in agreement. "Oh, our Phillip was very good in school, his teachers all liked him. He never got into any trouble. He was always a good boy, wasn't he, Roger?"

"Phillip behaved himself. He never got into trouble like some kids do, not at school or at home." Roger's arms were folded across his chest again, and Brady was beginning to wonder if the ex-military man ever relaxed his guard. "You see, we were always strict with both of them. They had their chores to do, they had bedtimes and rules and curfews. They weren't given too much freedom when they were teenagers. We always knew where they were going and with whom and when they'd be home." Roger cocked his head at his wife as if he weren't quite sure. "They both knew we had certain expectations, don't you think?"

Alice studied her hands, clasped neatly in her lap.

She's uncomfortable, Brady realized with surprise.

He turned his attention back to Roger. "Was Phillip rebellious about that? Did he seem to mind having strict parents?" he probed quietly. "Some kids chafe at that kind of thing."

"No, not really. We always had high standards in our home, and Phillip followed orders."

Brady scribbled *orders* onto his notepad and underlined it twice.

When he looked up, Brady saw that Roger was rubbing his chin thoughtfully. "The thing is, Phillip was always a bit of a day-dreamer. Kind of unfocused. He was never especially alert. Quite unlike his sister, I might add."

"Oh, Roger, that's not true. He was just very imaginative," his wife murmured softly. "Always jotting down little stories he'd come up with, and he just loved to read anything he got his hands on. Comic books for a while, and then when he was older, he discovered those wonderful King Arthur stories."

Brady saw a wistfulness in Alice's soft blue eyes as she recalled the little boy Phillip had been. "Remember how he loved that big *Knights of the Round Table* book someone gave him?"

"What I mostly remember," Roger bristled, "is how he played with dolls! What kind of boy plays with dolls?" he exclaimed.

His wife's face crumpled. Clearly, she had heard this before. "They weren't dolls, Roger. They're called action figures, and lots of boys collect them," she objected in a small voice.

He waved her off. "Look, Beth was only a year older, but so much more mature. She took her big sister role seriously, like he was her baby. To tell you the truth, I don't think the way she always babied him did Phillip a bit of good."

Alice made an effort to regain her cheerful spirit. She rose and crossed to the counter, returning with a small dish of oatmeal cookies. "Gracie helped me bake these last night. Would you like to try one?" She offered the dish to Brady.

He reached for it. "I'd love to." The cookies were soft and chewy, delicious.

She bit into one, too, and tried to explain. "You see, Mr. Brady, Beth was like a little mother to him. I always thought she bossed him around a little too much. When we went on vacation to Myrtle Beach, she wrote down a list of things for Phillip to bring with him, like his toothbrush."

Roger drew back in disgust. "What? I didn't know she did things like that."

"And remember our trip to Disneyworld at Easter when they were both in junior high? She packed his whole suitcase for him!" Alice's laughter tinkled through the room.

A look of distaste had settled on her husband's face. "See, when I was a boy, my sister never did anything like that for me. That's what I mean. Really, Alice, I think sometimes Phillip's head was stuck in the clouds." Roger turned to Brady. "And he was always losing things, leaving his jacket behind at the playground or forgetting to hand in his homework. He didn't always look where he was going when he was riding his bike." A distant memory suddenly flitted across his eyes, and he unfolded his arms to lean over and jab Alice in the fleshy part of her upper arm. "Remember that time he fell down the cellar steps and got hurt so badly? It was because he wasn't paying attention to what he was doing!" He shook his head in disgust.

"Oh, Roger, that's not true! He tripped over Beth's roller skates! That was just an accident," she exclaimed, eyeing him oddly. "Really, Roger, that's just not fair!"

Brady looked from one to the other as husband and wife glared at each other as if in a standoff, neither about to back down. He tried to get the conversation back on track. "What happened?" he asked.

"Beth had left her skates out, you see, and he just didn't notice them on the cellar steps," Alice explained. "I think the stairway light was off, and it was too dark to see well enough. Poor Phillip. He took a terrible fall and really hurt himself."

Roger cut in. "His wrist wasn't broken but it was bleeding like crazy, and I had to drive him to the emergency room. He got blood all over the seat and I had to have it specially cleaned. Phillip had a big gash and had to get stitches, and they made him wear a sling on his arm for the longest time." He held up his own arm to show where exactly the injury had occurred. "The gash left a big, jagged scar. A really ugly one, almost like a Z. It was on his right wrist, and he's right-handed. He had to do everything with his left. Made things damn awkward for a while."

"The poor kid, he was only six. It really wasn't his fault, Roger. It was just an accident." Alice turned to Brady, pleading. "These things happen with kids, don't they?"

Before he could reply, footsteps on the porch and the bang of the screen door interrupted their quiet conversation. Andrew bounded into the room and grabbed a carton of milk with one hand while rummaging through the fridge with the other. A variety of after school snacks began to populate the kitchen counters.

Alice rose to greet the kids, kissing the top of her granddaughter's head. "Hello there! How was school? Have a good day, you two?"

Gracie smiled from ear to ear. "I got 89 on my arithmetic test!" she announced, plunging a finger into the Nutella jar.

"That's wonderful, Honey!" She handed Gracie the soap dispenser. "Wash your hands first." She seemed grateful for the interruption and turned to her daughter-in-law. "Susan, would this be a good time to borrow the car? I thought I could pick up a few things for dinner, and Dad wants to stop at the hardware store. You all desperately need new light bulbs. We could pick up Halloween candy while we're out, too. Do you all get a lot of trick-or-treaters?"

Susan handed her the car keys and set Gracie's backpack at the foot of the stairs. Roger gathered up the papers in front of him and stuffed them into his briefcase as Alice went to get her purse. Hastily, they said goodbye to Brady as they headed out to run errands. He stood in the kitchen doorway, wondering if perhaps he should go, too. Susan wavered in indecision at the counter, a teapot in one hand and a highball glass already filled with ice in the other. Gracie began scooping up the crumbs left on the cookie dish, licking her fingers one by one. Susan pulled up a chair beside her, smoothing back her daughter's hair and refastening a dangling barrette.

"Any news on Dad?" asked Andrew, biting into a cold drumstick in front of the open fridge. "We haven't heard anything from the police." Peering over the chicken leg, his eyes were wide. "Have we, Mom?"

"No, not for a few days," she pursed her lips. "Unless Mr. Brady has some news?"

"Not yet, but I'm working on it."

Andrew wiped the grease from the corners of his mouth. "You know, I'm pretty sure I told him about my science fair project, but now I don't know if I did. Did I, Mom?" He lowered his eyes. "It's been so long, it's getting harder to remember stuff."

His mother reached over and rubbed her son's back.

Brady saw the boy stiffen in response. "Can I be excused? I gotta study. History test tomorrow."

"Of course. You go right on ahead, Honey." Susan had opted for the tea. Without missing a beat, she rose and poured a splash of brandy into her cup.

Gracie dawdled next to her mother, dropping uneaten Goldfish crackers one by one into a glass of milk. Susan pointed at the backpack at the foot of the stairs. "Why don't you get started on your spelling," she suggested.

The little girl beamed at Brady. "I got 100 one time on my spelling test," she told him proudly as she went to get her homework.

He smiled and sat next to Susan at the table. "How are you holding up?" he asked as soon as they were alone.

"Oh, you know, I have to keep going. The kids still need to go to school, they still need to eat. The laundry has to get done." She looked at him warily. "I see you've been chatting with my in-laws."

"That's right. Just trying to fill in some blanks."

"The thing is, it's just so strange not to know where he is." She jerked her head toward the calendar hanging on the wall. "It's been over a month now."

"I'm sure it's been really tough on you all." He placed his hand on hers. "You never told me how the two of you met."

"Oh, it was in college." A smile crossed her lips briefly. "It was my second year. Phillip was a senior. They had these mixers, you know, dances, so you could get to know each other. It was at the Homecoming mixer, pretty much right at the beginning of the year. I went with my roommate, and we were standing over by the punch bowl, waiting in line to get something to drink, and this rude upperclassman cut right in front of us."

Brady raised his eyebrows. "Phillip cut in line?"

She shook her head. "No, not Phillip, another guy. We didn't want to make a fuss, so we didn't say anything. But Phillip was standing off to one side watching us, and he came over and grabbed the fellow's elbow and told him he shouldn't do a thing like that. He just kind of joked around with the guy about what a bad impression he was making on these beautiful girls here, and then the guy stepped back and bowed down right in front of us, acting all chivalrous, and then he sprinted across the room. My roommate and I, we were just laughing at the whole thing. Phillip was so sweet. He helped us get our drinks and then he sort of looked at me, like he was shy, kind of, and asked me if I wanted to dance."

Gracie had joined them at the table, and Susan planted a kiss on her cheek. With her pencil poised over a list of spelling words, the little girl smiled as if she'd heard the fairy tale before.

"That's a great story," Brady chuckled. "A hero to the rescue and all. Phillip certainly sounds like a heck of a nice guy."

"Oh, yes, he really was," Susan gushed, "and so handsome. We liked each other right from the start. And then, of course, you know, the usual happened." She glanced down and placed her hands over her daughter's ears and whispered, "We had a hot and heavy romance, and one thing led to another. Somehow I made it through my sophomore year, although I was big as a house when Phillip graduated in June, and Andrew was born at the end of summer."

"Oh!" Brady's eyebrows shot up. "And so then you got married?"

"Right after his graduation. I mean, *right* after. The very next week."

Susan's memories had brought Brady a flood of his own as he stopped to recall the months of Pre-Cana instruction and the wedding at St. Peter and Paul in San Francisco with a couple hundred guests in attendance. The entire entourage had walked across Washington Square Park to an Italian restaurant where they'd feasted on a lavish celebration and been serenaded by violins. He imagined Phillip and Susan's wedding festivities had probably been quite different.

"Was the wedding a big one? Did you two go on a honeymoon?"

"We just went down to City Hall. It was a civil ceremony," Susan confided. "My parents had just left on a cruise, so they weren't even there." Silently, making sure Gracie couldn't hear her, she mouthed, "I didn't tell them, so they didn't find out we had done it until later."

"No kidding, really?"

"His parents stood up as our witnesses. They had flown out for his graduation. We were planning to have a big party later, but we never did. Because, you know, we just got busy…" she jerked her head toward Gracie and trailed off.

"What about a honeymoon?"

"We didn't really have one, but Roger and Alice did take us across town to the Fairmont Hotel afterwards to celebrate. The four of us had a lovely dinner up on the rooftop terrace, and then Phillip and I stayed overnight. It was amazing. I'd never been to any place that fancy before. The maître d' brought us a bottle of champagne, and the waiters made us feel so special."

Silence permeated the kitchen for a long moment until abruptly, Susan stood, turning her back to Brady. "That was 14 years ago. Where is he? What the devil is going on? More than a month already, I can't believe it." Brady saw tears of exasperation pool in Susan's eyes and watched her lower lip quiver. "I'm so confused, Tony, I'm all mixed up. I'm angry, I'm worried. I don't know what to feel!"

Brady squeezed her shoulder gently. "I know it's frustrating Susan. But I promise, I'm working on it. I'm hopeful we'll get a break soon. We just need to hang in there."

With trembling fingers, she reached into her pocket for a tissue to wipe her eyes, and he continued.

"Trust me, I know how hard it is, not knowing where he is."

Alarmed by her mother's sudden tears, Gracie ran to her side and yanked on Brady's arm. "Where's my Daddy? When is he coming home?" she demanded.

He turned to the little girl and looked into her eyes. "I don't know exactly, Sweetheart, but I'm going to do my best to find out."

He stood and offered Susan his hand. "It's time for me to get going, Susan, but I'll be in touch soon, I promise."

Gracie grabbed his outstretched arm. "Hey! What's that?" she asked, poking at the faded tattoo barely visible on the underside of Brady's wrist.

Hesitating for less than an instant, he replied in a low voice, "Those are the initials of my little boy. BSB stands for Brendan Stephen Brady."

Gracie shrugged. She returned to her spelling words, and the moment passed. Startled, Susan grasped Brady's outstretched hand, a look of confusion sweeping her face. Her fingers rested in his, and she stared at the inked initials for a long moment before she let go, dropping his hand as if she'd been burned.

"Gracie, Honey, your piano teacher will be here in a few minutes. Why don't you go warm up with your scales?" She pointed her daughter toward the living room. "Mr. Brady doesn't have time to be bothered by all your silly questions."

"No bother at all." He yanked his shirt cuffs down tightly over his wrists. "Nobody's questions are silly, and I'm happy to answer them."

CHAPTER TWELVE

Early Winter 2003

STEVE

The Desert Motel sat between a 7-Eleven and Manny's Taco Stand on a dry patch of land on the outskirts of the sleepy town of Rosamond. Behind the motel, Bobby's Aunt Millie shared a doublewide trailer with Gene, a man she referred to as her *gentleman friend* who hardly ever spoke. Bobby introduced him, and he dove in to pick up the ins and outs of his new desk clerking job.

Each toting his meager belongings, they had cleared out of the men's shelter and hitchhiked a ride to the motel, and from the moment they set foot on the place, it was obvious that without transportation, neither would be going anywhere any time soon. That suited them both just fine. Guests who frequented the quiet motel were mostly visitors who drove up from LA to test the horsepower of their new BMWs on the tracks at Willow Springs Raceway, or young families who came for the weekend to gape at the rare animals at nearby Windswept Ranch. Unremarkable in just about any way, the Desert Motel was unlikely to be much of a draw for travelers making their way through the desert valley of the Mojave.

Sixty on her next birthday, Aunt Millie had seen a lot of miles. The deep grooves on her wrinkled face revealed the effects of the dry desert sun, and her raspy voice had the rough quality that smokers or truck drivers seem to acquire. Steve watched her greet her nephew with genuine affection and thanked her for letting him help out at the desk, too.

"So what's it like in town? Anything going on?" he asked.

Aunt Millie crushed her cigarette in the ashtray on the front desk, leaving a ring of ruby red lipstick on the filter. "Not much. If you're up to it, take a hike down the road and see for yourself. Me and him usually drive in on Saturdays to pick up the mail." She jerked her thumb toward the doublewide out back. "He don't like to venture out much."

Heeding Aunt Millie's advice, Steve laced up his sneakers and jogged the two miles into Rosamond to take inventory. The downtown strip sat a couple of miles due west of the Desert Motel, just past two car dealerships and several drive-through fast food joints. On the main artery, two family-style diners, a pizzeria, an all-you-can eat Chinese buffet and a Thai take-out place drew a smattering of patrons. A deli with a sign out front advertised over-stuffed hero sandwiches. At the far end sat a Baskin and Robbins, a family-owned hardware store that was not part of any chain, and an old-fashioned hobby shop with kids' bikes on display in the oversized window facing the street. Big box stores hadn't yet arrived in Rosamond, and the local shops were kept busy. In a small public park off the strip, moms and dads on weathered wooden benches kept a watchful eye on the sandbox and swings.

Balancing a slice of pizza in his hand as he explored, Steve took in the scene and was pleased with his new neighborhood. Rosamond had the air of an earlier, simpler time that he found appealing. Across from the grade school near the park was a tiny public library, and though the industrial carpet inside was nearly threadbare, the gray metal shelves were piled high, and there was a real leather couch against the window. When he wasn't working nights or sleeping during the days, Steve planned to make the tiny library his home away from home. In Lancaster, he had been working his way through an entire volume of Ray Bradbury stories and hoped to tackle Asimov's *I, Robot* next.

As he had done in nearby Lancaster, he wandered the town on foot from top to bottom as the weather allowed, discovering that Rosamond's only other draw was a hole-in-the-wall card club with a Mexican-themed taqueria. He stopped in front of the club to read the sign pinned to the door indicating the restaurant had recently been shut down by the county health department. He poked his head inside, nodding at the uniformed guard stationed near the door.

"Hey, how come the taqueria's closed?" he asked.

The guard barely looked up as he shrugged. An older Hispanic man helping himself to free coffee to the left of the club's entrance stirred creamer into a Styrofoam cup. "Health department found rat droppings in the kitchen," the silver-haired patron shrugged. "Too bad, everybody loved Taco Tuesdays."

When he and Bobby had first arrived, Aunt Millie had shown them their accommodations at the back of the motel, a compact twin-bedded room with an unobstructed view of the broadside of her trailer. The roommates had each claimed one of the lumpy beds, dividing up the dresser drawers. An adjoining bathroom was so small it was nearly impossible to turn around. Opening the sticky accordion door of their shared closet, he spotted the clothes rod lying on the floor. A cigarette dangling from her lip, Aunt Millie reached in and picked it up. "Guess I'll send Gene over," she promised. "He'll fix that."

Somehow, the new night clerks managed to avoid bumping into each other inside the cramped room. Bobby volunteered to take the first two nights on duty, Steve took the next two, and from there, the schedule unfolded like clockwork. With a weakness for Hollywood movie magazines and cherry liquor chocolates, Aunt Millie wasn't especially chatty and didn't ask a lot of questions. As long as he and Bobby showed up for work on time, addressed the motel guests politely, and made sure there was hot coffee brewing in the office when she arrived each morning, she was happy.

Feeling restless one evening while Bobby manned the helm at the motel, he meandered around town and peered through the small window in the door of the card club. A memory of a trip he and Susan had once taken to Reno returned to him, and he scanned the crowd, expecting to find senior citizens nursing cocktails as they pumped their social security checks into hungry slot machines. In Reno, after he'd lost a handful of dollars, he'd shied away from gambling, never understanding how folks could part with their money so easily. Glancing around the brightly lit card room in Rosamond, he didn't see a single slot machine, and curious, he stepped inside.

The guard glanced up from his book of Sudoku puzzles as he walked in. The noisy crowd seemed to be having a good time. At oval-shaped tables covered in faded green felt, dealers shuffled decks of cards. The nervous fingers of hopeful players rippled through colorful betting chips. The lighting was much too bright, the piped-in music never let up, and in the stuffy cavern, there was no way he could even be sure if it was day or night. In spite of the garish atmosphere, he found himself drawn to the camaraderie he sensed. As he drifted from table to table, taking in the friendly games of Blackjack, Poker and Roulette in full swing, he listened and tried to make sense of what he heard.

"Twenty-one here," the Blackjack dealer wearing a shiny red vest announced.

Steve leaned closer to the table, trying to figure out whether *hit me* was the right call for a hopeful gambler with a ten and a six face up on the felt. Jovial ribbing and banter riddled with an unfamiliar lingo surrounded him on all sides.

"Pocket Rockets!" a man in a denim jacket with a *Metallica* logo on the back shouted, slapping two red Aces down triumphantly as his opponent answered, "Yeah? I got a Broadway Straight!"

Steve turned to his right to inch closer to the action at the Poker table. *What's a Broadway Straight*, he wondered.

Half an hour later, helping himself to a cup of watery black coffee, he was relieved that no one, neither employees nor patrons, had pushed him to part with any money or to take a seat and try his luck. He wasn't a gambler by nature and had never played games of chance, his only betting attempt when he'd bet his college roommate on the outcome of a football game and had to fork over his leather jacket when he'd lost. He really didn't know the first thing about how to join in, and that evening he was content to sip his coffee and simply observe, relaxing in the lively club while never spending a dime.

The following night, his shift at the front desk seemed never-ending. The neon sign outside cast its reflection on the lot where no more than a half dozen cars had been parked all weekend. The Desert Motel was quiet as a tomb. After all the guests had checked in, Steve figured that nothing much was likely to happen, and out of sheer boredom he began tinkering with an old desktop computer that had been shoved to one side. The clunky keys on the old Dell responded as if they'd been waiting for him. Reminding himself not to leave even the smallest digital footprint, he made sure no one would be able to track his activity. Checking e-mail didn't interest him, and he made it a point to erase his search history, playing it safe and revealing nothing when after a few attempts, he managed to get online.

Rooting around on the system, he stumbled on a veritable avalanche of casino games. "Free practice games," touted one website. "Casino games made easy," claimed another. Concluding after a few games that winning at Roulette was essentially just a matter of luck, he ventured a guess that the same was probably true of Blackjack, but he figured he'd give it a try. Mostly to amuse himself during his long shift, he taught himself how to play Twenty-one. Learning that *hit me* when the pair in his hand already totaled sixteen was unlikely to result in a win, he reasoned it would be best to hope for the dealer to bust. He made notes of what he learned, and for several weeks, his late night browsing on the Dell kept him entertained with free Blackjack games as he tried to out-wit the system. Occasionally he won a few hands, but usually, the electronic dealer managed to outsmart him, and he was forced to conclude that Blackjack, too, was largely a game of chance.

Might not be as interesting as it looked, he thought to himself, *unless Poker's a better game.*

With a journalist's tendency toward research, Steve clicked on an article in *Scientific American* and read about an adaptation of poker that had recently enjoyed a tremendous boom in popularity among card players around the globe. At three in the morning, he looked up bleary-eyed from a complicated explanation of game theory, and getting up to stretch his legs, he realized he'd been engrossed with total absorption for several hours. His shoulder muscles ached, and his backside had sunk deep into the stool behind the desk. He stood on cramped legs and walked over to the window, looking out at the parking lot where a single incandescent streetlight illuminated the blackness. With surprise, Steve observed that it was the first time in years that any activity had completely held his attention. For once, the daydreaming that was an integral part of his inner life had failed to distract him, and it was as if a light bulb had suddenly been switched on. He was fully alert, and despite the lateness of the hour, his brain tingled with an entirely new sensation of aliveness.

A few hours later when his shift came to an end, he headed back to the darkened motel room and silently undressed. He stepped over a pile of Bobby's clothes on the floor and crept to his side of the room, unable to prevent the bedsprings from creaking as he lowered himself onto the lumpy mattress. Too keyed up for sleep, he wondered if the library might have something on this intriguing new game called Texas Hold'em and began nursing the wild notion that playing Poker might provide a way for him to bring in some cash. After all, he reasoned, he'd never find a job without ID, and though he tried his best to be thrifty and most of his funds remained untapped, he knew the money couldn't last. He burrowed under the thin gray blanket in the shabby motel room, reflecting that if Steve Phillips was to survive, he'd have to come up with a way to produce some income, and it would be wise to consider all options, however unconventional they might be.

When he awoke the following day, it was nearly noon, and the room was empty. He padded to the tiny bathroom for a shower, drying himself on the towel he hung to dry on his side of the room. He walked the two miles to town to hunker down at one of the diners for the *$1.99 two egg all day breakfast special.* Sliding into a seat at the counter, he scanned the local paper over an unhurried cup of coffee before heading to the library with a mission.

The shelf of books he found on basic strategy revealed that in addition to Texas Hold'em, there were quite a few different games of chance, many with confusing names like 7 Card Stud and Omaha High-Low. He began working his way through a thick volume full of useful strategic advice, and as Steve made his way down the street after breakfast, he mulled over one of Doyle Brunson's insights on the importance of maintaining a poker face.

"Show me your eyes and you may as well show me your cards," the Poker guru had said.

Steve continued through the downtown streets, considering whether to invest in a pair of dark glasses to hide any possible *tells*, or revealing mannerisms.

By the end of November, the cheerful window of the local hobby shop no longer featured bicycles and had instead been decorated with colorful Christmas lights and toys, drawing holiday shoppers and hopeful children. An elaborate electric train loop, complete with flashing lights and bridges and a miniature depot, filled the main part of the shop window, and in the right-hand corner of the display sat a beautiful, large wooden dollhouse with an intricately carved gabled roof.

He stopped before the display and stood motionless on the sidewalk. As he peered through the window at the dollhouse and at all the tiny people sitting on the brightly painted furniture, his heart dropped with unexpected sadness, and Doyle Brunson's gambling advice evaporated in the chilly winter air. He felt a wave of regret wash over him, and without warning, tears clouded his eyes.

"Can you build one for me, Daddy?" Gracie had wheedled, hopping from one leg to the other. "One as nice as Ginny's daddy made for her? Please, Daddy, can you?"

His heart ached for the dollhouse his daughter had wanted, a dollhouse he had promised he would build and never had, but when he reached his hand to his face and felt the wetness on his lashes, he knew at once that remorse over the dollhouse could not wholly account for the unanticipated tears that stung his cheeks.

A pair of shoppers with packages in their arms glanced at him and hurried past. Suddenly self-conscious, he wiped the wetness from his face and shifted his gaze from the hobby shop window to the sidewalk below.

Get hold of yourself, he scolded. *Probably for the rest of her life, whenever Gracie thinks about me, the thing she'll remember is I didn't make that dollhouse for her like I said I would. She'll never forget I didn't keep my promise.*

He pulled his baseball cap lower over his forehead until it nearly covered his eyes.

Me neither. I'll never forget, either.

The cheerful morning lay in tatters. He hadn't wanted to think about the promise he'd broken, but the dollhouse in the window had awakened memories too painful to be ignored, and he knew why.

There was a secret he had carried hidden in his heart for eight years, and, as secrets often do, it held the power to erode all that it was meant to protect. The trouble with secrets, he knew now, is that they are very often not secrets at all. Nearly always, secrets fail to hide what everyone somehow already senses is true. With a child's trust, her face a miniature blonde and blue-eyed replica of her mother's, his little girl worshipped her daddy. She knew nothing about the secret, why it had ever been made or carefully kept for so long, but he had always known. Standing stock still in front of the hobby shop window, he could scarcely recall why he'd thought that keeping the secret was so important. With a sorrow that rendered him helpless, at that moment Steve knew that from the very start, he had not been able to love his little girl with his whole heart.

CHAPTER THIRTEEN

Winter 2003

BRADY

In the morning, the place was quiet since Shane had moved into the room he'd found on Craigslist, tight quarters he shared with a couple of guys in the Haight. After a hearty bacon and eggs breakfast, Brady carried his dishes to the sink. As he rolled up his shirtsleeves and plunged his hands into the hot soapy water, his eyes fell on the underside of his wrist and the inked initials that had caught Gracie's attention.

Soap bubbles clung to his skin, and he held his wrist under the tap to rinse them off. The tattoo had faded over the years, but the blue letters never failed to remind him of his freckle-faced boy. Brendan would be a man of twenty-four by now, if he were still alive, a possibility that Brady had begun to doubt. A classic middle child sandwiched between older brothers and younger sisters, the eight-year-old had always been the family's peacemaker, born with the uncanny ability to make everyone laugh.

The last time Brady had seen his boy had been an ordinary day in the middle of a busy week. Over and over, he'd replayed the images in his mind, recalling how that random Tuesday had turned into the worst day of all of their lives. The panic as his brothers in blue swept into the apartment, the frenzy as they scoured the neighborhood for hours on end, working overtime, with every detail burned into Brady's memory as if etched there by sulfuric acid.

That Tuesday, he had been working his usual beat in the Richmond District and hadn't thought twice when his wife announced she'd be taking the girls to the pediatrician. The two youngest had woken up with ear infections, a common occurrence in the Brady household. After school, eight-year-old Brendan and his older brother, Shane, had let themselves into the apartment as they often did, using the keys they wore around their necks. The boys were fixing themselves a snack when their mother had called home to say she was running late. She reminded them of their Boy Scout den meeting that afternoon at the rec center in the park, but Shane complained that he'd turned his ankle playing basketball during PE.

"That's why it took us so long. He was limping all the way home," Brendan had chimed in.

"Can't you drive us?" Shane had pleaded. "My ankle's all swollen and it hurts to walk."

His mother advised him to get some ice from the freezer until she could take a look at it and suggested they skip the Scout meeting this time.

To reach the rec center in their San Francisco neighborhood, the boys routinely crossed two residential streets, arriving in less than ten minutes. It was a quick, easy stroll, and Brendan begged for permission to set out for the den meeting on his own. He reminded Colleen that he'd often walked to the center with his brothers, and distracted by the two feverish little girls clinging to her side in the doctor's waiting room, the youngest now in tears, she'd hesitated for less than a minute before giving in. Later she said she knew it would be useless to try to reach Tony on his beat or Anthony at baseball practice at the high school. Hanging up the phone in the busy doctor's office, she consoled the little ones beside her clamoring for her attention, reassuring herself that Brendan was a responsible boy who knew not to talk to strangers.

That ordinary autumn day was nearly two decades ago, and the reliable eight-year-old had never come home again. Despite extensive efforts made by the local police force and eventually, even the FBI, neither Brendan nor his remains had ever been found. The boy's shattered father still yearned to know what had happened, even as he wondered if he'd be able to stomach the truth. Frustrated by false leads and dead-end searches, in time law enforcement authorities officially declared the case cold, but for Brady, it was a case that would never die.

As he scrubbed congealed grease from the skillet and stared at his child's initials, the ex-policeman wondered if the ink on his wrist could help him somehow make headway with the Lynch case. He dried his hands and opened his notepad to review the progress that had been made so far. Police had found the abandoned car in Lancaster, and he'd personally driven down and distributed flyers all over the surrounding area. He'd spoken to the Walmart store employees and circulated Phillip's photograph, but no one seemed to recognize the clean-cut, handsome reporter. At first, the rewards line had been inundated with tips from eager reward-seekers who'd reported sightings as far away as Seattle and Lake Tahoe. Some of the descriptions they gave weren't even close, but Brady diligently had tracked down every lead. As a former detective, he was well aware that as time drags on, the search for a missing person becomes harder and harder, the likelihood of success diminishing daily. He weighed the possibility that by now the missing man may have altered his appearance and paused to consider whether a follow-up trip to southern California was in order.

Feeling chilly, he slipped his San Francisco Giants sweatshirt over his head and turned the heat up a notch. The dry branches of the elm across the street reached upward toward the gray sky, and he saw that nearly all the trees had already shed their spindly leaves. As the winter holidays approached, Brady remembered all too well how miserable the first Christmas without Brendan had been. He feared it would be equally cheerless for Phillip's family, and with genuine sympathy, he picked up the phone to call Susan.

"Hey there, Susan. Just wanted to see how you're doing. Okay if I come by for a visit tomorrow?" he proposed.

"Sure, Tony, why not come over after lunch?" she replied in a dull voice.

He thought she sounded painfully low on the phone, and her mood hadn't improved when he showed up the following day carrying a bouquet of white daisies.

"Sorry," she apologized, shuffling into the kitchen in pink slippers and a robe. Her eyes looked bloodshot. "Having trouble sleeping lately," she mumbled.

Brady surveyed the messy room. It was 1:30 in the afternoon, but the morning's dishes were stacked in the sink caked with the remnants of breakfast, and an open box of cereal sat on the counter. He pushed an ashtray aside and took a seat at the kitchen table.

"Tough day?" he asked quietly.

She lit a cigarette and blew smoke from the corner of her mouth. "That's about right."

He chatted idly about the change in the weather while Susan smoked in silence until at last, Brady told her he had a confession to make.

He couldn't read anything by looking at her vacant face. She squinted, eyeing him directly for the first time since he'd stepped into the house, and he continued.

"The thing is, Susan, I know exactly how you feel every morning when you wake up, wondering where he could be."

She pursed her lips as if she didn't believe him. "How could you?"

Stumbling at first as he reminded her of the initials tattooed on his wrist, he explained about the blue ink etched into his skin. "I've never stopped wondering what happened or if he's even still alive," Brady confided, his face pinched and solemn, "and believe me, I know how painful that kind of uncertainty is. Not knowing what happened, well it's like a coat I wear wrapped around me every single day, like an old familiar friend."

After a moment's hesitation, Susan reached out to touch the letters on his forearm, murmuring softly, "Oh, Tony."

"I want you to know, looking for your husband is not just another case I'm working on. It's more than that for me, and I promise you, Susan, I won't give up."

The small kitchen seemed to expand as a bond stretched and filled the space between them. Abruptly, she busied herself with the coffee pot before changing her mind and reaching into the cabinet for a couple of glasses and a tall blue bottle of gin.

"My God. I had no idea." Susan opened the bottle and held it out to him. "Want a drink? I know I do."

She began pouring even before he'd answered.

"A small one, maybe. Some tonic, if you have it."

She found a bottle of tonic and wordlessly cut a lime into wedges. They sipped their drinks in a silence punctuated only by the hum of the fluorescent lamp overhead. Brady peered around the corner into the living room.

"In-laws out and about today?"

Susan seemed relieved to change the subject. "Alice and Roger have gone home. They said they had to get back before Thanksgiving. Things are less hectic here, for sure, but you'd be amazed how empty a house can feel with three people in it." She glanced at her hand wrapped around the tumbler of gin, frowning at her chipped fingernails. "I'm worried about getting through the holidays. You know, for the kids."

"The holidays can be tough, I know that," he agreed. "Maybe some counseling would help. For you and for them, I mean."

She grimaced. "Oh, no, I don't think much of that kind of thing. It's not for me. Phillip and I spent years in couples' counseling. Didn't do a thing for us, just wasted a lot of time and money," she complained with distaste. "I'll never do that again."

It was just the opening he'd been waiting for. "Was there something particular that sent you and Phillip into counseling?"

"Well, yes, after Gracie was born. We went for about a year and then just gave up. Every now and then we'd give it another try, but the problems we had never went away. In fact, everything kind of got worse." Susan twisted her wedding ring around her finger with a heavy sigh. "The truth was, Tony, Phillip and I weren't very happy. We hadn't been happy for a long time."

The fairy tale story she'd told him about how they'd met crossed through his mind. "When you started out, weren't you happy then?"

"You mean in the beginning? Sure, we were crazy about each other, and then Andrew came along. Everything was fine, we both loved having a little baby, even though we didn't get much sleep. It wasn't until I had Gracie that things got really bad."

Brady did some quick math. *There might have been miscarriages during that long stretch.* "The kids are, what, six years apart? That's kind of a big gap, isn't it?"

Susan got up to pour herself another drink and offered to refresh his. When he shook his head, she paused, as if she'd just at that moment realized she was standing beside him in her bathrobe and slippers. She patted her hair and tucked a curl behind her ear. "Oh God, Tony, let me go get dressed," she exclaimed, taking her drink with her as she took off up the stairs. "Be back in a sec."

Brady rubbed his eyes, wishing he'd opted for coffee instead of the cocktail. He carried his glass to the sink and squirted a stream of dish soap onto the cereal bowls caked with soggy Cheerios.

"Move over," she instructed as soon as she returned, slipping her fingers into a pair of rubber gloves. She attacked the dirty dishes with a burst of energy. He picked up a dishtowel and began to dry.

"See, what happened was, after Andrew, we just couldn't get pregnant," she explained. "We had to go to doctors and go through all kinds of tests. Kind of took the romance out of it, if you know what I mean. I had to mark the right days on the calendar and take my temperature and get shots and take pills, and oh my God, you name it. Not exactly real romantic." She held a juice glass up for inspection and handed it to him. "And then, surprise, surprise, it turned out the problem wasn't me at all. It was him." She rung out the sponge in her hand. "What was that awful thing he said? The doctor tried to explain with a bunch of diagrams on a pad of paper, but when we got home, Phillip said the problem was he was *shooting blanks*. What a terrible thing to say."

She cast a sideways look at him and clamped her mouth shut as if she suddenly realized she'd said too much. Her cheeks had turned bright pink. He wasn't sure if they were flushed from embarrassment or the gin.

"I don't think he ever got over that. And you know what, Tony? I've never told a single soul about this, not anyone. Phillip didn't want me to."

"I can certainly understand that. It's very personal," he nodded.

"That was when our problems really started, but we didn't go to counseling until after Gracie was born. The doctor said we had issues we needed to resolve. He was right, we did, but counseling didn't help."

"So I'm guessing if you couldn't get pregnant, you decided to adopt?"

They heard a car door slam outside, followed by footsteps on the porch.

Susan jerked her head toward the front door. "Carpool," she announced. "Let's not talk about it in front of them."

The kids burst into the kitchen abruptly, and their mother greeted them before turning back to Brady.

"Say, Tony, who runs your office for you? Do you need a secretary?"

"No, not really," he stammered, confused by the change in subject. "I run a pretty lean operation. I take care of that kind of thing myself. Why do you ask?"

"I figure I'm going to need to get a job, and soon. You know how rents are around here."

"A job, Mom? Really?" Andrew rifled through the fridge. "Where's the Snapple?"

"Look behind the 7-Up," his mother suggested. "I don't even know what kind of job I can get. I only had two years of college, and I've been taking care of you guys all this time." She held up an apple and offered it to Gracie. "We always depended on Phillip to make ends meet. He paid all the bills. I never even thought about money, but now that's all changed."

"You're going to go to work, Mommy? No way!"

Alarm appeared on Gracie's tiny face as she burst into tears. "Who's going to take care of me?"

A weary exhaustion spread across Susan's face. "I'm going to have to figure something out pretty soon, I guess."

Brady thought her eyelids seemed to have grown heavier. They looked half-closed in the late afternoon light streaming in the kitchen window.

Drinking gin so early in the day might not have been such a good idea, he thought to himself.

"Listen, I'd better go. Want to put these flowers in a vase before I take off?" he asked her, picking up the bouquet of daisies lying limp on the counter. He took a step closer to Andrew at the open fridge, where the boy was twisting the cap on a bottle of apple juice. "How are things going, Andrew?"

"Not bad. My Science Fair project won first place in the Behavioral Science category."

"No kidding! That's great!" He cuffed the boy's shoulder. "I bet you'll win next year, too!"

Andrew stole a glance at his mother before he lowered his eyes. "I might not go to this school next year. It costs a lot of money." Susan's face looked pinched. "I might switch to public."

"We'll see, we'll see," she cut in, peeling her daughter's arms from around her waist. "Come on Gracie, let's go find out if the ice cream truck is here. I'm pretty sure I heard the bell," she coaxed with false enthusiasm, guiding the little girl toward the front door.

Brady reached into the pocket of his jacket for his keys and began to follow them out. "Listen, kiddo, hang in there," he said to Andrew. "Something's got to break in the case soon. I'm gonna stay on top of it. Don't worry, we'll find your dad."

Andrew ducked his head. "I sure hope so, Mr. Brady. I just don't get it. There's no trace of him." His eyes grew larger as he seemed to search for the right words. "It's almost as if the earth opened up and swallowed him whole."

A familiar sensation, part fear and part grief, made it suddenly hard for Brady to catch his breath. A suffocating tightness clenched the contours of his heart as he recalled what he had felt when Brendan had seemed to vanish into thin air. Its unrelenting grip would only be relieved eventually by numbness, and even then, Brady knew, not completely.

CHAPTER FOURTEEN

Winter 2003

STEVE

He led an orderly life. Neatly laid out on the windowsill of the twin-bedded room he and Bobby shared were a comb and a plastic toothbrush in a cup. His tee shirts and shorts were stuffed into one dresser drawer, socks and underwear in the other. Shirts and a couple of pairs of pants had been hung on hangers in the closet. His sealed envelopes bulging with cash remained safely in a zippered flap in the Walmart backpack he rarely let out of his sight, each stuffed with the original bills that had been carefully counted out by the bank teller. Double-checking that the bag was within reach all the time wasn't exactly easy, and the soiled backpack had taken on a peculiar odor. It was time, he decided, to come up with a more permanent solution, one that presented itself on his way to the laundromat one Saturday with a pile of dirty clothes and a roll of quarters.

Between dryer loads, he ventured across the street to the Greyhound station on the corner. The terminal wasn't busy, and he noticed that hardly anyone seemed to be waiting for a bus.

Behind the newsstand, a teenage attendant sporting a Lakers jersey rearranged a stack of newspapers, and behind the ticket booth, a middle-aged clerk was talking on the phone. Taking inventory, Steve saw several rows of lockers, each about the size of a small duffel, and a couple of vending machines offering candy and gum in a waiting room outfitted with faded blue plastic chairs. An old TV set mounted on the wall was tuned to a local news channel, the sound barely audible. Steve positioned himself in front of one of the vending machines and leaned forward as if to study its selections intently, glancing left and right and scrutinizing the place to assess its security. A single overhead camera faced the ticket booth where the sole attendant had hung up the phone and was now thumbing through a magazine. Steve couldn't tell whether the camera was on, but he could see that its lens faced the empty waiting room and away from the lockers.

He slid a few coins into the candy machine with intentional casualness. A Snickers bar thudded noisily down the chute, and suddenly ravenous, he tore open the wrapper and bit into the nutty chocolate before drifting over to the rows of lockers. He tugged softly on two combination locks that held fast. The chocolate in his mouth tasted stale, and he tossed the uneaten bar into a nearby receptacle.

That very afternoon, as his clothes tumbled rhythmically in the dryer, Steve's thoughts wandered in quiet meditation until he settled on a plan that would simplify his life.

A cardboard box he'd saved from a recently purchased pair of bedroom slippers made the perfect container for the cash-laden envelopes, and once the box was securely locked in place, he spun the combination several times before leaving the bus station. Nervous at first, he returned every day for a week to rotate the shoebox in and out of three different lockers, but no one took notice of him. Satisfied that his assets were secure, he visited his bus station locker only when it was time to insert another handful of quarters.

After Steve discovered the free online casino games on his night shift, he staked out a corner of the library and immersed himself in Doyle Brunson's enormous *Super System*, systematically setting out to learn the nuances of proper bet sizing and determined to get a handle on pot odds. In the early afternoon before swarms of noisy middle schoolers burst through the doors, the study table in the library was a haven. On his first day there, the only other patron was a young woman jotting down something she'd found in what appeared to be a book of recipes. They exchanged a friendly nod as he asked, "What are you reading about?"

She held the book up. "*The Moosewood Cookbook*," she smiled sheepishly. "Trying to get my kids to eat vegetables."

He chuckled, opening the small spiral notebook he'd brought with him for note-taking. With the ambitious goal of mastering the game of Texas Hold'em, he energetically set about committing everything he read to memory, grateful for the pile of books in front of him on the long table.

The first thing he learned was that each player was dealt two cards that only he could see, and these were called *hole* or *pocket* cards. During betting rounds, the dealer revealed a total of five cards face up on the table, and these were known as *community cards*. The player who won the hand was the one who used these five, along with his hole cards, to make the strongest possible combination. As play rotated around the table, bettors proceeded to make their decisions. They could *check*, or they could raise someone else's bet, or they could fold their hole cards and decline to play the hand.

But what's the strongest possible combination?

Steve thumbed through the index until he found the hand-ranking chart, a kind of roadmap every one of the books seemed to feature as part of its appendix. He learned that Three of a Kind, even lowly Deuces, beat Two Pair, and Two Pair of anything was always better than even the highest single pair, Aces, commonly called *Pocket Rockets*. That much was easy enough to remember, but he wasn't certain whether a Flush (five cards, all of one suit) was better than a Straight (five cards of any suit in consecutive numerical order), and he was pretty sure that Four of a Kind, or *Quads*, beat them both. With his index finger poised on the ranking chart in the back of Doyle Brunson's tome, Steve's concentration was broken at that moment by a man leaning on a walker nearly shouting at the librarian.

"You recommended *Captain Underpants* last time," the elderly man announced, "and my grandson loved it."

She beamed at him. "I knew he would, Mr. Cunningham!"

Steve returned his gaze to the ranking chart. There were so many details to memorize, and he doubled down on his focus, but in the back of his mind a nagging voice warned him that reading about Poker was not the same as actually playing the game. Every part of him began itching for a chance to try out the strategies he was learning, but he cautioned himself to wait for the right time, and meanwhile, to keep studying.

In the days that followed, Steve read on with passionate intensity. He devoured everything he could find by Mike Caro and David Sklansky. He made notes, he played practice hands on the computer in the office, and he spent hours at the card club observing. The regulars were usually confident young men in their twenties, slick and eager, or gray-haired retirees with time on their hands and money to burn. He speculated that the small town's men and women in their thirties and forties were too busy juggling their jobs and kids. Armed with his notebook, he scribbled notes to himself as delighted winners scooped up piles of chips from the center of the table and losers busted out in disgust. He watched seemingly never-ending games in which players came and went at will, opening their wallets again and again to peel out twenties as their chips were swept up by rivals.

"That's it for me, I've had it," he heard a player sporting a trim white goatee complain in annoyance as he rose from the table. "These cash games are killing me. I'm holding out for the next time there's a tournament."

Beside him, one of the club regulars, a heavyset fellow who introduced himself as Troy, said he shared the older man's opinion and commented that playing tournaments was a completely different ball game.

Do I have to learn two completely different strategies? Steve wondered. He didn't want to reveal how green he was by asking and instead, jotted down his questions. *Tournament play – different strategy? How much bankroll needed?*

Manning the motel desk late at night, he channel-surfed. Catching television reruns of past tournaments, he heard announcers dissect players' betting decisions and weigh their variable odds. One night, he watched as an amateur young player with the unlikely name of Chris Moneymaker took home a huge trophy and a couple million dollars. Staring at the TV in the corner of the lobby, Steve was spellbound, and his mouth hung open as he gawked. Equally awe-struck, the television commentators and the wildly cheering audience celebrated the 28-year-old player's incredibly good fortune.

He was so keyed up that night he barely slept at all, and at the card club the following day, he struck up a conversation with two regular players who looked like they might be brothers.

"Yeah, that just happened this summer! Chris Moneymaker won over two million bucks, and get this. The guy's real name? I'm not even kidding, it's actually Moneymaker!" crowed the younger man, outfitted in a deliveryman's blue jumpsuit with *Dave's Appliances* on the back and *Mikey* emblazoned over his pocket.

"No kidding? I thought for sure someone made that up," Steve laughed.

"I know, right? The guy was basically an accountant with some boring day job, and then he just got unbelievably lucky. Amazing, huh?"

Steve found out they really were brothers. The older one said the accountant had been working at a mid-level office job when he had unexpectedly fared quite well in a local tournament, so well that he'd automatically qualified for a seat in a much larger competition. That larger contest turned out to be the Main Event of the World Series of Poker. New to the gambling world, Steve had never even heard of it, but Eric claimed the WSOP was the gold standard for Texas Hold'em tournaments, the event of the year for players around the globe.

His younger brother Mikey emptied the creamer bowl into a Styrofoam cup of tepid black coffee. "Tastes like dishwater," he complained with a grimace. "See, the tournament's been around since the seventies, but now that it's on TV all the time, it's gotten hella well known. Everybody's into it now, even people who barely know how to play."

It turned out the lucky accountant had bought into the smaller tournament for a mere $86 just looking to have a little fun. When he won the coveted first place trophy at the WSOP, the guy took home a staggering $2.5 million. It was exactly the kind of classic rags-to-riches success story that captivated the attention of just about everyone in the poker-playing world, professionals and amateurs alike, but especially wide-eyed newcomers with outsized dreams, and Steve Phillips was no exception.

"Could happen to anyone, I guess."

"Sure, why not?"

$86. He couldn't stop thinking about it.

If a total amateur had been able to pull it off, why couldn't he? He was smart, wasn't he? How hard could it really be to win a little money?

It's time to start playing some hands, Steve decided. *Time to get in the game.* And on his next day off, he headed downtown with a roll of twenties bulging in the pocket of his Walmart jeans as he stepped jauntily into the windowless cavern.

"$200 worth of chips, please." He slid ten bills under the cage, and though his heart was beating so loud he could almost hear it, he tried to sound as if the request was one he made every day.

"Sure thing, Hon. What's your name?" The blue-haired cashier popped her gum without looking up from behind the window, her pencil poised on a hand-written list.

He'd used the name for three months and responded without hesitation. "Name's Steve Phillips."

She counted his bills and added his name to her list. "I'll let you know when a seat opens up, Hon."

He pocketed the receipt she handed him and stepped back from the cage, his heart pounding inside his chest.

In the early afternoon on a weekday, the club was nearly empty. He heard his name called on a crackling loudspeaker almost immediately and took his seat at one of the tables, trading his receipt for a clear plastic tray of red and green chips. Someone had left a small pillow on the back of his seat, and he leaned against it gratefully. As he stacked his chips, he saw that up close, the faded green felt looked frayed and there was a rip in the vinyl border. It was his first time playing a hand, and Steve wasn't sure what to expect. He played conservatively and took down a few pots, and at once his confidence climbed up a notch.

It's not so hard, he told himself, feeling smug. *Guess all that studying is paying off.*

He leaned forward and began to make more aggressive wagers. A guy with a huge stack of chips limped into the pot, and Steve, thinking the fellow's hand must be weak, raised with half his stack. *After all,* he thought, *a pair of Jacks has to be good.* Turned out the more experienced player had an Ace and a Queen in his hand and promptly paired his Queen, outflopping him just like that. Half of Steve's stack disappeared in a heartbeat. The misstep rattled him, and a few minutes later, he lost another big bet, even though the middle pair he'd been dealt had better odds pre-flop than his opponent's hole cards.

Everything happened so quickly, and it was all so confusing. Guys on either side of him ribbed each other with banter and friendly insults. The music coming from the speakers seemed to get louder and louder. He struggled to tune it all out and follow the action at the crowded table and found he had trouble remembering the strategies he'd so carefully studied. Panic mounted inside him, and within minutes, Steve was on tilt. His chip stack shrank to a dangerous level, and he waited until he was dealt what he thought was a monster hand, busting out when his pair of Queens ran into a Straight.

His rival had played him as easily as a fiddle.

"Tough luck, man. I had you from the flop," his opponent, wearing a Dodgers cap, explained, referring to the first three cards the dealer had placed face up on the table. "I was holding eight-nine, and then seven-ten-jack came up on the flop."

Steve flushed with embarrassment. "Really? You flopped a Straight? Wow. I kept betting my Queens! I thought for sure I had you," he complained. "It was the best hand I'd had since I sat down."

"Gotta be careful with Queens. Those ladies look pretty but they can go either way. If they hold up, people say they're a top ten hand. A good hand to shove all-in with in a no-limit tourney. Not so great in a cash game, though."

Steve peeled away from the table, nursing his confusion with another cup of free coffee and tried to figure out where he'd gone wrong. When he circled back to the table, the Dodgers fan had pushed all the chips he'd won into the pot. Unable to contain his excitement, a young kid barely out of his teens flipped over his hole cards, shouting "Full House!"

"Wow," Steve mumbled as the man in the Dodgers cap rose from the table with a shrug and caught his eye.

The losing player removed his cap and swabbed his brow with a neatly folded white handkerchief. "You new here?"

"Is it that obvious?" he extended his hand. "Name's Steve. Steve Phillips."

The man who had trounced him shook his hand firmly. "I'm Rob. Hey, nice to meet you."

Rob seemed to know everyone. As the two of them drifted away from the table where another round of betting was already in progress, Steve watched him wave to someone on the other side of the room.

"This game's a lot harder than it looks. I've been playing just about every day since I retired from the store," Rob told him. With a broad, open face and a salesman's friendly demeanor, he checked his watch and continued. "My wife runs the homework club at the middle school most afternoons. I come here to get out of the house, have some fun, try my luck." Comfortably, Rob kept up a continuous stream of conversation. "Sometimes I win, sometimes I lose. I guess I come out about even."

"Even's not bad, but eventually I'd like to come out ahead," Steve commented. "You know, make some money at it."

"Wouldn't we all?" Rob laughed. "I think I do better playing no-limit tournaments than cash games."

Steve couldn't mask his confusion, and Rob went on to explain.

"See, this game's called limit poker. There's a limit on how much you can bet." Rob peered over his glasses at Steve. "Didn't you notice that?"

"No, not really."

"Tournaments are no-limit, see. You can bet everything you've got if you want to and try to steal the pot. But you have to pace yourself, 'cause they go on and on. If you play tournaments, you gotta last. If you bust out after the end of rebuys, you can't buy back in. You're out for good." Rob glanced up to see if Steve was following. "It's kind of like single elimination tournaments in sports. You ever play sports?"

"Sure, when I was a kid. Baseball, basketball. Not all that well, but sure, I played. How about you?"

"Baseball. I played catcher. As a boy, I used to love those tournaments. Loved the threat of single elimination." He cocked his head. "Thought I'd get to raise some kids and see 'em do all that, but we never had any. You?"

The salesman's outgoing manner had drawn him in, but the innocence of Rob's question caught Steve off guard, and almost imperceptibly, he winced.

"Yes," he stammered, "Well, no, no. That is, I used to, but not anymore."

Rob raised his eyebrows and sighed knowingly. "Divorce, huh? The curse of the times, ain't it? It's tough on us guys."

Steve managed a silent nod, and Rob glanced down at his watch again, asking, "So, you coming back tomorrow?"

"Maybe. I think so. It was fun playing, but man, it's way harder than it looks. There's so much to learn, so much to remember."

"Ain't that the truth, man? I play all the time, and I'm still learning, myself." Rob laughed and gestured toward the door. "Time for me to head out. See you around."

Steve lingered at the club to watch a few more hands. He began to sense a rhythm to the play, noticing when bets were raised, when cards were mucked and chips swept up in triumph. He tried to tune out the playful ribbing between players and to get used to the constant clink of chips riffling through their fingers. After sacrificing the wad of cash he'd come in with, in the days that followed, he retreated to lick his wounds in the library's study room. Piled high beside him was a dog-eared stack of poker manuals and spread out on the table in front of him, a deck of Bicycle playing cards.

CHAPTER FIFTEEN

Winter 2003

BRADY

It had been months since there had been any trouble, so when his son showed up with a duffel bag stuffed with what looked like everything in his closet, Brady answered the doorbell with surprise.

"Hey, buddy. I wasn't expecting to see you tonight. Something happen?"

Shane shuffled inside and with a grunt, heaved the bag from his shoulder to the floor.

"Oh, yeah, something happened all right. Only this time it wasn't my fault."

Brady cocked his head and held back the questions tumbling through his mind. Whose fault it was when things went wrong was always a loaded subject with Shane, and he wasn't sure he wanted to touch it.

The duffel bag and faded denim jacket Shane had tossed on top of it lay in a heap, and he kicked it out of the way.

"Why do these things always happen to me, Dad? The vet's place got robbed. Whoever did it totally trashed the place and took all the money out of the register. Anthony's buddy said he had to let me go 'cause he's gotta close the place down for a while, but I'm pretty sure he thinks I had something to do with it."

"Oh, boy. I thought things were going so well over there."

Shane caught his eye and held it.

"Dad, I swear I didn't have anything to do with it."

"Of course you didn't." He gestured toward the kitchen where he'd been sorting through a stack of files. "Come in and sit down. Have you eaten?"

"Not hungry." Shane slumped into the closest chair.

Ignoring his son's protest, Brady puttered about, throwing together a makeshift supper. He heated up a couple of bowls of thick clam chowder and tore a loaf of sourdough into chewy hunks. The two of them slurped their soup for several minutes. When he'd finished eating, Shane wiped his mouth and pushed back from the table. His eyes fell on the pile of manila folders Brady had shoved to the side.

"What's all this stuff? You working on something?"

Brady dipped a crust of sourdough into his bowl and scooped up the last of the chowder. "Yeah, a lead I got on the case I took on back in September. You know, the TV reporter?"

"I remember you talking about some guy who just up and disappeared." Brady thought Shane seemed relieved to discuss something other than his own problems. "You think it's a good lead?"

"Could be. Someone down in Lancaster, you know, where the car was found, well, a guy called into the rewards hot line. He remembered seeing someone who matched the description we put out. Says he saw him at a nearby men's shelter." He gestured at the thick stack of folders. "I'd already gone through copies of the registers for all the shelters within twenty-five miles. I looked at every listing for the past few months, but there's no mention of my guy. I might go down there again and meet up with the tipster in person. It's not much, but at least it's something. It's been a tough case to crack, not a single break all this time." He looked over at his son. "It's been really hard on the guy's family. You know how that is." Brady paused. "The cops have just about given up."

"The cops," Shane scoffed. The smirk on his face spoke volumes. "They give up pretty quick, don't they? If they can't figure it out like that," he snapped his fingers, "it's over for them."

Reluctantly, Brady had to agree. The police effort so far had been lackluster. "Thing is, I promised the family I wouldn't give up, but believe me, without a single break, I'm pretty frustrated."

"Think maybe the guy has changed the way he looks, or made up a whole new name for himself?"

"Anything's possible, I guess." Pleased his son seemed interested, he ruffled Shane's hair. "Good instincts, kid. You thinking about becoming a PI like your old man?"

"Not a chance." An involuntary shudder seemed to run through his son. "I don't know what I would do if I found someone who'd been kidnapped or murdered. Seriously, you'd have to have nerves of steel. I couldn't take it."

Brady cleared their dishes, reflecting on the path Shane had travelled since the twelve-year-old had twisted his ankle that day his brother went missing. Brendan would be twenty-four by now, and everyone in the family believed that if he had somehow managed to survive, surely he would have surfaced by now. In the interim, the kids had all grown up. Anthony Jr. was a father himself, and Bridget was engaged to be married. After a rough handful of years during their teens, each of the others seemed to have accepted the loss of their brother and moved on with their lives.

Except Shane, who still believed he was to blame. In and out of rehab, he'd had a history of skirmishes with the law, and Brady suspected he sometimes used street drugs. For years, he'd urged his son to get the help he needed, offering to pay for it and keeping his fingers crossed that Shane wouldn't become another family casualty.

"Stay as long as you want, 'til you're back on your feet again. You'll see. Things will get better."

"I don't know, Dad. Seems like every time I try to make it on my own, I get shoved down again. You're the only one who still has faith in me. Mom doesn't even answer the phone when I call, and I can't keep getting Anthony to bail me out."

Slumped in anguish at the cramped kitchen table, a young man still broken after nearly two decades, Shane suffered powerlessly under the yoke of self-inflicted guilt. Brady knew the wound was still fresh, even after all this time, and the pain he heard in his son's voice made him want to weep. A cloud of uncertainty still hovered over Brendan's disappearance, deepening their torment and making closure impossible for them all. It had just about broken Brady's heart when Bridget, his youngest, had confessed she couldn't really remember her brother, couldn't picture his face anymore. She had blurted out that innocent admission just a couple of years after Brendan had been gone, and he had ached for his daughter then, just as tonight he ached for the son who sat before him, struggling to hold himself together.

Both lost in lonely sorrow, Brady thought he saw something flit across Shane's clouded eyes. "Hey, Dad, remember that time the cops thought they'd found his bones in the woods up north? What a bungled-up job they did," his son snarled with disgust. "Man, they were so friggin' clueless."

"I remember," he replied softly.

"I didn't know whether I wanted it to be him, or if I didn't," Shane confessed. "When you took off with them to check it out, I was terrified what you'd find."

Brady remembered the cold, gray day as if it were yesterday. Flanked by a half dozen of his brothers in blue, he had trudged into a remote wooded area in the fog. Fear clutched his heart, icy fear that the bones would be Brendan's, and then came the plummeting letdown. Despite a hopeful start to the expedition, forensic authorities later traced the remains to a four-year old Mendocino girl, another lost child who had never made it home.

"It's such a weird feeling. You know he couldn't possibly be alive, but you kind of want to know what happened." Brady thought Shane's voice had suddenly grown husky.

"I know what you mean," he replied. "Because if it was him, then at least we'd finally know something. Maybe it would have helped us all move on."

"Yeah, but Dad, that was the worst thing about it," Shane groaned. "If it was him, then we'd have to imagine him getting killed. That's what drove me crazy. Sometimes I used to think if he did get killed, I hope he died fast, so he didn't suffer."

Brady leaned in close. "I'll let you in on a secret," he confided. "It's nuts, but sometimes I used to let myself think maybe he was taken by a family who didn't have any kids but really wanted one, and maybe he was off having a happy life somewhere." A flush of embarrassment crept over his face at the naked hope he'd revealed. "I know it was stupid. It's just something I told myself on some of those really dark days. Especially in the beginning."

Shane tore at his thumbnail. His cuticles were raw, and Brady wondered how long he'd been making them bleed like that.

His son continued. "I can't stop thinking about that first night. I kept looking out the upstairs window, hoping I'd see him coming down the sidewalk. Mom made the girls go to bed, but I don't think I slept at all that night."

They'd been full of hope all through the bleary-eyed hours, waiting for Brendan to return any minute with a story of what had delayed him. He and Colleen had clung to that hope in desperation long past what was reasonable, fiercely unwilling to let it go.

"We were like zombies, all of us," he said. "Your Mom and I drank pot after pot of black coffee. We were so wired on caffeine, we didn't eat, or sleep. Every time the doorbell or the phone rang, we just about jumped out of our skin."

"Yeah, and I was mad at you and Mom for making me go to school the next day. I wanted to go look for him instead, but maybe you guys wanted us out of the house for a while." His son turned to him. "Was that it, Dad?"

"Honestly, I don't know. I guess we tried to make things as normal as we could for the rest of you kids."

He'd been a cop, painfully aware that most kidnapping victims were killed within a few hours. Sleep-walking through the first forty-eight, overly caffeinated, he'd remained vigilant, fearing the worst while at the same time reassuring everyone that Brendan was somehow safe.

With effort, Shane hoisted himself out of the kitchen chair and drifted into the living room. He peeled back the curtain, peering out on the street where a gang of teenagers sailed past on skateboards and watched them egg each other on to try more and more daring moves.

"You know, for years there were times I thought I saw him somewhere and I'd try to follow him, and then I'd see it was just somebody who looked kind of like him. Man, it really killed me whenever that happened."

Brady joined Shane at the window. "You two were good buddies."

"He was my little brother, tagging along on everything I did. My friends thought he was a pest, always hanging around and bugging us. Then when it happened, it was like everything changed in the family. Nothing ever felt the same, did it?"

Brady stood silently beside him as they contemplated the busy street below. Dusk had fallen, and the streetlights had switched on. The apartment was grown chilly, and he shivered, wondering if he should turn the heat up. Losing Brendan had been a pain he could scarcely bear at the time, and Shane's struggle with the demons that still plagued him re-opened the raw wound in Brady's heart. He draped his arm loosely around his son's shoulders. "Each of us lost so much when we lost him. I think maybe we all clung to each other just to survive," he murmured in a low voice.

Almost imperceptibly, Shane gave a tiny nod.

"Then for a long time, none of us could bear to even speak about him, and we all grew apart. I don't know which was worse." Brady's voice was nearly a whisper. "But the thing is, we've got to go on. We've got to keep putting one foot in front of the other, we've got to try to make something of ourselves." He tightened his grip on Shane's shoulder. "Our lives have to count for something. That's why I do what I do. It's the only thing I *can* do."

Brady knew even as he said the words that what he told his son was only part of the story. It was true that he continued pressing on, but again and again, especially alone in his apartment late at night, shooting tendrils of familiar pain coursed through him without mercy. It was then that the grieving father rose from his bed to pore once again over his missing son's case files, grasping for a clue that had somehow gone unnoticed. Only recently had it begun to occur to him that the mystery might never be solved and that the freckle-faced boy might never be found.

Bit by bit over the years, the hope he had nurtured had been slipping away, until now, there was almost none.

CHAPTER SIXTEEN

Winter 2003

STEVE

In no time at all, they'd become poker buddies. Playing low stakes hands, Rob and Steve began meeting at the club whenever they could to try to improve their luck. Steve found that playing those hands turned out to be a quick way to put what he'd learned into regular practice, and it wasn't long before he began to acquire some chops and with them, a modest degree of confidence.

On Thanksgiving, he'd volunteered for the desk shift at the motel so his roommate could join Aunt Millie and Gene for a turkey dinner in town with all the trappings. Alone in the office, he'd passed the holiday watching a rerun of *It's a Wonderful Life* on TV. After that, the days between Thanksgiving and Christmas flew by in a flurry of tree lightings and carolers, and the weather turned chilly, warranting the purchase of a warm winter jacket. Steve guessed the holidays could become a minefield for someone who didn't want to get swept up by the past. He cautioned himself to squash the memories that threatened to crop up as recollections of Andrew and Gracie in soft flannel pajamas and the sweet smell of cinnamon rolls in the oven lurked at the edges of his mind.

Bobby offered to man the desk on Christmas Eve, and when Rob extended an invitation to a home-cooked dinner, Steve jumped to accept it.

"Every year, we have a holiday party. The wife likes to invite anyone she thinks doesn't have other plans," Rob explained in between bites of the frosted angel-shaped cookies someone had set on a plastic tray next to the coffee dispenser at the card club. "She rounds up all the strays she can find. I said you might have folks who expect you, but she told me to ask anyway."

"Nope, I don't have any plans. I'd be happy to join you. Let me bring some wine." Steve smiled as he turned to face his new friend. "Listen, man, there's something I want to explain." He ducked his head. He'd been wanting to clear the air, and with no more than a moment's hesitation, the words spilled out of him. "Remember when I said I don't have a family now, but I used to?"

Rob took a sip of coffee. "Figured you just got divorced, and she took the kids. Happens all the time."

"Yeah, well, the thing is, it's kind of complicated."

"What, did she take 'em clear out of state?" Rob squinted up at Steve from the corner of his cup. "She take you to the cleaners, too?"

"Nothing like that, man," Steve stammered. "See, there was a car accident, a head-on collision. It was a drunk driver. The accident ... well, the thing is, no one survived." He looked away as he heard Rob draw a sharp breath. "I don't like to talk about it," he added in a low voice.

"Oh my God, that's terrible."

Neither spoke for a long moment. A young man in a Cal State Fullerton sweatshirt reached between them for a fistful of cookies. "'Scuse me, guys," he said.

Steve watched Rob's normally ruddy complexion turn to chalk. "Oh man, I'm so sorry. I had no idea," his friend replied, his right hand covering his heart. "I never even asked you what happened."

Steve felt as if he were on stage, an actor in a play, and he stepped into the role and cast his eyes downward soberly without a word. Never before had he told such an outright lie, not to anyone, and at once he saw how much easier it was to lie than to camouflage the truth. As a boy, he'd been brought up to be honest, and suddenly he realized what others seem to know instinctively, that lying quickly solves so many problems. The thought occurred to him in a flash of recognition that the ease with which he had deviated from the truth had something to do with the habit he had recently acquired of bluffing at cards. Playing poker, he had become comfortable telling lies. The moment the lie left his lips seemed not quite real, and he felt lighter, as if a burden had been lifted from his shoulders.

He turned to Rob with an appreciative smile. "It's nice of you to invite me, man." He did his best to affect a normal tone of voice. "What time? Should I bring one bottle or two? What size crowd are you expecting?"

Two bus rides transported him to Rob and Judy's home, sitting snugly in a row of single story houses on a small suburban lane. Brightly color lights were strung across porches, and an inflatable Santa surrounded by reindeer adorned the lawn of the rancher next door. Steve dug into the pocket of the trousers he'd purchased for the occasion to check the address Rob had scrawled on a scrap of paper. A wooden ramp led to the front door. He straightened the tie chafing at his neck and shifted the wine to his other hand to ring the doorbell.

Stepping inside, he heard holiday music playing and saw that the fireplace mantle in the living room was decorated with fragrant Christmas greenery. Guests mingled around a festive table that sparkled with tapered candles in polished silver candlesticks. Rob pulled him into the warm room, announcing, "Hey, everyone, say hello to my buddy, Steve."

He began to enjoy the first social outing he'd gone on in months. Rob ceremoniously carved the golden-brown turkey, and the dinner table soon boasted platters of candied yams, cornbread stuffing and homemade cranberry sauce. The wine Steve had brought was declared a welcome addition, and Judy handed him a corkscrew and asked him to do the honors.

Everyone was dressed in their Sunday best, and he was glad he'd thought to wear a tie. Rob took up residence at one end of the table, and his bubbly wife bustled at the other. Seated to Steve's right was Ira, a dapper gentleman with a neatly trimmed white goatee he'd seen a few times at the club. Ira confided that this was to be his first Christmas since his wife had passed, and his only son worked clear across the country on Wall Street and couldn't make it home for the holidays. Across the table, Judy's great aunt Ellie told Steve about the assisted living home she'd recently moved into. She said she appreciated the wheelchair ramp Rob had installed for her so she could visit the house. Steve found himself thinking that Ellie's cheeks glowed with a slightly unnatural tint. *Maybe she applied too much rouge or blush or whatever women her age use,* he thought as he listened to her monologue politely. His eyes drifted to the far end of the table where a young woman with a head full of golden curls was laughing at something Judy had said.

Waving a forkful of turkey breast in the air between Steve and Ira, Rob interrupted his gaze. "So, listen to this, guys, big news down at the club! I just got wind of a Texas Hold'em tournament they're hosting on New Year's Day." Rob's face was flushed with excitement or perhaps the wine he'd been drinking. "You guys want in? The buy-in is only fifty bucks."

"No kidding! I've been dying to try playing in a tournament," Steve replied with genuine interest. "Tell me what it's like. I mean, how's it gonna be different?"

At their end of the table, the conversation grew lively. Between bites of drumstick and mashed potatoes smothered in gravy, Ira and Rob began to tell poker stories with great animation and backslapping laughter, each describing hands they'd won and lost. They filled Steve in on strategic differences required for playing tournaments and spouted advice on how to size a bet and when to shove all-in. By the time the pumpkin pie topped with dollops of whipped cream arrived at the table, he had decided to join the men and play his first poker tournament with them on New Year's Day.

Judy rose to clear the dessert dishes, warmly shooing them all away, and the group retired to the living room. Rob opened an expensive looking bottle of brandy and poured the golden nectar into a collection of delicate glasses, setting them carefully onto a silver tray.

Such a fancy party, Steve thought, surveying the room. Rob and Judy's friends seemed as spirited and outgoing as their friendly hosts. The pretty blonde he'd spotted across the table with Judy was standing against the wall beside the upright piano, leafing through a pile of sheet music with interest. He selected two glasses from the silver tray and ferried them across the room, introducing himself as he held one up to her.

"Thank you," Jackie murmured with a shy smile.

"Cheers," he replied, bringing the delicate glass to his lips. "How do you know Rob?"

"Honestly, I don't, really," she answered. "I only just met him. Judy and I work together. We run the homework club at the middle school."

"You're a teacher?"

"I am, actually. I'm credentialed in Special Ed, but I just moved here and I had to get a job in a hurry." She spoke so softly that Steve was forced to lean his head in close to hers. "I managed to get work after school at the homework club right away, but I'm trying to get hired on for next year in Special Ed." She took a dainty sip of the golden liquor. "I mean, after all, it's what I was trained in, and I miss it."

She seemed a bit fragile, he thought, and he wondered why she'd had to get a job in a hurry and what had happened. "Had to. I just came out of a messy divorce." She pursed her lips daintily. A trace of coral lipstick edged the dainty glass. "Mmm, that's nice."

"Rob broke out the good stuff, didn't he?" he smiled, looking into her violet eyes and thinking they reminded him of the deep part of the ocean.

"How about you? What kind of work do you do?"

"Oh, I had my own business up in the Bay Area, before the dot com bust," he replied, purposely vague.

"Uh-huh. I heard that affected a lot of people."

"So, after that, I came down here thinking I'd start something new, and that's when I ran into Rob at the card club. We got to know each other playing a little poker together. I'm new here, too and don't know a lot of people yet." He glanced at her sideways, wondering about the messy divorce. "You have kids?"

"No, thank goodness. We were only married a couple of years." A nearly imperceptible sigh escaped her lips. "It's a story I'm sure you've heard a hundred times. We were high school sweethearts, and we got married way too young, right out of college. It's lucky we didn't have kids, it would have made leaving so much harder. We were going to, but then things started falling apart. He'd have made a terrible father." With a shudder, Jackie steered the conversation away from herself. "How about you? What's your story? Do you have a family?"

Forcing himself to look away from her probing eyes, once again he found it surprisingly easy to repeat the story he'd invented, the words spilling out effortlessly as he recounted the details. When he looked back, he took in the way her bouncy curls formed a frame around her face. The brandy had made her skin glow, and despite not having once imagined being drawn in by a beautiful woman again, with almost no warning, Steve felt something inside him begin to stir. The skin on her smooth white neck was nearly translucent, and a handful of barely discernable freckles graced her pink cheeks. Something about this girl seemed as helpless as a wounded bird he immediately wanted to protect. Illuminated as if by an inner light, something about her roused Steve in a way that hadn't happened in a long time.

A memory of the heat of first love and of Chloe flitted through his body, and suddenly, his collar felt warm and damp. He unbuttoned the top button of his dress shirt and loosened the knot on the new tie.

She had listened in silence, and now he saw her eyes, large and round, grow wide with genuine surprise.

"Oh, I'm so sorry," she murmured in a gentle voice. With her cool fingers, she reached out to press his forearm. "What a terrible thing for you to have to go through."

He produced a lopsided smile. "Here's to moving on." He lifted his nearly empty glass in a solemn toast. "Something it appears we both need to do."

Tentatively, almost shyly, she raised her glass to touch his.

"To moving on," Jackie repeated, and they both felt the heat of the brandy as it burned a little going down.

CHAPTER SEVENTEEN

Spring 2004

BRADY

By spring he'd made several trips south to speak with the Walmart store staff members. When he stumbled across a security guard who insisted that the man he'd dropped off on Palmdale Boulevard was indeed the one featured in the poster he'd circulated, Brady thought he'd finally hit pay dirt.

About time, he muttered under his breath.

The guard directed him to a men's shelter a few miles away in nearby Antelope Valley where Brady interviewed an employee and worked his way through yet another guest register. It was entirely possible, the harried attendant conceded, that Phillip Lynch had stayed at the shelter at some point, although he could not be sure, pointing out that so many rudderless men drifted in and out, it was nearly impossible to keep track. Once again Brady scoured the area around Lancaster in every direction, lingering in restaurants and this time, visiting the local library. The head librarian recognized Phillip's photograph right away, recalling that she'd noticed the nice-looking gentleman almost daily that winter before his visits had seemed to cease abruptly. She told Brady that she'd thought it odd that, despite hours spent reading by the fire, as far as she could tell, the man had never checked out any books.

"I don't think he had a library card," she suggested, peering over her bifocals.

Undeterred, Brady decided to beef up his search with a few new investigative tools. Some of the younger PIs more familiar with the new technologies had begun using a forensic database to gather information. Efficiently combing through publicly available resources online, these subscription-only databases were able to uncover obscure details that helped solve cases. Access was afforded only to law enforcement officers, forensic experts and private investigators, and he gave some thought to signing up for a subscription. When Carlos Salcedo revealed in his weekly phone call that recent budget cuts had slashed the missing persons squad back to one over-burdened full-time detective, Brady knew his prediction had been spot on. Barely six months after the man he was looking for had gone missing, local police didn't exactly call the case cold, but clearly, they had moved their investigation to the back burner.

Brady stopped by the precinct unannounced one morning and found Salcedo knee deep in a small mountain of cases, complaining that his supervisors had kept up a constant shuffling act of departmental priorities while every day, new files landed on his desk.

The detective reached down to stuff a folder into the cardboard box at his feet. "Sorry about the bad news, Brady. You know how it is. I'm two weeks behind on my reports," he'd gestured, indicating the pile of paperwork in front of him. "Listen, if we get any new intel, we'll take another look at it."

The detective's lackluster reassurance left Brady with the sour taste of disappointment in his mouth. Bracing himself for what lay ahead as he rode the Muni back to his apartment, he plotted his next steps, starting with a phone call to his client to break the news.

From the other side of the country, Roger had steadfastly continued to retain the investigator's services, wiring a healthy stipend to Brady's bank account on the first of every month. He had insisted all along that he wanted to keep the investigation going, although lately he'd begun to sound less convinced that the effort would pay off.

"This thing is taking its toll on Alice," he confessed. "She hasn't been sleeping well. She's just not herself. She's at sixes and sevens, and she misses Phillip terribly."

"Of course she does," Brady sympathized. "I'm really sorry to hear Alice isn't feeling well. Please give her my best, would you?"

Distracted, Roger didn't seem to have heard him. "To tell the truth, Phillip's disappearance is taking its toll on everyone. I talked to my daughter this morning. Beth has been so worried she's having a hell of a time concentrating at work. There's some kind of restructuring thing going on with her company, and now she's afraid she's going to lose her job. There wasn't much I could think of to cheer her up, and now you tell me the police are ready to call it a day."

Even as far away as San Francisco, Brady could almost picture Roger pacing back and forth and had no difficulty imagining the grim look on his face. His client's despair was palpable, and Brady struggled to reassure Phillip's father with a detailed report on his most recent trip south.

"I know how hard this is on the whole family, Roger, and I'm doing my best to find your son. Trust me, I'm not going to give up."

"Frankly, Brady, it's hard for me to believe nobody has stepped up to try to get that reward money, for Christ's sake!"

"Doesn't seem like it, not yet, anyway." He tried to inject a measure of professional calm into his voice. "I've just completed another sweep through Lancaster. Checked out the surrounding area in every direction and picked up the guest register from a nearby shelter Phillip may have stayed at," he reported. "Trouble is, the cops continue to maintain that the parking lot where the Volvo was found is where the trail goes dead. Without any surveillance video, every single one of those Walmart cameras have turned out to be useless."

Brady knew that in any investigation there was always more digging that could be done, and it was his opinion that law enforcement's decision to dismiss Walmart as a potential source of clues had been overly hasty. Working on a theory that someone must have seen Phillip, he'd spoken not only to the librarian but to bartenders and bank tellers, mothers pushing strollers and teenagers shooting hoops in the park, all the while hoping that someone's memory would be jogged. Patiently waiting for that person to come forward, he had to admit he was growing frustrated, and he knew his client was, too. As they hung up the phone, Brady assured him that finding his son was only a matter of time and perseverance.

Law enforcement may have shoved the case files into cold storage, but he wasn't about to give up.

In his heart, Brady knew he would not stop searching for Roger's missing son, because he was still searching for his own. He knew all too well that the aftermath of any tragedy has an immeasurable and long-lasting impact on those left behind.

For years, each member of his family had agonized over what they could have done to alter the events of the fateful afternoon that Brendan had disappeared. Colleen blamed herself for allowing her eight-year-old son to walk to the youth center. Decades later, Shane was still punishing himself for not accompanying his little brother to Scouts. Brendan's innocent little sisters had immediately acquired the nervous habit of looking over their shoulders, lest they too might be snatched away, and they'd grown up regarding the world around them with unnatural suspicion. Each of the children had been wrenched from the carefree purity of childhood, and their parents' marriage had not been able to withstand the fallout. Every single member of the family had been traumatized to the core.

The tentacles of the aftermath had been far-reaching. Brady transferred to detective work, thinking he could solve his missing son's case from within. Born and raised a Catholic who'd practiced faithfully his whole life, he'd turned his back on his religion. Even now there were days he wished that he could still believe and envied those who did, but his faith in a benevolent God had been permanently shattered when Brendan had vanished without a trace.

Computer-aged sketches of at first, a teenager, and now, a full-grown man, had taken the place of those early pictures of a freckle-faced eight-year-old. Brady shook the sleep from his eyes every morning with a familiar hollow heartache. Cocooned under a soft blanket in the fog of those first few minutes of consciousness as scattered rays of dim morning light crept through the blinds, he remembered that he still did not know what had happened. The anguish that never left him always took him by surprise. Nestled beneath the comforter he considered whether he should remain in the paralyzing stupor he felt or get out of bed and throw himself into more hard work.

Keep going, he rallied himself time and again. *It's not what's already been done. It's what hasn't been done. Think about that and get back to work.*

Somehow, every morning Brady managed to convince himself to try once more to put an end to the relentless uncertainty that had taken up residency in his gut.

CHAPTER EIGHTEEN

Spring 2004

STEVE

When he sat down to play on New Year's Day, Steve soon learned that tournament poker was a beast of another color. Squeezed in shoulder to shoulder at a table with eight other hopeful club regulars, he'd quickly surveyed the circle, recognizing brothers Mikey and Eric right away. His betting chips, organized by color into tidy stacks when the Tournament Director called out "shuffle up and play," had begun to shrink almost from the start, holding out just past the first hour of competition. Rob fared much better, managing to take sixth place and more than double his initial buy-in. Later, when they reviewed the hands Steve had lost, he tried to learn from his mistakes.

He admitted he'd been more than a little nervous at first, and his pulse had quickened when he was dealt a premium hand, two shining one-eyed Jacks. Bested by a pair of Kings, he kicked himself for having fallen in love with his cards and not laying them down. Moments later when his King-Ten hit Two Pair on the flop, he'd confidently raised and re-raised, despite the Ace on the board warning him to take it slow.

"Even if he paired his Ace, I already got Two Pair," he smiled slyly, his hand covering his mouth.

But as Steve soon learned, the poker gods can be cruel. An unassuming Eight on the flop had turned his opponent's matched pair of Eights into a set, and referencing the hand-ranking chart he'd committed to memory, Steve had forked over what remained of his chips. Miffed as he conceded his mistake, he learned the hard way that Three of a Kind will take down Two Pair all day.

Later when he reflected on his loss, he concluded he'd better hone his skills playing smaller tournaments before returning to a multi-table contest. The pulse of the competition had been unmistakable, demanding such single-minded concentration that he hadn't once thought of anything else, including his family or the fact that at home it was still Christmas vacation. He'd been grateful for the distraction, apprehensive that the twin daggers of guilt and doubt might have the power to unsettle him. Through the remainder of the lonely holiday week at the nearly empty motel, he'd passed most of his time playing free practice hands on the internet and heating up cans of Campbell's Hungry Man soup in the microwave oven in the lobby.

The days began to grow longer as spring approached. He got to know some of Rob's friends at the club, and they happily shared all kinds of advice. At two and three-table tournaments, he began experimenting with different strategies, searching for ways to prolong the stretch of time he remained in the game. *"Seems like luck is a huge part of it,"* he observed, and he vowed to become more patient and to wait for opportunities to capitalize on good luck when it arrived. He discovered that his people-reading skills were well-suited to the game, and soon he found he could almost always hold onto his chips long enough to make it to the Final Table, the group remaining at a tournament's end. When he'd routinely begun placing fifth or fourth or sometimes even third, he set his sights higher and sought out larger, more challenging contests.

One Friday evening, Steve stepped out of the motel shower onto the grimy bathmat and began to prepare for his date with Jackie. The steamy bathroom mirror hid the beard he'd let grow in, and with a threadbare towel, he wiped off the mirror and began trimming the few stray hairs he'd found. Lately he and Jackie had been spending nearly all their free time together. Tonight they planned to catch the new Jim Carrey movie in town. Rummaging in the back of the closet he shared with Bobby in search of the new shirt he'd hung there, he stumbled on a crumpled shopping bag tucked in the corner. Uncertain whose it was, he peeked inside and discovered a new pair of size eleven Michael Jordan sneakers with the tags still attached. He lifted the bag out of the closet to take a closer look. Behind the bag on the floor of the closet sat two iPods, one still housed in its original packaging, and a couple of men's wristwatches in velvet jewelry boxes.

What the hell is this? Is all this stuff stolen? What's Bobby been up to?

An alarm bell in Steve's brain began to chime, urging him to put everything back just the way he'd found it, and he sat down heavily on his bed as he tried to make sense of what he'd seen.

This is really bad. Steve's mind was racing. *If he's been stealing, it's only a question of time 'til the cops bust in here and start asking questions.* He felt his chest tighten with panic and reminded himself to breathe. *I can't let that happen.* He told himself to calm down, returning to the closet for his new shirt. He reached into a dresser drawer for his favorite sweater and peered into the rusty mirror to drag a comb through his wet hair. Glancing at the clock on the chipped wooden nightstand, he realized he'd need to hurry.

Okay, buddy. The gig here is over. Caput. Time to move on. No way the cops can find you here, sharing a room with Bobby. Time to get the hell out. He stuffed his room key into the pocket of his trousers and stared at himself in the mirror. *But where can I go?*

On the dresser, a torn receipt lay nestled between a Bic lighter and pack of Marlboros. Holding the crumpled paper up to the light, he squinted trying to make out the faded letters. The only word he could decipher was *pawn.*

First thing tomorrow, I'll take a look at Craigslist. He'd heard there was a market for house sitters and even pet sitters now. *Fingers crossed, maybe I'll get lucky again and find another place that's rent-free and leave this crummy motel in a heartbeat.* Steve pulled the door shut behind him. *I'll spend more time with Jackie,* he smiled despite his concern about what his roommate was up to. *Bet she'll like that.*

They met downtown and picked up slices of pizza as they strolled through the park before the movie. Afterward, they stopped for ice cream in the cool night air, licking each other's cones. Jackie suggested they go on a picnic that weekend, and on Sunday, she packed a wicker basket full of all the things she knew he liked.

He spread a blanket over the spongy grass in a secluded corner of the park.

This feels great, he mused, lying back after they'd eaten the sandwiches she'd made.

"I bet you were a knock-out in high school," he teased, his fingers running up and down the freckled skin on her bare arm and pausing at the hollow beneath her elbow.

A rosy flush appeared on her neck, and she laughed. "No, not really. I studied a lot, and my girlfriend's mom got me a job after school."

"Oh yeah? What kind of job?"

"It was in the childcare room at the Y. My friend worked there, too. We just played games with the kids and watched them on the playground. It was fun, and we got paid for it."

"Didn't you ever sneak out of the house to meet some guy or get in trouble for breaking curfew?"

"My sister did that, but not me. I was always home on time. She was the wild one, I was the good kid."

"I was the good kid, too," he sighed. "My sister and me, we were both the good kids."

She laughed. "Are you and your folks close? I was thinking of going home for a visit, maybe Mother's Day. Bakersfield isn't that far from here. Want to tag along?"

"Sure," he replied. "I'd love to." He propped himself up on an elbow to gaze at her.

"Had enough to eat? she asked, smiling. "Full?"

"Very full." He patted his belly. "Everything was delicious." He leaned in close. When they kissed, her lips were warm and smooth on his, and her hair had the faint scent of spring flowers.

When she pulled away, he lay back again and clasped his hands behind his head, shutting his eyes against the afternoon sun breaking through the trees overhead. It had been a long time since he'd lain beside a woman, and the one on the blanket beside him was unlike any he'd ever known. *For one thing, she's not making any demands, and she hasn't asked where things might lead.* He opened one eye. *What's she thinking? Is she picturing us together down the road?* Discomfort rippled through him briefly. *It's way too soon to think about that. Technically*, he reminded himself, *I'm still married.*

Steve had never thought about asking Susan for a divorce, even after the months of couples' counseling that had failed to fix things between them, and he found himself wondering whether opening himself up like this was risky. *How am I gonna keep Jackie from learning the truth?* Against his will, his lips curled into an uneasy scowl.

Jackie's finger traced the glower that had creased his face. "You okay?"

He looked at her. The pretty woman sitting cross-legged beside him wore a genuine expression of concern. Her khaki shorts were cinched at the waist by a thin belt of braided red leather, and with pleasure Steve noticed the dimples in her bare knees.

"Sure, I'm fine. It's nothing."

She bent over and kissed him. He tasted orange soda on her tongue and kissed her back, their mouths slightly open, their eyes closed. She wanted him. He saw it in the flush of her face and felt it in her mouth and in the way she pressed her warm body against his. The back of his neck grew wet with beads of perspiration as desire fluttered through him, as necessary as air to breathe.

Arousal stirred him like an old friend.

It wasn't Susan's memory that came to him now, but Chloe's, her hand on his thigh and the sudden electricity racing through his loins when her fingers inched upward toward his groin.

"How about we head back to my place?" Jackie murmured in a husky voice, pressing close enough to Steve to feel his heartbeat.

Every inch of him answered *yes*.

They hurried to pack up the remains of their picnic, clumsily folding the fuzzy blanket and leaving a trail of crumbs for the geese hovering nearby. As they made their way back to her car, she shyly slipped her small hand into his, and he realized how much he'd missed a woman's touch.

He squeezed the delicate fingers that held his thick ones. "What are you thinking about?"

She didn't answer right away, leaning over to brush his cheek with lips warm from the sun, or from the heat between them. "You really want to know?" she asked, handing him the car keys.

He looked at her quizzically. "Sure."

"I'm thinking that maybe," Jackie whispered, "maybe I'm falling in love with you."

CHAPTER NINETEEN

Fall 2004

BRADY

The Giants had taken the field to start their warm up. Seated behind third base, Brady passed a printed program over to Andrew. "America's pastime," he quoted from the brochure. "Baseball's such a great game, isn't it?"

"Hang on a sec." Andrew was bent over, reaching into the backpack at his feet for a creased leather mitt, freshly oiled that morning and smelling faintly of rawhide. "Never know if you'll catch one," he grinned, his face shiny with anticipation as he craned his neck and looked around. "These seats are perfect for foul balls."

"You're right about that."

The season was well underway, and it had turned into the kind of crisp, cloudless day in San Francisco he remembered from his own childhood. Balancing paper plates of garlic fries in their laps, they bent their heads over the program to compare batting averages. Andrew bragged that he knew the names and jersey numbers of most of the home team players, and to prove it, he began to recite them. In their bright orange and black Giants caps, the two of them seated shoulder to shoulder looked as if they might have been grandfather and grandson enjoying an afternoon in the sun together.

Last Sunday, Brady had stopped by the house with a box of Krispy Kreme donuts for the kids and a bouquet of fresh flowers for Susan. He'd also brought a couple of game tickets a client had given him and offered to share them with Andrew. Now the boy set the plate of garlic fries on the empty seat beside him and slid the fingers of his left hand into his glove, pounding the pocket with his right fist.

"My dad gave me this mitt a couple years ago. It's a little small for me now, but it still kind of fits."

Brady knew how much the boy missed his father's attendance at his ball games. "Hey, what do you think of your team this year? How's the JV season starting out?"

Andrew enthusiastically described how he'd gotten on base twice last weekend, once on a walk and once with a double. "Line drive all the way to left field." With animation, he shared a funny story about the crazy pre-game drills the coach had the team doing right up until game time. Brady flagged down the hotdog vendor for a couple of chili dogs. Hungrily biting into his, Andrew asked, "Say, Mr. Brady, you want to come to one of my games? We're playing at home next weekend."

"Sounds like a great idea," he replied warmly, scribbling the details of the invitation onto the back of his ticket stub.

The public school Andrew had transferred to for his second year of high school was sprawling, but Brady easily located the game behind the gym and slipped into a seat beside Susan and Gracie in the home team bleachers. The grassy playing fields had been freshly mowed, and the straight white lines between the bases looked as if they'd recently been painted. Boys of all sizes wearing pin-striped uniforms and batting helmets crowded around the dugout in front of the bleachers. Brady checked the tall green scoreboard in right field and saw with satisfaction that Andrew's team led by two.

He turned to Susan to ask how things were going with the new part-time job she'd taken. Dark glasses hid her eyes, and the corners of her mouth were pinched. With a grimace, she responded that the take-home pay wasn't enough to cover their expenses.

"I'm looking for a boarder to bring in some cash," she confided in a voice that carried over the crowd.

Squirming beside her, Gracie groaned. "What's a boarder? Am I gonna have to share my room?" *Her voice is also too loud,* Brady thought, as spectators beside them turned their heads. "What about the bathroom? Gross!"

The poor kid is worried, he realized. *Can't say I blame her."*

Scanning the area next to the bleachers, he spotted three girls that looked to be about Gracie's age. They were happily jumping rope, and he asked if she wouldn't like to join them. She shook her head vehemently, inching closer to her mother, and began rhythmically kicking the metal seat in front of her. A woman decked out smartly in a sequined sun visor turned around to glare at the disturbance before moving to a different seat. Neither Gracie nor her mother appeared to notice the people seated around them. The two huddled together at the far end of the stands, separate and alone. Spectators cheered or groaned as the game went on, and after a few futile attempts to engage Susan in conversation, Brady gave up. When the game was over, he swung down from the bleachers and dusted off his trousers. Barely managing to high-five Andrew as the JV team swarmed out of the dugout, he heard the coach call a huddle. "Good game," Brady called out over the confusion. "I'll try and stop by later this week."

He didn't have a free moment until Wednesday afternoon. When he finally made it over to the house for a visit, he wasn't even sure anyone was home. The curtains in the living room window were drawn, and the house looked dark when he rang the bell.

"It's open, come on in," he heard Andrew yell from inside.

Opening the unlocked door, Brady found the boy at the kitchen table leafing through a paperback copy of *The Catcher in the Rye*.

"Hey, how's it going, kiddo?"

Andrew polished off the apple in his hand in three large bites. "Hi, Mr. Brady. Doing alright," he mumbled, juice running from his lips. He wiped his mouth with the sleeve of his flannel shirt and got up to grab a couple of sodas from the fridge. "Looking for quotes to use for my English paper. You ever read this?" He held up the book so Brady could see the cover.

"Ah, yes, Holden Caulfield. J.D. Salinger was a great writer, wasn't he? I loved that book when I was in school. You know, back in the Civil War days."

Andrew chuckled appreciatively. "Coke or 7-Up?"

"Coke. Frankly, I'm glad they're still teaching that book. My kids really liked it, too." Happy he'd found Andrew in a talkative mood, he continued. "How about you, what did you think?"

"Great book, the best. I'm thinking about writing about his sister, Phoebe. We have to pick one person to analyze, but it can't be Holden. My teacher calls it a character analysis," he explained. "I like Phoebe because she's still an innocent little kid. See, Holden's the older brother, kind of like me, and Phoebe's kind of like Gracie. She's the little sister, and she's kind of got this innocence." He handed Brady the soda and tore open a bag of Nutter Butters. "Phoebe's too little to have been messed up by life yet, you know what I mean? Nothing really bad has happened to her yet. Plus, she's pretty much the only person Holden actually likes. He hates everyone else."

"I got it!" Brady snapped his fingers. "I read it a long time ago, but I remember that Holden kept calling everyone a *phony*. Everyone except his sister, that is. Right?"

"Yep, that's him all right. So you remember Phoebe?"

A memory at the back of Brady's mind tumbled forward. "Kind of. Mostly though, I remember Holden. And that red hunting cap he wore. Wait, doesn't Phoebe give Holden her Christmas money?"

"That's right, she does! The thing is, when she does that, it makes him cry. It really gets to him. That part of the book is pretty amazing, no kidding. Hang on a sec." Andrew began flipping through pages. "Look, I marked this paragraph to use in my paper. Think this is a good quote to use?"

Brady took the paperback from Andrew's outstretched hand and studied the highlighted passage. "You know, you're right, this is fantastic. J.D. Salinger was something else, wasn't he?" He leaned back, enjoying the friendly exchange. "Nice work, Andrew, finding that passage. I'm sure your paper is going to be first rate. You a sophomore this year?"

"Yep, second year."

"You enjoying your new school, then?"

He saw a muscle begin to twitch in Andrew's cheek as the boy twisted the tab on his drink. "Not really. I like my English class, and Social Studies is okay. At my old school, I used to like everything, even math and science, and you know, all the sports." His voice trailed off. "It's all different now."

There had been a lot of changes, Brady knew. That fall, Andrew had transferred from a small college prep to the huge public high school down the block. He hadn't complained and seemed to have taken it in stride, and Brady knew he was proud he'd made the baseball team. To him, Andrew seemed more mature than most kids, but he knew that without a dad around, it wouldn't be hard to fall through the cracks.

"Listen," he suggested in what he hoped was a fatherly way, "if you're having trouble with anything, like Math or Science, don't be afraid to ask your teachers for help. Maybe get some one-on-one help after school if there's something you don't understand."

Pressing his lips together tightly, Andrew folded his arms over his chest.

"Really, I mean it. Don't be shy about asking for help," Brady went on. "You don't want to let yourself get behind."

"Yeah, maybe," Andrew grunted. "See, it's mostly Biology. The class is huge. In my old school, we had fifteen kids at the most. Here's it's more like forty, and it's so noisy and disorganized, sometimes I can't even hear what the teacher's saying."

"Hang in there, it's still only the beginning of the year. Sometimes it takes a few weeks for things to settle down."

The boy seemed to bristle, and Brady wondered if it was a mistake for him to offer fatherly advice. Andrew began gathering his books together, saying he'd better get started on his paper. Brady reached out cautiously to detain him.

"Before you head off, tell me something, how are Gracie and your mom doing? I could barely get a word out of either of them at your game the other day."

Andrew shifted the books to his other hand and seemed to choose his words with care. "The thing is, Mr. Brady, Mom really hates the new job. She says all she does is empty bedpans. She complains a lot."

"Couldn't she get some kind of office work instead? Something more skilled?"

"I don't know, I think she took the first job she could find." He shrugged with irritation. "And Gracie cries at just about anything. No kidding, the kid doesn't have one single friend! Aren't little girls supposed to play with Barbie dolls or Beanie Babies with other little girls?" He looked puzzled. "You know what, Mr. Brady? Gracie isn't anything like Holden's sister Phoebe, now that I'm thinking about it. Gracie isn't like anyone's sister I can think of. She's, I don't know. Gracie's just different."

Brady hesitated. "Listen, kiddo, I know it's tough with your dad not around and all. It's hard on everyone. She's probably having a tough time, too." He made a mental note to suggest counseling to Susan once again, if not for her, then for her daughter.

Andrew looked down at his shoes. "She says it's her fault that Dad left. She thinks she got on Dad's nerves or made him angry. I told her it's not her fault. But you know what? Gracie always thinks everything is her fault, even before this. She doesn't have any, what do you call it? Self-confidence. She never did."

"How does she do in school?"

"I guess she has a lot of trouble sitting still. Dad used to tell her to stop fidgeting and pay attention. I learned to read when I was five, but she could barely manage those Easy Reader books in second grade. She's just kinda slow. Mom said she didn't care, she said everyone learns to read, but Dad always seemed like he was getting fed up with Gracie."

"Think things have gotten worse this year?"

"Yeah, probably. Mom keeps getting calls from the principal. After it happened, I went back to school right away, but Gracie wouldn't go. She just wanted to stay home with Mom. I think a lot of times she faked being sick."

It was getting late, and Brady could see that Andrew was itching to head upstairs. "Hey, Mr. Brady, I gotta get started on my paper." Halfway out of the room, he turned back. "I don't know what's going on with Mom. She started smoking again, and I don't remember exactly, but I don't think she used to drink this much booze." As he reached the stairway, Andrew paused as if he suddenly realized maybe he shouldn't have said so much, especially the part about his mom's drinking. A hooded look came over his eyes, and Brady could sense the boy begin to pull back into himself.

"I guess we all think it's our fault Dad left."

"You, too? Do you think that?"

"No," Andrew breathed softly, "not really." His boyish chin quivered. "You know, sometimes I'll go a whole day without even thinking about him." In a voice so low it was nearly a whisper, he asked, "Do you think that's weird, Mr. Brady?"

At the foot of the stairs, he reached out to squeeze the boy's shoulder.

"No, it's not weird."

The heart can grow callous when filled with unspeakable loss, and Brady ached for the teenage boy before him struggling on the precipice of manhood. He wanted to tell him that each of us must travel a lonely journey without the aid of a roadmap, a solitary journey through sorrow and anger in order to one day arrive at acceptance. But the right words eluded him, and the moment in which to speak them passed. The best he could manage was to feebly clasp the boy's shoulder. He knew how inadequate the gesture was and mourned that he could not do more for him. For Andrew, the process of forgetting had begun to set in, and Brady knew that acceptance was still very far away.

CHAPTER TWENTY

Fall 2004

STEVE

Don't be hasty, don't jump the gun, Steve reminded himself again for what seemed like the millionth time. *Gotta do things right. Take Bobby out for a drink first. Maybe pick up some flowers for Aunt Millie. A plant for the lobby. Brighten the place up a little before I go.*

Although he'd be the first to admit that the Desert Motel had been a lifesaver when he'd needed it, now he was apt to break out in a sweat every time he opened the closet door. There was no question about it, Bobby's stash had grown larger. Chowing down on breakfast at the diner, he scribbled a list on the back of a paper napkin, and one by one Steve began checking off the boxes.

A sweet second-hand motorbike turned up on Craigslist, and he dug into his poker winnings to buy it. The bike required a Class M1 license to make it street legal, and that meant standing in line all afternoon at the DMV with two pieces of mail addressed to him and sweating through a written multiple-choice test. The test was peppered with trick questions, and he failed it on the first try and had to return and stand in line all over to try again. At the bus station, he removed the bulging shoeboxes stuffed with cash, and armed with the motorcycle license identifying him as Steve Phillips, he opened a brand new bank account, tossing the tattered boxes into the nearest receptacle.

Transportation, check. License, check. Bank account, check. First month's rent and security deposit, all set. Just as he was beginning to relax, he realized he had no idea how to solve the next problem and scratched his head thoughtfully.

Any landlord is gonna need proof of employment.

Feeling queasy lately about bunking down in the motel room he shared with Bobby, Steve had started staying over at Jackie's so often that Rob, with a knowing wink, asked if the two were living together. No, Steve confided, it wasn't something he or Jackie had talked about, and he wasn't sure what he'd say if she brought it up.

"Jackie is one of a kind, man. She's the least demanding woman I've ever known," he told his buddy. "Doesn't even seem to mind when I play cards into the wee hours."

He wasn't ready to make any promises about the future, preferring to take one day at a time. With his stomach grumbling already as he stood in line at their usual taqueria, he scanned the menu idly. His mouth watered as he ordered the Tacos al Pastor, and he debated picking up extra guacamole and salsa for Jackie. She wasn't an especially big eater, but he knew she had a weakness for those salty Mexican chips. They were celebrating tonight. She'd finally nabbed a full-time position with the school district as an itinerant Special Ed teacher. He'd helped her line the back of her car with file boxes full of learning resources so she could visit schools all over the county to help struggling kids access the services they'd been promised.

"The state is required to provide these services," she'd explained. "That's what's so frustrating." A lot of the kids Jackie worked with couldn't read well, mixing up the letters and the words on the page. Some relied on medicine to stay focused, and all too often their parents forgot to get the prescriptions filled. Last night, Steve had watched her comb through a huge stack of papers she told him were IEPs, Individual Education Plans.

"What are you looking for?" he'd asked, peering over her shoulder.

"I'm matching each student's needs with the services I know are there for them," she'd told him.

Jackie loved the kids, especially the youngest and most vulnerable and seemed to be especially fond of the ones with more than one problem. "What I do is really not that hard," she insisted. "And I love helping them." The frailest kids were her biggest weakness, and she knew she had to guard against the urge to swoop in and rescue them all.

Steve opted for the extra guacamole and salsa and managed to squeeze everything into the bike bag he carried. Smiling appreciatively as he entered the apartment, he saw that Jackie had set the table and lit a fat yellow candle. Samba music played on the radio.

"Have a good day?" he asked as they polished off the juicy tacos and worked their way through a couple of beers.

"A busy day, that's for sure! Two meetings back-to-back after school. Oh, and Mr. Will, the principal I told you about, remember? The one I like so much? He just announced his retirement."

Steve's thumb peeled the corner of the IPA label on his bottle of beer, listening with only half an ear. He pointed at the remaining taco, reaching for it when she shook her head. He spooned the last bit of guacamole over the taco. He'd been planning a trip to the club later to take some easy money from the amateur players who drank too much and played fast and loose. *Fish*, he'd heard them called.

Dipping a chip into salsa, Jackie chattered away. "They're throwing a surprise going-away party for Mr. Will. He and his wife are going to Europe on some kind of fancy tour group trip. They're starting in London and then going to a whole list of countries. I guess they'll be gone for weeks! Or maybe it's months, I forget. Oh my gosh, they're so excited! He said neither of them have ever been outside the U.S." She sighed wistfully. "I've barely set foot out of the state. Never been to Europe. Have you?"

"Nope, never." He licked the salsa from his fingers. "Something to look forward to when we're that age, right?" Scooping up the empty wrappers, he grinned at her. "Right?"

Jackie pressed her lips together. Each dreaming silently of something in the distant future, they sipped their beers.

An idea had begun to form in the back of Steve's mind, and he pushed his plate to the side and turned to her. "So, this principal and his wife, you think they need somebody to housesit or maybe pet sit while they're away? Someone to take care of the mail? Where exactly do they live?"

"No idea," she shrugged, looking puzzled. "Somewhere nearby, I think, maybe Willow Springs?" She cocked her head and squinted at him. "Why? You want me to ask him?"

"I mean, if it seems like there's a good moment, sure, that'd be cool." He tried to sound casual. "I'd love to help out, if they need it."

Steve's sudden idea turned out to be a brilliant stroke of timing. Jackie was good at her word, and after a phone call to the principal, that weekend they drove over to Willow Springs so she could introduce the man she had assured Mr. Will was so trustworthy. Pulling into the driveway, Steve had to pinch himself. The sprawling ranch house, painted a hue that reminded him of coffee laced with real cream, looked like it belonged on the cover of *Home and Garden*. A trail of tiny yellow roses graced the cheerful wooden trellis a few steps from the sidewalk, and bougainvillea of every shade hung from the eaves on the veranda where two white Adirondack chairs flanked a small table. A row of flower boxes lined the bay window facing the street, and a welcome sign hung from the brass knocker on the front door.

"Nice place," he whispered as Jackie leaned on the bell.

Tall and trim, a mustachioed Mr. Will answered the door. His wife met them in the living room holding a glass pitcher of iced tea. "Please, have some, won't you?" she offered, setting it down on the coffee table with a tray of tall glasses. "I'll be right back with the lemon tarts. They just came out of the oven," she smiled warmly.

Moments later, leaning forward eagerly from his seat on the couch, without planning to, Steve automatically donned his reporter's face, open and reliable, and assured Mr. and Mrs. Will that helping them out would be his pleasure. He held his breath as he watched them look him up and down and wondered secretly if he was about to get lucky again.

"It'd be great to have someone clip the roses, and we like to get the dogs out for a walk every day. I'll arrange to pay bills in advance, but maybe you could sort through the mail and forward anything that looks important," Mr. Will proposed. "We'd already been thinking about hiring a gardener and putting the dogs in a kennel, so you'd actually be saving us money."

His wife touched his arm. "Couldn't we offer a small stipend in exchange?"

"Oh, no, I wouldn't hear of it. I'm happy to make myself useful," Steve objected, helping himself to a second lemon tart. "May I? These are so good, Mrs. Will." He rolled his eyes appreciatively. "Delicious." He wiped the corner of his mouth with the cocktail napkin Jackie had passed to him.

Mrs. Will beamed. "I'm so glad you like them!"

"Listen, you two should relax and enjoy your trip to Europe without worrying about things back home. Sounds like a once-in-a-lifetime vacation. After all these years, I'm sure you've earned it!"

"I have been kind of worried about my English garden," she confessed. "It's taken a lot of work, but it's finally just about perfect."

The arrangement was settled quickly. While staying in the Wills' guest room, Steve promised to walk the two rambunctious golden retrievers and tend the orderly garden, to keep the spiky bougainvillea in check and mow the lawn every couple of weeks. Wasn't it lucky, the soon-to-be retirees asked themselves, that the friendly new Special Ed teacher had such a trustworthy boyfriend willing to do them this favor?

"I'll sure miss you," Jackie said fondly as Mr. Will bent down to graze her cheek. "But I know you guys are going to have a great time." She grasped his wife's outstretched hand. "Be sure and send us postcards, won't you?"

The weekend after he'd packed up and carted his things to Willow Springs, glossy new posters appeared near the cashier's cage in the card club. "Save the date! Join us for Tag Team Poker!" the posters announced in bold letters, and on Monday, Rob cornered him, pointing at the wall behind the coffee table.

"Listen, tag team is crazy fun. Let's sign up together!" Excitement shone in his ruddy face. "It's a good way to keep working on our skills, and it'll be wild!"

Skeptical, Steve frowned. "I don't know. What is tag team poker, anyway? I've never even heard of it. How does it work?"

"I've only played it once, but I'm telling you, it was a hoot. You sign up together with a buddy. Each guy forks up half the entry fee and you share a stack of chips. You can tag out anytime, then the other guy takes over. It's back and forth like that." Rob threw a friendly arm around Steve's shoulder. "It's way more fun than a regular tournament. Everyone is more relaxed, more casual. Trust me, you're gonna love it."

Steve hesitated, squinting. "But how do you figure out who plays and when? Do you split the time evenly?"

"Not necessarily. Usually teams do something like twenty minutes on, twenty minutes off, but one guy could end up playing more, I guess. I've seen some partners use the good cop, bad cop routine. You know, one guy is the bully, the other guy plays tight." Grinning, Rob leaned in close and poked him in the ribs. "We could decide on a strategy going in, or we can make it up as we go, either way. Come on, man, it'll be a gas!"

Steve admitted that lately he'd been making great strides and his poker game had been getting better and better. He'd begun to feel relaxed at the table and had been having fun, engaging in lively banter with the other players. He stroked his beard thoughtfully. "I don't know. I'd feel bad if I blew it on some stupid bet and lost all our chips. It's not like I have a ton of experience yet. Maybe I should wait 'til the next time this tag team thing comes around."

Rob shook his head. "Who knows when that's gonna be? Listen, you're playing just about every day now and winning a lot," he argued. "Right? Haven't you been taking down tons of pots? You're as good as I am. I think maybe we're about even. We even play the same style. C'mon, we'd be great partners," he wheedled.

Still unconvinced, Steve held back. "When is this supposed to happen, anyway?"

Rob glanced around the card club at the oversized posters staring down at them from all sides. "What, are you blind, man?

Everyone's talking about it," he cuffed his friend lightly. "Where've you been? Look around you!"

He surveyed the familiar club. A buzz seemed to have filled the contours of the cavernous space overnight, and even the bored security guard working his Sudoku puzzles at the front door was engaged in an animated conversation with a couple of regulars.

His buddy wasn't about to let up. "Next Saturday, it's a one day event. Look, we'll play all day, and then you and Jackie can come over to our place after. Judy'll pick up some ribs, and we'll barbeque. You and me, we'll man the grill," he coaxed. "Come on, buddy, it'll be a blast!"

Crowding noisily into the club in pairs, over two hundred hopeful partners signed up for the event. It had drawn a noisy assortment of couples, a few father-and-son teams, even a pair of identical twins. Partners flipped a coin to see who would play first, and Rob slid into a seat at one of the oval tables, packed with a spirited group of aspiring gamblers. Steve recognized Ira, and a friend at another table waved and mouthed "good luck." He saw Mikey in his usual blue jumpsuit seated at a table near the cashier's cage and his brother Eric standing nearby.

For the first twenty minutes, Rob sat back and scrutinized the action on the faded green felt. Steve watched his partner go to work projecting the image of an overly cautious player while trying to spot the inexperienced players, the *fish*. Over and over, as opponents called and re-raised him, Rob tossed his cards into the muck. By the time he motioned for Steve to take over, about a quarter of their starting chips had disappeared.

"Sorry, Buddy, not a great start," Rob leaned in to whisper in Steve's ear. "The good news is, I've got them thinking I'm super tight."

"I'll see what I can do to change things up."

The plan they'd agreed on called for Steve to take the more aggressive stance, and waking up with Kings almost as soon as he'd sat down, he three-bet and took down a good size pot. He raked in the winning chips, and Rob, grinning, shot him a thumbs up. Steve rolled up his sleeves and stacked his chips neatly in front of him. Many inexperienced players were eliminated early from the competition, and roughly every half hour, teammates swapped places with each other. At the break, he and Rob each dug hungrily into their jackets for the snacks they'd brought along.

"What do you think? Should we change up our game?" Rob asked, his mouth crammed full with a Cliff bar.

Steve had already devoured half of a lukewarm sausage muffin in two huge bites. "Yeah, maybe we should sit out more hands now, let some of these guys take each other out. Things are about to change."

Rob knew his partner was referring to the momentum shift that happens when players begin to take bigger risks, shoving chips into the pot and hoping others will fold any hands that might otherwise beat them. "I think so, too. A lot of teams are about to bite the dust," he agreed. "Let's dial it back and try to make it to the Final Table."

He and Steve cut down on the percentage of hands they played just as the other teams began increasing theirs. When the dust had settled two hours later, they found themselves one of nine teams still alive.

"Congratulations, players," called out the uniformed Tournament Director, stepping into the circle to oversee the action more closely. "Welcome to the Final Table! Good luck, ladies and gentlemen!"

The blinds and antes required to play each hand were sky high by then, and players with short stacks began to take do-or-die risks. Trying to steal pots, gamblers shoved all their chips over the betting line and held their breath, hoping to convince their opponents to stand down.

Many of the big risk-takers busted out and grudgingly bumped fists in a gesture of good sportsmanship as they left the table. Patiently, Rob bided his time, waiting for position and playing only the blinds, until just two other teams were represented at the final table. A young woman and an older Filipino man nodded warily at him from behind dark glasses, and Rob craned his neck to look at Steve.

By that time, fatigue had set in, affecting them all. Onlookers shouted encouragement to their friends, and a weary Rob signaled his partner for relief. Steve had just downed his fourth cup of the watery coffee the club kept brewing when he squared his shoulders and took his seat and began arranging the chips he'd been left with. Before he had a chance to ask what the blinds were, he felt a light tap on his shoulder and turned his head.

"How about a chop?" The older Filipino man beside him spread his open palms to include the trio of teams that had lasted this far. "Everybody agree?"

The suggestion that they split the winnings and call it a day was not unreasonable, and Steve paused to consider making a deal. A quick assessment of their chips revealed that his and the woman's stacks were very close in size, while the man proposing the three-way chop had curled his left hand protectively around a dangerously low stack.

Steve figured that since the fellow was short stacked, he was likely to shove everything he had into the next pot, and there was no telling how that might go. "Give me a minute," he replied, rising from his chair to consult with his partner.

Rob had immediately raised his eyebrows. "I wouldn't advise going all-in against the short-stack." He covered his mouth with his hand, whispering, "but you know what? I think *she* will. I've been watching her." He jerked his head to indicate the young woman riffling her chips on the felt. "She's pretty aggressive. She's gonna try to take him out. The guy figures he's got nothing to lose, so he'll shove, and she'll take the bait."

"Exactly what I think, too," Steve whispered.

"If that happens and she knocks him out, then you and she will be *heads-up*." Rob locked eyes with his buddy. "And you know what? I think you can take her down."

Steve's stomach churned, and he slowly returned to the table and took a deep breath, pausing to reflect. *Poker is a lot like life. You never have all the information you need to make good decisions. You've just gotta take your best shot.* He slid back into his seat as the other players scrutinized him closely. *And face it, you've got to have some luck.*

"I'm fine with a chop," the woman offered.

Any decision to chop the pot has to be unanimous, and in a quiet voice, Steve politely demurred. "Let's play on," he suggested, and the three settled down for the final battle.

As Rob had predicted, within seconds, the short-stack shoved all his chips over the line. Steve quickly folded his Eight-Ten off-suit and sat back in his chair to watch what the aggressive woman player would do. Sure enough, without hesitation, she called the bet, and just like that, the Filipino man and his partner busted out when their pair of Sevens failed to hold up against her Ace-Nine offsuit.

The winner removed her sunglasses and offered the loser her hand. "Good game," she said, and the two remaining players spread out for the endgame known as *heads-up*.

Many late nights after playing round after round of poker, Rob and Steve had debated and finally agreed that *heads-up* is a beast of another color. Because victory is so clearly black and white, status and ego are at stake just as much as the winnings, and a strategy for domination is more important than ever. Quite often even before any betting takes place, the outcome is determined because a player has committed to a certain degree of aggression, independent of the cards that are dealt.

Once the woman had knocked out the Filipino man, she took on the position of chip leader at the table. Her boyfriend, less consistently aggressive than the woman, stepped in to relieve her, and Steve found himself in trouble as he tried to adapt to the new player's style. Dark glasses obscured the man's eyes, and a hooded sweatshirt hid most of his face. With increasing alarm, Steve watched his own chip stack begin to shrink. At last he stood and gestured for his partner to spell him.

"It's not happening for me," he shook his head. "It's up to you now, Buddy."

At the midday break, he and Rob had discussed what their strategy might be if they were lucky enough to arrive at this point.

"Heads-up hands are won mostly by a high card or a pair. Hardly ever with Straights, Flushes, or even Two Pair. I say at that point, we just go for it," Rob had suggested.

"Be aggressive, force the other guy to fold," Steve had mused, thinking how unlikely it was that their tournament lives would even last that long.

Now that moment had arrived in earnest, and without delay, Rob set to work on the strategy they'd agreed on during those late night debates. Looking to intimidate the other player right off the bat, he made a couple of risky bets to test the waters. The younger man sprawled on the felt, his elbows resting on the table. He removed his dark glasses and for a long moment deliberately stared Rob down. Steve watched the man's eyes zero in on the steady pulse he could see throbbing in Rob's neck. Finally, his opponent folded his cards and tossed them into the muck. "Good fold," Rob commented as he turned over two shining Jacks to reveal the strength of his hand. Then barely glancing at his cards, several hands in a row, Rob made outsized bets, four or five times the big blinds, forcing his rival into folding, until finally the player's chip stack had been reduced to a fraction of what he'd started with. Squirming uncomfortably, the young man knew he was in big trouble now, and in desperation, he leaned forward and wagered all he had left. With a smug smile, the all-in player sat back and awaited Rob's reaction. Shrugging as if to say he could afford to take a chance with a hand or two, Steve's partner called the bet. His opponent flipped over a monster hand, the suited Ace-King of Spades, the odds-on favorite to win. Steve heard Rob draw a sharp breath as they waited for the dealer to place five cards one by one face up between them.

All at once, the contest was over.

On Sunday morning, when the residents of Rosamond shuffled out to their front porches in slippers and bathrobes to collect their morning papers, they were greeted by a front-page photograph of Rob grinning from ear to ear as he held up the winning hand, a pair of red Threes.

CHAPTER TWENTY-ONE

Fall 2005

BRADY

Brady looked up from the bank statement in his hand hoping the ringing phone meant that Roger was returning his call.

An unfamiliar voice greeted him. "Mr. Brady? It's Kevin Moffat here. I'm the guidance counselor at Eastmont High. I found your name listed in Andrew Lynch's file."

"Yes, he asked if he could include me. I guess you could say I'm a friend of the family. Everything ok? Is there some kind of problem?"

"No, I don't think so," the disembodied voice continued. "I'm calling about the college essay Andrew submitted. Are you familiar with it?"

"No, is it an assignment he needs help with?"

"Nothing like that," Mr. Moffat quickly reassured him. "The essay is a personal statement, an important part of his college application package. Our English teachers advise the kids to write about something personal, and Andrew has submitted a rather curious composition about his father, who he claims vanished into thin air a couple of years ago."

Brady thought the counselor sounded as if he doubted the accuracy of Andrew's account, and he did his best to maintain his composure as Mr. Moffat continued. "Frankly, the essay was quite disturbing, and I had to read through it twice. I wasn't quite certain it was true." He cleared his throat. "I have to admit, Mr. Brady, the level of raw emotion expressed in the essay is pretty unusual for a teenager, especially a boy."

"I can assure you that Andrew's story is completely true," Brady replied. "It's been a very difficult situation for the family."

"Undoubtedly. Anyway, after I'd read it, I sent the boy a note to come see me here in the guidance office. I had a hunch maybe he could use a good listener."

The counselor seemed to be taking an inordinate amount of time to get to the point, and Brady was anxious to hear back from Roger. "That was kind of you. It's always good for a young person to have someone to talk to."

"Yes, I agree, and that's why I'm calling, Mr. Brady. It sounds like you and he have also developed a nice rapport. He says you've taken an interest in his schoolwork and sports and that you've consistently been someone he could talk to about things."

Glancing at his wristwatch, Brady tried to wrap up the call. "Is there something I can do for you, Mr. Moffat?"

"Well, as you might imagine, Andrew and I have spent a lot of time talking about college. You see, that's my role here at Eastmont. His grades will probably be good enough to qualify for some kind of scholarship, but he's going to need some help filling out the financial aid forms." The counselor lowered his voice and went on in a conspiratorial tone. "I've tried reaching out to the boy's mother, but she doesn't appear to feel up to it. If you could lend a hand, I think it would be of great service to the family."

At last, he's getting to the point. "Sure, go ahead and send the forms home with Andrew. I'll see what I can do," he promised, shaking his head as he returned to the stack of bills waiting for him. He paid the Pacific Gas and Electric bill and had forgotten about Mr. Moffat when Roger's call came through.

His client's manner lacked its usual clipped urgency. "I'm afraid I have bad news, Tony."

Brady immediately picked up on Roger's despair on the other end of the line. "What's wrong?" he asked.

"I'm afraid things have gone from bad to worse here. It turns out what Alice has is an especially aggressive form of cancer. The damn thing has spread everywhere, and the doctors don't think there's much more they can do at this point." Solemnly, he described his wife's surgery and subsequent treatments, adding that the revolving door of healthcare attendants they'd had to hire was putting a significant crimp on their finances. "Turns out these aides aren't covered by our insurance, and the bills mounting up are through the roof."

"Oh, Roger, I'm so sorry for all your troubles," Brady replied with genuine concern. "Please tell her I'm praying for her, will you? Let her know I'm sending my best."

"The bottom line is I'm afraid I can't afford to keep you on. Look, you gave it your best shot, but I'm beginning to think the police may have been right all along."

Brady began to object, but his client quickly cut him off. "It's no use, Tony," Roger repeated sadly. "I'm afraid it's entirely possible Phillip wanted to disappear."

Stunned by how quickly Alice had deteriorated, Brady tried to make sense of the sad news as they hung up, struck by the speed with which bad news can alter everyone's lives with indiscriminate vengeance. Suddenly grasping the financial consequences of Roger's decision, he realized how much he'd come to rely on his client's backing. Years of experience had taught him that any ongoing investigation depends on having an adequate bankroll, because there is always more to do, and he was painfully aware that unless there is money to do it, the case will fade into history like so many cases have.

Brady's downcast eyes fell on an open box of posters on the coffee table beside him. Fresh from the printers, the new batch featured a computer-enhanced image of Brendan recently produced by a forensic artist. A combination of his and Colleen's features stared back at him, revealing a handsome young man in his prime. The strong, straight nose was a mirror image of Shane's, and the shape of the jaw bore a distinct resemblance to his own. Brady had been about to head out to all the usual haunts to distribute the updated posters, a process he'd found more therapeutic than just about anything else. When news of a possible abduction had been fresh, images of the freckle-faced boy had been circulated to police departments across the country in an effort to cast a wide net, as the FBI had advised at the time. Brady held one of the images up to the window to examine it, asking himself whether everything that could have been done had, in fact, been done. The father who had never learned what had happened to his child stood at the window of his one-bedroom apartment, wondering how he was going to pay his bills.

He flipped through his checkbook to take stock of his finances. Hopeful for any break in his cases, he had just laid out a hefty yearly premium for access to the forensic database his PI buddies had recommended. The subscription was expensive, and he'd been counting on Roger to fund it, and yet, grudgingly, Brady had to admit that money wasn't the real issue. His police department pension more than covered his thrifty lifestyle, and he didn't expect to find himself out on the street any time soon. Since the day he'd hung out his shingle, he had proudly solved upwards of a dozen cases, but the lack of resolution in his last two remaining cases continued to plague him. He felt that grief so deeply that the glow of any earlier successes paled, and he knew it was that very grief that had served to propel him forward.

Could I continue working if I don't get paid? The answer came to him surprisingly swiftly. He knew that if he could discover what had happened to Brendan, finding closure would be payment enough. As for Phillip Lynch, it remained unfathomable to him that a man would purposely walk away from his family.

How could anyone willfully destroy the lives of those who loved him?

Mr. Moffat's odd request finally returned to his memory, and Brady put away his checkbook with a heavy sigh and dialed the number at Phillip's home.

"Is Andrew around?" he asked when Susan answered. "Okay if I stop by?"

Up in Andrew's bedroom next to an empty bottle of Snapple and a handful of candy wrappers, two tall stacks of college catalogues stamped *Eastmont High School* sat on the cluttered desk.

"Ten more and I'm done," the boy grunted from the floor where he was doing pushups.

Brady took a seat at the desk and leafed through a *Barron's Guide,* pausing at a page marked with a yellow sticky note.

"Looking at colleges, eh? Anything specific you're looking for?"

"I don't know, I always get good grades in English, but the guidance counselor at school has been telling me about things like Sociology and Anthropology. I've never even heard of some of this stuff." Andrew flipped one of the catalogues to a page the counselor had marked. "Listen to this: *Aberrational Human Behavior.* Or how about this one, *Gender Politics?*"

Brady peered over his shoulder. "Lots of interesting choices."

"Mr. Moffat thinks I might be able to get a scholarship, but I don't know, Mr. Brady, what's the point if I don't have a clue what I should study when I get there?"

Brady tried to recall what it had felt like to be a high school student contemplating what lay ahead. "What are some of your classmates thinking about studying?"

"Some of the guys say their dads want them to go into law or business. A couple of 'em want to make movies or design video games. My friend Jack, he's on the varsity football team. He says if he gets recruited, he's going pro as soon as he can."

"Maybe your guidance counselor can help you decide, Andrew. And once you get in, you can get advice from the college's career office. Those folks know a lot, it's their job. I bet they'll help you figure things out."

Andrew jammed his hand into the pocket of a pair of dirty jeans as he began pacing the room. As he passed close to him, Brady was surprised at the soft fuzz he saw on the boy's chin. *He needs to start shaving,* he realized with a start. *Maybe he needs someone to show him how.*

"One thing's for sure." Andrew gestured to the application papers littering his desk. "I can't ask Mom for help with any of this."

As if on cue, down the hall they heard a door slam. "Leave me alone! And don't come in!" his sister was shouting from behind the closed door.

"And another thing, Mr. Brady." Andrew's shoulders sagged. "Gracie. She's like that a lot. No one's really paying attention to the kid. Mom's at work, and I've got a ton of stuff to do, baseball practice after school and all this college stuff, and now I'm bagging groceries a couple shifts a week. The thing is, see, Gracie still doesn't have a single friend. I told her to sign up for some clubs at school, but she didn't do it." He toyed with a scab on his elbow, and a trickle of blood appeared. He looked up at Brady with a defeated expression. "Doncha think it's bad for a kid her age to be by herself so much?"

Brady frowned and rubbed his chin. More than once he'd suggested to Susan that her daughter might benefit from some therapy. He had witnessed the child's behavior first-hand and observed that Gracie was quite unlike the pre-pubescent girls he'd seen who giggled and already batted their eyes at neighborhood boys. He wasn't a psychologist, but he was pretty sure that Andrew's little sister suffered from a fairly low opinion of herself.

"Anything different going on here at home lately?"

The boy paused for a minute to consider. "I guess Mom got more hours at work so she's not home as much. And you know that new guy she rented the garage to?"

Brady cocked his head. Word was the boarder was a student somewhere. He'd seen someone who looked to be in his early twenties sporting a greasy ponytail and a bushy moustache that needed trimming. Recently, he'd noticed an old pick-up truck with a broken taillight parked in the driveway.

"See, this guy is around here all kinds of random hours. I can't figure out his schedule, if he even has one, and I smell weed on him. The school bus drops her off after school, and a lot of times, no one else is home." Andrew's voice rose. "Geez, Mr. Brady, she's just a little kid. Mom used to always be here when we came home from school. When I was her age, I never got left by myself with some random guy smoking weed!"

Brady sighed. He was beginning to feel more and more responsible for this tattered family. "Let me see what I can do. Maybe we can get Gracie some professional help. I'll try talking to your mom again," he promised. "And listen, hand over those financial aid forms and let me take a look," he added, pointing to the applications stacked on Andrew's desk. "I filled out a lot of these things for my kids."

Heading outside to the weathered sedan in the driveway, he slid into the driver's seat and leaned his head back. Closing his tired eyes, he clenched and unclenched the fists of both hands. That pesky arthritis was acting up again. Silently, he made a mental note to pick up a razor for Andrew and reminded himself to talk to Susan about Gracie. *None of this would be happening if their father were still here,* he speculated. *On the heels of this kind of trauma, just about everyone's life takes unexpected turns.*

He peered into the rearview mirror, asking himself once again if it wasn't time to close the books. *Hadn't Roger's announcement been permission to put an end to it? And anyway, how could it possibly help anyone if I did manage to find him, if he doesn't even want to be found?*

Brady turned the key in the ignition until the motor caught.

And what about Brendan? If I ever find out what happened, could it bring any of us peace?

Looking both ways, he released the brake and inched the car into the street.

"I can't give up," he declared out loud as if hoping to convince himself, "because when I do, that's when it ends. When I stop, no one else is going to go on looking for either one of them."

PART III

JAGGED SCARS

CHAPTER TWENTY-TWO

Winter 2005

BRADY

Brady hopped from one foot to the other on the sidewalk in front of the nursing home as he waited for Susan's shift to end. The evening air had turned crisp, and he thrust his hands into his coat pockets and wished he'd worn gloves, his fingers stiff with the cold. When she stepped outside, he couldn't help noticing she'd put on a few pounds, or maybe it was the puffy down jacket she wore.

"Thanks for meeting with me," he greeted her. Taking her elbow, he led her in the direction he hoped to find a Starbucks, thinking he'd beat the chill with a warm drink. "How'd it go today?"

She shrugged. "Who could possibly enjoy any part of cleaning up after old people?" Her voice was without inflection. "It's whatever, but at least my paycheck just about covers the rent."

Brady tried to inject a note of optimism into the conversation. "Glad you're making ends meet. New boarder helping out with expenses?"

"Danny? Oh, he's great. So much nicer than the last guy. Pitches in whenever he can to help around the house, too."

Foot traffic on the city sidewalk had begun to pick up with the five o'clock office exodus. Together, they strolled past a pizza-by-the-slice stand with a line forming out front. A skateboarder flew by, barely avoiding a collision with a businessman in a suit, a leather briefcase clutched to his chest. Two short blocks from the nursing home, Susan paused beside Al's Cocktail Lounge and jerked her chin toward the bright neon sign flashing in the window.

"Brrr, I'm freezing, Tony. What do you say we stop in here?"

He hesitated. A dimly lit bar wouldn't have been his first choice, but he followed her inside and waited for his eyes to adjust to the darkness.

"Good evening, Suse. How're you doing? Getting chilly out, isn't it?" The bartender drew a wet rag across the counter and motioned to two empty barstools. "The usual?"

"You know it." She slid onto a stool and patted the seat beside her. "What would you like, Tony?"

Brady wondered how often she stopped in for a quick one after work. "I'll take a beer, whatever's on tap," he replied, abandoning his secret longing for a cup of hot tea.

The familiar bartender set down a couple of cardboard coasters and a dish of peanuts. Susan piled her coat beside her in a way that suggested they'd be staying for a while. When her drink appeared, she speared the olive and took a good-sized sip. "Any news?" she asked.

Brady wasn't sure how much Susan knew about his financial arrangement with her father-in-law. "In a way, yes. Roger called to update me about Alice's medical situation. Sounds like things have been rough back there."

"Oh, I know. It's really hard on them. Seems like it came out of nowhere, the cancer. I guess it's pretty aggressive."

She reached for a handful of nuts and chased them down with another swallow. "The whole thing is just terrible. And poor Alice, she's honestly one of the nicest people you'd ever meet. This thing has really kicked Roger in the gut, on top of everything else." Susan took another sip. "They're good people. I feel bad for them."

"Me too." Sipping his beer, he scanned her face. "You knew, didn't you, that Roger has been paying me all along, right? To keep me on the case."

"I guess I did know that, but I don't know how much or anything. Roger never said. He sure as heck knew I couldn't pay for it. I figured for you to keep looking for Phillip had to be costing plenty."

Brady realized he'd have to break the news. "The thing is, Roger says he can't keep me on retainer any longer." He saw Susan's face fall right away, and her sagging shoulders spoke volumes. "I wasn't sure if he'd told you."

She drained her cocktail, motioning to the bartender for another round. "So is that it, then? Is this the end of it?"

Still nursing his beer, Brady waved his hand over the top and sent the barhop away.

Susan went on. "Two years already, and you never found him," she clucked her tongue. "You know what? Lately I've started to think Phillip meant to leave on purpose. I mean, everyone says so. If that's true, then he really didn't love me, did he?" She twisted the wedding band on her ring finger. "Maybe the police were right, Tony, and he really did run out on us. Maybe it's as simple as that. I've been such an idiot hoping for him to come home."

Brady swiveled to face her. "See, that's partly the reason I wanted to talk to you, Susan. Okay, so Roger can't keep me on, but I'm not ready to give up. I wanted to come tell you in person. I'm not about to stop looking for him." He looked directly into her eyes. "I'm prepared to keep going, Susan, and don't worry, you won't have to pay me to do it."

The relief written on her face was the confirmation he'd been hoping for. She tilted her head and squinted up at him. "But isn't it kind of hopeless?" She plucked the olive from her second martini.

He shook his head. "Not to me it isn't, and I'll keep trying to find out what happened, no matter how long it takes."

Brady watched Susan slump heavily on the stool beside him and almost slip off the barstool. Even in the bar's dim light, he could make out the new furrows etched into her forehead, and he thought he saw something different in her eyes, a blank despair he hadn't noticed before. The months her husband had been absent had begun to take their toll.

"Why did you say maybe the police were right? Was there a reason Phillip would want to take off? Is there something you haven't told me? I know it's personal, Susan, but the thing is, I need to know."

With a click, the electric heater on the wall switched on, and a blast of warm air encircled them. He loosened the knot on his tie and unbuttoned his jacket. Wordlessly, Susan had begun to cry. He hadn't been expecting tears, and after a moment's hesitation, he reached into his pocket for a white cotton square folded neatly in two. She took the handkerchief from him and dabbed her eyes, blotting the streaks of mascara trickling down her flushed face.

"It was Gracie," she stammered when at last she began to speak again.

Brady arched his bushy gray eyebrows. "Gracie?" The abrupt turn in the conversation caught him off guard, and he placed his arm around her. "What about Gracie?"

The gentle pressure on her shoulder seemed to comfort Susan, and she began to confide what she admitted she hadn't ever planned to reveal, not to anyone. "Remember I told you about the trouble Phillip and I had getting pregnant? I mean, after we had Andrew?"

"I remember."

She went on. "When we first got married, we used to talk about having a whole bunch of kids. In those days, neither of us had any idea how much kids cost or how to support a big family, but when we were just starting out, that's what we used to say to each other."

He willed himself not to interrupt.

"I think I told you, after Andrew, we tried for a long time, until the doctors finally figured out that it was Phillip who was the problem. They said there was no way he was going to be able to get me pregnant. So everyone told us we should try adoption."

Brady nodded. He had figured as much. *But so what*, he wondered. *So Gracie's adopted. Plenty of kids are. Why the big secret?*

"You asked me about counseling, remember? Well, we sat on that counselor's couch for months trying to figure out what to do. What a waste of time! By then we really didn't see eye to eye on anything. Phillip even said he didn't know how I'd gotten pregnant in the first place and maybe Andrew wasn't really his." She shook her head in disbelief. "Oh, things got nasty all right."

From the corner of his eye, Brady glanced at his wristwatch. He knew the kids would be expecting their mother at home soon and figured he'd better not keep Susan out too long. He signaled the bartender to ask for the check. "So, you and Phillip went with adoption?"

"No, we didn't. The wait list for a baby was years, and anyway, I really didn't want to go that route. Andrew was in kindergarten by then. I didn't want to wait, and besides, I wanted my *own* baby. I mean, there wasn't anything wrong with *me!*" Her voice rose as she pointed her thumb at her chest. "It was his fault we couldn't get pregnant! It wasn't *my* fault."

Afraid he'd say the wrong thing, Brady pursed his lips together tightly and noticed an elderly patron at the far end of the bar looking at them strangely.

Angrily, Susan resumed her tirade. "The way I saw it, we just needed some sperm that could get the job done. So we ended up going to a clinic and just picked a guy from a list. The whole thing took about five minutes in a doctor's office, and just like that, bingo, I was pregnant." She snapped her fingers. "I'm not kidding, it happened just like that. Worked like a charm, I guess because I'd already had all those shots." She peered over the top of her drink at Brady. "And that really set him off, how fast the whole thing worked with another guy's sperm."

Both their glasses were empty now, and Brady reached for his wallet. "Okay, I get it. So Phillip isn't Gracie's natural father. So what? He's still her Dad, isn't he? After all, he's the one raising her."

Susan lowered her head. "See, that's just it. Phillip was never okay with it. He made me promise not to tell anyone ever, and by God, Tony, I never did tell. He thought if we told people, they wouldn't treat Gracie the same as Andrew. Back then, no one talked about that kind of thing. It was all hush-hush. And at the clinic? They just told us to go home and forget about it. So we never told a soul, not even our families, and even between ourselves, we just never talked about it." She gazed into the empty bowl of peanuts between them, her voice barely a whisper. "We acted like it never happened. It was almost as if we'd made some kind of silent pact."

"And were you able to forget about it like the clinic advised? Was he?"

Tears pooled in her eyes as anger gave way to despair. "I tried to, but no, I don't think Phillip ever forgot. Gracie was a colicky baby and cried all the time. No matter what we did, she never seemed to smile. She was downright miserable morning, noon and night and wouldn't let him give her a bottle. Sometimes I'd catch him just staring at her with a funny look on his face."

"It must have really bothered him that someone else's sperm is what worked." Brady paused to consider whether he'd have had the same reaction.

Susan's voice had grown thick. "And Gracie had so many problems! She wasn't anything like Andrew. She just couldn't seem to get the hang of things. You know, like jumping rope or roller-skating, all the things most kids can't wait to do. I love my daughter, but to tell you the truth, she's still kind of a weird kid," she complained in an overly loud voice.

Their tab appeared in front of them on a plastic tray with a couple of breath mints, and Brady slid a handful of bills down the bar. "I think we'd better go," he told her, reaching for the jacket folded neatly on the stool beside him.

But Susan couldn't seem to stop talking. "The poor kid is near-sighted. They told us she couldn't see the blackboard, and then her teeth came in all crooked and they said she needed braces." She threw up her hands. "Andrew has perfectly straight teeth, and guess what, none of us wears glasses! Gracie was always just different." Susan twisted her wedding ring again, gazing at her left hand as if it belonged to someone else. "Phillip and I were fighting all the time. Oh, sure, we'd go back and see the counselor once in a while, but frankly, I think it just made everything worse. We never told anyone about the donor, not even the counselor. It was just this big secret that kind of hung there between us, and the more we tried to tiptoe around it, the worse it got."

She swiveled on her stool. "What's that thing people say? *Like an elephant in the room?*" Brady helped her to her feet. "That's right. The thing everyone notices but no one wants to talk about."

The day suddenly felt very long. "Listen, it's getting kind of late, Susan. We should get you home. The kids will be wondering."

Teetering, she found her coat and tried to wiggle one of her arms through a puffy sleeve.

"That's the whole thing about secrets, isn't it?" he said as he helped guide her arm through the sleeve of her jacket. "We keep secrets to protect someone, or maybe to protect ourselves, but what happens instead is the secrets eat away at us inside, like some kind of disease. The things we work so hard to keep hidden? Those are the things that end up destroying us."

She swayed uncertainly, and he wasn't sure she'd even heard him. "You know, Tony, I've been holding onto this secret all this time, and it's weighed me down. I'm just so damn tired."

He saw she was on the verge of tears again and suggested he drive her home. "Please let me give you a lift. It's on my way, really."

"No, no. I'll be fine. Just need some fresh air," she insisted as she shuffled past him into the evening chill.

They made their way down the sidewalk, retracing their steps to the nursing home. He hoped the crisp night air would buoy Susan's spirits and that her melancholy mood would lift. All around them, men and women clad in winter coats and scarves headed to their cars or bus stops on their way home to dinner with their families. Holding her arm as they neared the parking lot, Brady remembered his promise to Andrew.

"There is something I've been wanting to talk to you about," he began tentatively in what he hoped was a well-meaning tone of voice.

Susan fished in her purse for her car keys and held them up triumphantly. "Got 'em!" She opened the car door. "What about?"

He wasn't sure she was sober enough to understand, but he took a deep breath and blurted, "It's about Gracie. Seems like the kid is having a hard time. I know I've suggested it before, but have you given any thought to getting her into counseling?"

She narrowed her eyes and snapped at him with uncharacteristic displeasure. "On my God, Tony. My husband left me without a word, and I'm barely managing to put food on the table. Now you want me to shell out for some quack so my daughter can contemplate her navel? Gracie just needs to buckle down and stop getting into trouble. And she needs to help out a little. Maybe even clean her room and stop answering back and slamming her damn bedroom door. A good swat on the behind'll do the kid more good than an hour in any shrink's chair, believe me."

Susan tossed her bag into the car, glancing sidelong at him as she plunked down heavily in the driver's seat. "Gracie needs to stop driving me crazy," she declared, struggling to attach her seat belt. "That's what she needs, and frankly, it's what I need, too."

CHAPTER TWENTY-THREE

Fall 2006

STEVE

With the toe of his sneaker, he inched the apartment door open carrying the gallon of milk she'd asked him to pick up and found her standing in the kitchen in a daze, a large manila envelope clutched in her hand. The envelope's contents lay scattered on the counter, and when he followed her tear-streaked gaze to the heap of legal documents, Steve knew without being told that Jackie's divorce had come through at last.

The ugly blindside when she'd discovered him cheating with one of her girlfriends was a story he'd heard her tell often, right down to the predictable detail about the sorority sister who had moved into the conjugal bed and replaced Jackie lock, stock and barrel.

"So much for the bonds of sisterhood," she'd spat the first time she'd told him about it.

Setting the container of milk down, he wrapped his arms around her and pulled her close, gently prying the envelope from her hand and laying it on top of the papers that had paralyzed her. She buried her face in his shoulder with a soft whimper. The front of his shirt grew damp, and her tears left a trail of dark mascara across the faded flannel. He thought she looked so fragile at that moment, and in a sudden swell of tenderness, he murmured, "We knew this was coming. It's what you wanted, isn't it?"

"I know, I know," she sniffled. "I just didn't think I'd feel so bad when it did."

He tucked an errant ringlet behind her ear, breathing in the familiar scent of apples as he kissed her forehead.

"Honestly, it's kind of a relief, but it's sad, too. Like the death of something."

"Uh huh." His arms tightened around her. "Life's complicated, isn't it?"

She didn't deserve to be treated that way, thought Steve protectively. Jackie was so sweet, so considerate, always thinking of everyone else, never of herself. Her students adored her, and her colleagues liked and respected her. Best of all, he knew she loved him exactly as he was, asking for very little in return.

Rocking her in his arms, he couldn't help remembering how his own marriage had unraveled, and how quickly. After Gracie had arrived, when couples' counseling clearly hadn't changed a thing, he and Susan had both tried to pick up the pieces. For his part, he'd made every effort to keep the ball rolling as the marriage had spiraled into its collapse. He'd tried to pretend they were a family like any other, but eventually he'd had to admit that everything about it was a façade, and he blamed himself.

What kind of father cannot find it in himself to love his only daughter?

Nagging questions he could never answer plagued him every time he looked at the little girl. It was his fault, his low sperm count, and his guilt and misery just seemed to grow worse as the years went by and he never seemed to forget that Gracie wasn't really his.

Holding Jackie as she buried her face against his chest, he wondered how such a delicate bird had wound her way into his galvanized heart. He thought it was against all odds that she'd fallen in love with him. Sympathetically, she'd grieved over the tragic loss of his family and set out to make him whole again. When she suggested he move into her apartment after the Wills had returned from their trip, it was merely as a practical matter.

She suggested that moving in together made economic sense.

"But we're still getting to know each other," he argued, worried that it might would ruin everything that was good between them. He thought he'd better not point out how much he had been enjoying his new liberty. But Jackie, patient as Job, brought up the suggestion only once. She never applied any pressure, and eventually, Steve agreed to give it a try.

His guarded "yes" he said, was dependent on a few ground rules.

It was Saturday night, and they had been standing shoulder to shoulder in her kitchen, washing and drying the dishes after the delicious shrimp scampi she'd fixed for dinner. Half a bottle of chilled wine sat open on the table behind them, and he looked forward to finishing it off later watching a movie he'd rented.

He began with as much delicacy as he could muster, deftly placing a kiss on the hollow at the back of her neck. "Sweetheart, you know I'm crazy about you, and I want to move in, I really do."

Jackie's gloved hands were plunged into a sink full of dirty dishwater. She kept her back towards him. "You do?"

"I do. I really do." He reached around her and set the dish he was drying into the cupboard overhead. "I love you, Jackie. Don't you know that?" His hand landed at her slim waist, and he turned her around to face him. "Don't you?"

"I guess so." He followed her eyes and saw her gaze was focused on a spot on the wall behind him.

"And I'm over here all the time anyway, so it totally makes sense. But I need you to understand. Living together, okay. But marriage, well, I just couldn't do it again." He dropped his chin and looked away. "It's just not in the cards for me."

He knew it wasn't the first time she'd heard him say he never wanted to be married again but felt he'd better squash any expectations she could have that a wedding might be on the horizon.

Jackie slipped off the soapy rubber gloves. "I know that. You've never said anything different. I get it, Hon. Look, getting married isn't everything, and believe me, I don't have any illusions. Trust me, the way things went the first time didn't give me any ideas about marriage being permanent."

He raised his face and his lips grazed hers, savoring the fruity aftertaste of the rosé they'd been drinking and whispered, "Can you live with that?"

She gave an almost imperceptible nod. "I don't need a ring on my finger to feel like we're in this together. I just want us to be here, living our lives with each other. That's what matters to me. That's more important than someone who makes promises he can't keep."

What have I ever done to deserve this woman? Steve asked himself. Still, he wanted to be as straightforward as possible. "And kids? Well, I just don't think so. I'm not sure I could go through that again, either. I know I'm being selfish, and it's not fair to you, Babe. You might want to have kids someday, but I just think it would be too much for me, going through all that again."

When she tipped her face up to his, he felt himself sinking into the liquid pool of her deep blue eyes. "Frankly, I don't know if this is such a good deal for you, Jackie. I'm not a very good prospect. Maybe there's someone else out there who would be better for you. Maybe you ought to think about it."

Her damp hands slipped beneath his shirt, and she pulled him in close. The coolness of her fingers on his bare skin made a sudden shiver run through him.

"I don't need to think about it. We've both been through some tough times, haven't we? I'm just glad we found each other. Pretty lucky, right?"

She stood on her tiptoes and smiled. Her warm mouth met his, and her full lips parted. The two of them clung together for a long moment before he pulled back and gripped her shoulders with both hands.

"Are you sure this is what you want, Babe?"

Her eyes shone with softness. "Sweetie, we don't have to figure it all out right away. Let's just take it a day at a time."

It wasn't long before Steve loaded up his motorcycle with the few things he owned and carted them over to her apartment.

"Is that all you've got?" Jackie asked, her eyebrows raised in surprise. "I moved everything out of the front closet to make room for you. Where's the rest of your stuff?"

"Most of it's still in storage," he shrugged, "but this is all I need. I like to keep things simple."

"Is it up in San Francisco? Maybe we can drive up and get it some weekend and you could show me around." She warmed to the idea quickly. "I'd love to meet some of your friends."

"Sure, we'll do that some time. No rush."

Slowly at first, they began to settle into a rhythm. Everything about their life together felt new to Steve, and he realized that he'd never lived on his own with a woman before. His marriage had begun with a baby almost immediately, and for a long time, he and Susan and little Andrew had been a family of three before Gracie had joined them. Living as a couple now, he became attentive to Jackie in a way that hadn't been possible when children filled the home. On the couch thumbing through his poker books with the radio tuned to a jazz station they both liked, Steve took in the sight of her sitting beside him reviewing her students' IEPs, and he beamed with contentment. It felt right.

When Jackie went to work, he headed for the card club. Ever since he'd discovered Texas Hold'em, an addictive anticipation fueled by raging neurons swam through his brain, and his fervor for the game had not subsided. Most of the time, he couldn't stop thinking about it. A thrill unlike anything he'd felt before pulsed through him as soon as the dealer began shuffling the deck and cards were in the air. In that moment, the surge of adrenaline made Steve recall the excitement of falling in love, and he asked himself how something as simple as a game of cards could make him feel so alive.

It's crazy! How could outwitting a rival on the felt be as addictive as falling in love?

No, he knew gambling wasn't love, but the endorphins the game released seemed to produce the same acute sensation, the same tumbling rush of emotion, and before long, a very clear, intense addiction to it began to change Steve in ways he could never have anticipated. He'd become pretty good by then, pricing his bets just right and bluffing when he sensed another player's weakness, and he was delighted he could make decent money doing something he loved. Winning gave him the same satisfying sense of self-worth he'd achieved when as a journalist, he'd won awards and accolades, and he found he didn't miss his old avocation a single bit. Absorbed in every detail when he played, his whole being hummed with aliveness. Without workplace demands or parental obligations, it became easy to focus, and his game improved almost daily. His wins outpaced his losses, and he began to imagine himself battling it out with big time movers and shakers on the tournament circuit.

Steve was in deep. So deep that when he heard the news, he was instantly sucked in. In sleepy little Rosamond there was to be an opportunity to win a seat at the most prestigious tournament in the poker-playing world, the World Series of Poker.

"Isn't that the one you said is in Las Vegas usually?" Jackie asked innocently when he came home carrying a couple of entry forms.

"That's right," he replied with obvious excitement, setting aside one of the forms for Rob. "But there are games that lead up to it, satellite games with small entry fees so anyone can sign up. See, if you win one of those, you don't have to pay the hefty fee to play the Main Event."

Jackie had been brushing her teeth at the bathroom sink. She rinsed her mouth with mouthwash, and Steve went on.

"The thing is, anyone who can win a satellite can play against the heavyweights in the WSOP that way, and if you beat those guys, that's the big time. What's amazing is, for the first time, they're gonna have a satellite right here at the club. Think of it!" He lifted her off her feet. "It's a chance to be the next Chris Moneymaker!"

Winning a satellite just like the one about to take place in Rosamond's local card club was precisely what had happened to the now famous amateur Steve had spotted on Aunt Millie's TV back at the Desert Motel. The idea that any novice player could compete in the WSOP Main Event and maybe win the big money, along with a great deal of celebrity, was a notion that fed every player's wildest fantasies.

The club was buzzing with excitement when Steve showed up the next day. He thrust an entry form into Rob's hand. "What do you say it's time to move up to the next level?"

"Oh, you know it is!"

Together they joined the line at the cashier's cage to sign up. Already twenty-deep, the line full of local players snaked through the club.

Steve's initial optimism evaporated almost as soon as the two friends, along with sixty-five other hopeful entrants, sat down to play the satellite game. They'd never seen the club so crowded. The bodies packed in shoulder to shoulder at tables that had been added to accommodate the throng barely left enough room for them to stretch. Steve managed to last to number thirty-nine before being knocked out, and by then, Rob had already busted out. Despite being eliminated early, they vowed to try again the following year, and drowning their sorrows later that night, they pledged to make the satellite game an annual event.

At the bar and grill next door, they each ordered steaks, speculating after a couple of drinks about how they would take down the tournament next time.

"That was brutal," Steve declared with a mouthful of prime rib. "Feel like I haven't eaten in a week."

"Yeah, I'm famished." It was late, nearly closing time, and the restaurant was empty except for a couple of strays nursing whiskeys at the other end of the bar. Rob flagged down the only waiter still on duty to ask for more bread. "Can you imagine what it would be like if we both won a seat at the WSOP? How great would that be, man?"

"You bet I can imagine it." Steve doused his dinner in steak sauce. Another round of beers arrived in front of them, and he paused before he took a swig. "The thing is, buddy, I really need to go up against the big guns. I feel like I'm treading water here, playing local games. I don't know, maybe I've hit a plateau. You know what I'm saying?"

"Yeah, I get it." Rob slathered butter onto a roll. "It's kind of like if you ever played golf or tennis. If you want to get better, you gotta play with guys better than you. I mean, if you really want to nail your game, right?"

Steve gestured with his fork. "I mean, it's one thing to take down some of these local yokels, but the thing is, I don't really know if I'm up to playing with the heavyweights. I gotta find out if I really could go pro at this, or if I'm just kidding myself," he mused aloud. "I gotta know if I'm really any good."

They chewed their steaks in companionable silence before Rob spoke up. "Hey, I told Judy about all the comps they give you if you win. She couldn't believe all the free flights and hotel rooms and stuff."

"Yeah, I heard they give Moneymaker the penthouse suite now."

"Nice! Judy always complains we never go anywhere for a real vacation. Man, Vegas would be perfect," Rob dreamt with a wistful look on his face. "I've always wanted to take her on one of those gondola rides, you know, at that hotel they've got that looks like Venice."

"The Venetian. Pretty sweet." Steve pushed his plate away and signaled the waiter. "Of course, you and me, we wouldn't have time for sightseeing, we'd be slaving away at the tables, trying to bring home the bacon and make our women rich!"

"Ah, that'd be so amazing." Rob drained his beer. "Nice to dream about it, anyway."

"Trust me, eventually, we're gonna make it happen," Steve clinked his bottle against Rob's empty one. "We just need to stay with it. You and me, we've got what it takes." He burped and patted his full stomach. "Patience, man, that's the key. Patience."

Rob slapped a credit card onto the bar, and Steve reached for his wallet. "Let's hope so. One of these days, man, one of these days."

CHAPTER TWENTY-FOUR

Fall 2008

BRADY

Brady slammed the instruction manual against the table in frustration, cursing the meaningless diagrams along with the salesman who had made it look so easy. Over waffles last Sunday at Blanche's Diner, his old friends Joe and Charlie had warned him that the new database wouldn't work on his woefully out of date computer, so Brady had just spent half a day at Best Buy and come home with a brand new laptop. Now if he could just manage to boot it up, he'd be able to download the pricey new forensic software he'd subscribed to.

Intending to take a deeper dive into the open cases that remained on his docket, he'd cleared his schedule for the week ahead. As he looked down at the twisted cables snaking through his fingers, he wondered if there were someone he could call, someone computer savvy enough to figure out why the expensive system refused to boot up. *A college kid could set this whole thing up in about two seconds,* he fumed. Immediately, Andrew Lynch came to mind.

"Come over here and help this old geezer out," he coaxed over the phone. "I'll spring for a pizza."

Andrew laughed and said fine, he'd bring the drinks. The San Francisco State sophomore had recently declared his intention to major in Psych, and enthusiastically he'd called Brady to share the news. "After I get my Bachelor's, I'll apply for a scholarship and go to grad school. I'm thinking maybe I'll be a family therapist, or a child psychologist, something like that. Some kind of counselor. I think I'd be good working with kids," he'd confided, and Brady had agreed with him.

The pockets of Andrew's high school letterman jacket bulged with the cans of soda he'd grabbed from the fridge, and Brady saw at once that his handsome face was drawn tight with uncharacteristic irritation.

"What's up? I hope I didn't tear you away from studying. Anything wrong?"

Tersely, Andrew described the scene he had just left at the home he still shared with his mom and sister. He'd gone into the kitchen to wrangle the drinks and stopped in the doorway when he saw Danny pass his mother a lit pipe. Sniffing the air, he knew the aroma wafting through the room wasn't incense.

"I thought maybe Gracie could smell it upstairs."

He'd taken in the usual bottle of vodka open on the counter and his mom's hand wrapped around a tumbler, and he watched from the doorway as she pushed Danny lightly on the chest with her other hand. When she stepped over to the oven, Danny had sidled closer, sliding his arm around her waist in a familiar way that made Andrew feel sick to his stomach.

"They must not have heard me come down the stairs."

"Did you speak up? Say anything to them?"

"You bet I did! I reminded them Gracie was upstairs. I wanted them to know they weren't alone. Danny just laughed, and Mom said dinner would be ready soon, but I said I had to go." Andrew's eyes flashed with fury. "I just grabbed a couple of sodas out of the fridge and left." He looked like he wanted to punch his fist through the wall. "I had to get out of there, Mr. Brady. I thought I was going to throw up. They were acting so flirty, and the guy still had his arm around Mom."

Brady told him that he hadn't been aware that things had become romantic between Susan and the boarder, but Andrew said he'd seen it coming.

"Danny spends way too much time hanging around, and I'm telling you, the house stinks of weed. He's always leaving spliffs or a pipe lying around somewhere. Isn't it against the law having it in the house? What if the police come by?" Andrew sat down heavily, his face flushed. "It's not like they ever do any more, but what if they did?"

Brady slid a box of piping hot pizza from the oven. "It's definitely a problem having drugs in the house, especially with Gracie around," he agreed, clearing space for the box on the table.

Andrew reached for a slice, and it disappeared into his mouth in two hungry bites. Tomato sauce trickled down his chin, and Brady handed him a roll of paper towels.

"Mom drinks so much lately, she's almost always looped. I haven't seen her smoke Danny's weed, but I'm sure she does. Thing is, Mr. Brady, I'm not home much anymore. I'm either in class or in the lab, and the bookstore just gave me Saturday hours. But Gracie's there a lot, and I'll bet she knows what's going on."

Last month when Andrew had laid out his plans to become a therapist, Brady had reflected that the only good to have come from his father's disappearance was that the kid had somehow managed to find his calling without the aid of any parental guidance. He knew that Andrew had been forced to shoulder a lot of responsibility growing up and wondered if a little help from a relative might be in order.

"Any chance your grandpa could come out for a visit? It's been a while, hasn't it?"

Andrew shrugged. "When Grandma died, Grandpa started going on trips with this tour group he hooked up with. It's called something like Seniors Abroad. I think he's in Italy right now, or maybe that was last month."

He reached for the instruction booklet and spread the pages open before them on the table. The fluorescent light overhead buzzed as he consulted the pages and Brady sipped his drink. After a moment, Andrew pushed his plate to the side and set to work connecting the modem and the printer, rapidly swapping discs in and out of the drive.

"What about your aunt, the one you said you liked? And don't you also have some relatives in Colorado?"

Andrew untangled a rat's nest of cables and snaked them together neatly. "You mean Aunt Beth? She checks in every now and then. She got a job in New York and sent me a postcard with a picture of Yankee Stadium. And my mom's sister in Colorado? Uncle John has a lot of heart problems. He's in and out of the hospital all the time."

He switched off the power and pulled the warranty card from the box. "That should do it. Let's give it a minute to make sure everything's working." He flashed Brady a grin. "Got to make sure the customer is happy. We'll get your internet up and running, too."

Brady cuffed his shoulder with affection. "You just saved me a bundle." He rummaged through the cupboards for a package of cookies. "Gracie is what, thirteen now? Is she still getting into trouble at school?"

He saw Andrew's eyes flicker with interest at the sight of the Nutter Butters, just as they had when he was a boy. "These are the best," he mumbled, his mouth full as crumbs landed on the front of his shirt.

"You're the one got me hooked," Brady laughed.

Andrew grabbed another handful of cookies and passed the package back. "Yeah, Gracie's in trouble at school all the time. Last week she got caught smoking in the bathroom and got sent to detention. Seriously, I don't know what's wrong with her. I don't think I got sent to detention even once," he shook his head. "Mom got her a cell phone, and you should see how fast the kid types just using her thumbs. It's crazy."

"I guess all the kids are pretty good at that now."

"Yeah, but I don't know who she could be texting because seriously, she has no friends. Maybe she's playing a game or something." He stood and walked to the kitchen window. "I don't have a clue what thirteen-year-old girls are into."

Andrew powered the new laptop back on and stepped aside as Brady entered his password. The two of them watched the flickering screen for a long moment. "Seems like it's running okay now," he announced with satisfaction, draining his soda and crushing the can with his fist.

"Hey, thanks so much, pal. Sorry to steal so much of your time. I probably pulled you away from your studies, right?"

"Stats homework. I'm organizing the data I got from observing the preschoolers on campus. There's a one-way mirror at the child development center and you look through it to watch them play. It's pretty cool." Andrew got to his feet. "I better take off. Still have to make the graphics for a PowerPoint presentation for class on Tuesday."

Still plenty worried about his little sister, Brady thought, wiping the table with a damp cloth. He began to load software onto his new system, speculating that teenagers as young as Gracie might already be visiting social media sites online, and as forensic database files began to populate his hard drive, he wondered if he could repay Andrew's favor by finding out what the girl was up to.

Conducting background research on someone he wanted to know more about was nothing new for Brady. Properly doing his job had always depended on using a variety of different methods, and the internet had proven to be a versatile tool, magically turning up a small avalanche of data with merely a couple of keystrokes. He began by running a bevy of innocent searches and was surprised when those queries led him onto websites he'd never even dreamt existed, websites that instantly alarmed and saddened him. Drilling down for hours, Brady found himself held hostage to his keyboard well into the night, dumbfounded by the abundance of information readily accessible to anyone persistent enough to hunt for it.

Early in the morning, he hit pay dirt. Innocent of the danger of revealing too much online, Gracie hadn't bothered to disguise her name, and as Brady scanned the pages of websites favored by her peers, he tripped over pictures of the girl's bare midriff, her upper body clad in scanty halter-tops. Heavily made up eyes cast seductive glances at the camera lens. The blonde hair piled loosely atop her head in a sophisticated French twist afforded her an older, alluring look, and examining her user profile, he saw that she had listed her age as sixteen. In the upper right corner of the site, she'd claimed her interests were "having fun with boys, especially older ones."

The pages Brady had stumbled on worried him, and he was hypnotically drawn to keep looking, well into the night. After no more than a few hours' sleep, he rose from the computer to make himself some breakfast. Opening the windows of the stuffy apartment, he hungrily sucked in the fresh morning air. On the sidewalk outside, mothers pushed strollers toward the school on the corner as children with backpacks trailed alongside. A Mexican churro cart playing a cheerful jingle pulled up at the intersection. The scene outside painted a stark contrast to the grittiness of Gracie's profile page on the popular social media website he'd logged onto, and in the fog of sleeplessness, Brady rubbed his bloodshot eyes and wondered what he could possibly do.

She hasn't broken any laws. Sure, the kid may be about to fall through the cracks, but really, is it any business of mine?

On the sidewalk below, a gray-haired woman in sweatpants stepped into the vestibule of his building. Leaning over to peer out the open window, he could see what looked like a Nike duffel bag hanging from her shoulder. *Martha something,* he thought as he tried to recall his next-door neighbor's name.

I mean, really, were we all that different when we were teenagers? he asked himself, suddenly recalling that his own sister used to sprawl across her bed for hours on end with Jefferson Airplane blasting from the radio while she scribbled furiously into a little notebook with a locking clasp. If her pesky little brother ever dared to intrude, she'd slam the diary shut, shooting daggers at him as if he'd poisoned her cat. *Typical adolescent behavior,* he shrugged and abruptly recalled Gracie, huddled over her pink diary, tearfully clutching a stubby pencil.

I wonder if there's some kind of online version the kids use now.

Using two thick fingers, he typed a few keywords into a new browser window, *teenage girls* and *online journal* among them, and in less than a minute, Brady tripped across something called MyDiary. In the site's pull-down menu was a user directory, and he found that Gracie had not only created a chronicle much like an old-fashioned diary, but she had once again identified herself with her actual name. Amazed at how easy it was to uncover, Brady began clicking through a series of entries painfully detailing the ups and downs of the teenage girl's life.

Most of what he found was routine. Someone at school had snubbed her. She'd snatched a twenty from her mom's wallet and gotten away with it, skipped class to smoke a cigarette in the bathroom. Many of Gracie's entries were uneventful and he scrolled through them until one grabbed his attention.

"Danny is so cool! He fixes stuff around the house and last night he cooked hotdogs outside like Dad used to. Mom doesn't even know how to work the grill. She likes him BIG TIME." Beside the capital letters, Gracie had inserted a red heart with an arrow. "What if Danny turns into my new Daddy? HAHAHA!"

He read that she knew about the boarder's drug use.

"Danny does coke and he said he'll give me some. Not the drink haha. He says he has something cool called molly. That sounds fun, right?!"

He saw that Andrew's fears about Danny's bad influence were justified, and Brady continued scrolling, wondering if he'd find any reference to the girl's missing father.

"Everyone at school is so mean," she'd written. "Someone wrote SLUT in red lipstick on my locker. I bet it was Chelsea, or maybe that bitch Brianna. When I'm 16 I am so quitting school."

Typical teenage angst, he thought, until finally, she mentioned Phillip.

"When I crashed my bike that time at the park, Daddy got so mad at me. It got all scratched up. He said what the hell is wrong with that kid. I felt so bad I wanted to die. I guess my Daddy doesn't really love me."

Brady had raised four teenagers of his own and knew that adolescents could be painfully awkward and self-absorbed, but the sadness in Gracie's diary had a kind of hopeless quality to it, and it broke his heart.

"I used to wish Daddy would come back but I don't even care anymore. Anyway everyone says he ran away from us on purpose," she had scribbled in girlish purple ink. "I bet it was my fault. It was me Daddy didn't love. If my own Daddy didn't love me then I guess no one ever will." She'd even drawn two teardrops beside her entry. "Maybe I'm not loveable."

What a terrible thing for any child to think, Brady breathed wearily, shutting the lid of his laptop as he stood up. *Poor Gracie. She could be headed for real trouble.*

He rummaged through the bathroom cabinet for a bottle of drops for his burning eyes, strained from surfing the web all night, and waited as the drops soothed the ache below his eyelids. *I ought to let someone know*, he thought to himself, but he couldn't think of anyone to tell. Standing at the sink with his eyes shut, he tried to imagine what kind of advice a professional might give him and wondered if he even knew anyone he could ask.

Wait a second. Wasn't Martha a social worker or something for the county? Didn't she do some kind of child welfare job? Once when Shane was in trouble, she had given Brady the name of a reliable rehab facility, and he had always been grateful for the tip.

He fumbled through an old address book stuffed in the drawer of his nightstand. *Martha, Martha something*, he muttered, flipping through the tattered pages in vain. The clock beside his bed read 8:30 as Brady padded across the hall in his slippers, and he was relieved when his neighbor responded to his knock.

"This is a surprise. What can I do for you, Tony?"

Martha Feldman, he remembered as soon as he saw her. *That's it.*

"Problem with your son? Come on in," she invited. "I've just put the kettle on for tea. Join me?"

"Thanks, Martha. Shane is doing well, thank goodness. Clean and sober for a while now." He stepped inside. Her apartment was a mirror image of his, and he felt disconcerted.

Recently retired, Martha reminded him that she had indeed been a social worker for the county. Deep lines around her spectacled eyes attested to the years she'd spent dealing with troubled teenagers in the system, and she listened quietly as Brady told her about Gracie's disturbing journal entries.

"The pictures I found online are rather troublesome. I'm afraid of what might happen if I don't step in and tell someone, but if I do, things could get worse, couldn't they?"

They spoke for a while about the rise of social media platforms and the easy access they provide to troubled and lonely kids. Although Martha cautioned Brady that she couldn't be certain, she agreed that what he'd discovered might well be cause for alarm. She drew up a list of resources to help point him in the right direction, and they talked about what would happen if Child Protective Services were to step in.

"You're not wrong, the provocative pictures are worrisome," she agreed. "Is there any indication the girl has been active in chat rooms?"

"I... I don't really know," he stammered. "A chat room? What do you mean?"

She explained that it was common for adult men to troll chat rooms specifically to target underage girls and that it was a legal transgression, as well as a moral one.

Shaken, Brady asked, "How do I even find these chat rooms?"

She directed him to a few of the most popular sites, warning him that he was likely to be shocked at what he might find. "Some of this stuff is pretty appalling," Martha warned him. "This is sex trafficking, Tony. Some of these girls are even younger than thirteen. And it can be underage boys these men are after, too."

Stunned by what he'd learned in just a few minutes of Martha's time, he thanked her for her advice and headed across the hall. He brewed a pot of fresh coffee, extra strong this time, and stood watching the inky black liquid drip through the grinds. Martha thought if Child Protective Services got wind of things, they might even break up the family, and Brady was afraid to do anything to make matters worse. He glanced at the stack of case files piled on the kitchen table and knew they'd have to wait until he figured out what to do.

He took a sip of his coffee before it had cooled and winced when the hot liquid burned his lip. Opening one of the files, his eyes fell on a reward flyer with Phillip's face printed on it, and he cursed the man for the havoc he'd wreaked in his little girl's life when he'd left her behind.

CHAPTER TWENTY-FIVE

Fall 2008

STEVE

A pencil tucked behind her ear, Jackie stapled a 3x5 index card to a poster board that had taken over the dining room table. In June she'd submitted her thesis for her PhD, and last week she'd signed on as head of Special Ed for the county. This afternoon she was putting together a workshop for teachers of students with multiple disabilities. The new job was a huge step forward for someone who had once been an itinerant teacher, and Jackie loved everything about the assignment. She'd be training other teachers to do the job she used to do and best of all, she'd be passing on the knowledge she'd gained in the process. "It's a chance to pay it forward," she'd told Steve, beaming.

He knew that working one-on-one with the kids had been a journey full of surprises for Jackie. Sometimes, on frustrating days she'd spent coaxing reticent students to give long division a try, or reminding distracted third graders about the workbook pages that lay crumpled at the bottom of their backpacks, she swore she didn't miss having kids of her own. But on those happy days when a shy kindergartner presented her with a flower picked on the way to school, she confessed she dreamt about the perfect children he and she would be sure to produce. In quiet moments of pillow talk, she told him that since she'd been a little girl, she'd vaguely pictured the distant day when she'd become someone's mother. With the self-righteous conviction of the very young, she was certain that she'd always be fair and compassionate with her own children. She'd never forget to pack a lunch, never miss a conference with the teacher, never lose her temper over a jacket forgotten at the playground or a bedroom door slammed in adolescent frustration. Snuggling under his arm in bed, she assured him she'd never be the kind of parent who did any of those things.

Steve kept his silence and let her talk, but he didn't budge, maintaining all along that he wasn't interested in starting another family. He suggested that the two of them could use a little more space, and that winter he and Jackie had transplanted themselves from her tiny apartment to a bungalow on the edge of Willow Springs. They hadn't decided yet whether the extra bedroom would be an office or a guest room, and Jackie hadn't mentioned a nursery, but he found he relished their new domesticity, and he surprised her by planting a vegetable garden where his tomato plants had thrived all summer long.

Jackie stopped mentioning the possibility, and for a long time, she insisted that other people's children were more than enough for her. Grateful to have landed on her feet after the brutal dissolution of her marriage, she said that things between them were so good she sometimes had to pinch herself. A photo she'd taped to the door of the fridge, taken at graduation on the day her

PhD with Distinction had been awarded, reminded her every day of his faithfulness. He had surprised her with a bouquet of roses just moments before Judy had snapped the picture. In it, Steve's arm encircled Jackie's waist as he lovingly kissed her cheek. He reassured her often, and she'd never had any reason to doubt him.

And yet late at night before drifting off to sleep, or waking before him in the early morning, Jackie was occasionally visited by vague and indistinct doubts. Judy had let it slip once that she'd confessed she sometimes found him oddly inscrutable. Jackie had told her friend she didn't have a clue what working in the dot.com business really meant and wondered how an English major who read all the time managed to find himself in that line of work. Every now and then, she probed Steve gently for more details, and each time, he deftly sidestepped her inquiries.

"You're so mysterious," she'd purred playfully in bed one Sunday morning.

She had often shared stories about growing up in her hometown of Bakersfield, about pillow fights with her sister and camping trips when her dad pan-fried the trout they'd caught. He'd laughed out loud hearing of her first kiss at a middle school dance when a chaperone had delivered an embarrassing lecture to the red-faced twelve-year-olds. She told him how she'd met her ex-husband and described the unraveling of their marriage in lurid detail. Filling him in on everything important or funny that had ever happened in her life, Jackie claimed to be an open book and held nothing back from him.

"I hardly know anything about you before we met," she pouted. "Come on, tell me, who are you, Steve Phillips?"

"You know everything that's important," he murmured, sliding the strap of her nightgown down and nuzzling her bare shoulder. He looked into her eyes reassuringly. "You know I love you, and you know I'm not going anywhere. To tell you the truth, Babe, I was a pretty boring guy before I met you."

"Huh. You mean to tell me no racy love affairs when you were a young Casanova? No family drama with the parents in your wild youth?"

"Nope." Steve kicked off the covers and swung his legs out of bed. "Sorry to disappoint you, but literally, everything that happened was absolutely ordinary and dull. I just followed the script. Went from high school to college to work, got married and had kids right away, and never once stopped to think about where I was headed or if any of it was what I really wanted."

Steve reached for his jeans and turned back to Jackie, still warmly cocooned in the down comforter, her wheat blonde hair splayed out on the flowered pillow under her head.

"Absolutely nothing special happened. That is, until right around the time I met you."

He grabbed yesterday's tee shirt from the bedpost and held it to his nose before poking his head through it. "That's when my real life began. I mean it."

As usual, his grin was contagious and his pleasure persuasive, and Jackie couldn't help smiling back at the handsome man getting dressed at the foot of their bed.

He kept Jackie in the dark about his past, but he kept himself in the dark, too. He preferred not to think much about his life before they'd met, mouthing his oft-repeated mantra and managing to convince himself that Phillip Lynch didn't exist anymore. *Don't look back. Keep moving forward*, he continued to chant inwardly nearly every single day. The lie that Phillip Lynch no longer existed was a story he began to believe. He bought the story hook, line and sinker, stepping into the role of Steve Phillips in the present with a great deal more interest than he'd ever had in remaining Phillip Lynch in the past.

In the present, the woman he loved made him happier than he'd ever been, and despite her occasional attempts to wheedle him about his past, when he held her in his arms at night he could picture the two of them together far into the future. He suspected that Jackie still mourned the absence of children in their lives and felt sorry that he'd robbed her of that joy, but he told himself that all that really mattered was their deep and satisfying connection to each other. She completed him, and he knew that married or not, he was committed to her with an intensity he had never felt with Susan. That his happiness was based on a lie was, to him, a mere technicality that had long ago ceased to matter. Their life together in the present was a good one, a happy one, and he wasn't worried about it. Instead, Steve began to focus seriously on his goal to become a professional poker player, and most of the time, the intensity of that focus left little room for anything else to occupy his thoughts.

He was driven to become an expert at poker and had already become convinced that the mental game was as important as mastering the fundamentals. Raking in a fair number of good-sized pots on a regular basis, he set out systematically to uncover additional strategies he could employ to outwit his rivals and soon made an unexpected discovery: a convincing bit of play-acting was often all that was needed to take down an opponent whose chips greatly outnumbered his own.

It's all about projecting a believable image and getting people to believe what you want them to believe. You've got to paint a picture of what you want the truth to be and put it out there on display.

Early on, he had bought into the idea that bluffing was the key to a gambler's success, and he'd fallen into the typical beginner's trap of bluffing far too often. It had been an especially easy trap to fall into; after all, a bluff is simply an act of deception, and the whole of Steve Phillips' existence was essentially based on a falsehood. After numerous failed attempts to represent his hand to be more valuable than it was, he realized that aggressive bluffing wasn't likely to produce the desired effect, and that a successful bluff depended on the ability to back up the lie he was trying to tell. If his opponents suspected he was a loose player who always claimed to have the best hand, his bluffs would fail to convince anyone that the story he was telling was true. If on the other hand, he was seen as a cautious, conservative player, his occasional bluffs were far more likely to work.

To succeed, Steve knew he would have to figure out how to project a convincing narrative, and he became fixated on the idea. If he could give himself over and truly step into and fully inhabit his own narrative, then the story he projected would be infinitely more believable. If he allowed himself to be completely swept up in the deception, whether a bluff or an outright lie, persuading others that what he said was, in fact, the truth would become nearly effortless.

Isn't that exactly what I've spent the last five years doing anyway, making sure not to slip and say the wrong thing?

It was as if the floodlights had just switched on, and everything was instantly illuminated. To succeed, he knew he had to play the part to absolute perfection, and that taking pains to always be careful and consistent, the picture he painted both at the poker table and at home had to be one that was believable.

This unexpected insight immediately transformed the way he played his cards, just as it changed everything else about his life, and Steve knew at once exactly what he had to do.

CHAPTER TWENTY-SIX

Spring 2011

BRADY

The pain medication had made him drowsy, and Brady had been dreaming fitfully when some time after midnight, the first message, rambling and incoherent, was left.

"Tony, it's Susan. Gracie's gone! What should I do? I found a note she left and she says to leave her alone and don't try to find her. Call me as soon as you get this! And wait 'til you hear this, turns out she hasn't been going to school for two months. No one ever called me! Not once! That school is so damn big, nobody there cares, that's why. If you ask me, they totally dropped the ball."

The second message, speculating that a boy had to be involved, appeared just before dawn. By then, Susan was sobbing, and her words were slurred.

"You know how fifteen-year-ol' gir's get. Boy-crazy, used ta call it. But Gracie nev' brought *anyone* 'round here. No boys *or* gir's! Never even heard her ona phone wi' anyone," she'd cried. "Where th' hell is she? Why won' you call me?"

Most of her third and final message was garbled by uninterrupted hiccups. "I know, I know. You tried ta warn me! Andrew
says I shoulda paid more attention, he's been saying that f'years.
Ah, what does he know? Been damn hard raising kids by m'self!
Wadn't sposed ta be this way! I'm all alone here! Tony, where th'
hell are you?"

He'd overslept and woken up groggy from the medication,
and it wasn't until late morning that he finally noticed the blinking
light on the answering machine. Even after listening to the alarming
messages, Brady didn't feel well enough to respond. He puttered
around the apartment, washing yesterday's dishes and taking out
the trash. He leafed through the *Sunday Chronicle* and then he'd
returned to his bed with a mug of chamomile tea and an electric
heating pad he'd found buried in the hall closet. He took two more
pills, dosing off and on most of the day, speculating that the pain in
his back that had kept coming and going all weekend had probably
started when he'd lifted his grandson up at the monkey cage at the
zoo, or maybe when he'd lugged the stroller in and out of the trunk
that last time. When he woke up around dinner time, woozy from
pills and so hungry he couldn't think straight, he stepped out of
bed and immediately noticed the swelling in his ankles. Promising
himself he'd call the doctor first thing Monday morning, he opened
a can of Dinty Moore stew.

When he'd satisfied his hunger, Brady lay back on the couch
with a family-sized package of frozen peas saddle-bagging his feet.
It had depressed him to hear Susan's messages, but he hadn't been
especially surprised. Lately her panic-stricken messages had been
arriving on an almost weekly basis. He'd heard from her when a

supervisor had reduced her hours at the nursing home because she'd been late again, and after the second DUI, when the court took away her license and ordered her into treatment. After Danny had moved on, she'd called more than once to complain about the revolving door of boarders who failed to pay the rent on time. Brady had grown tired of responding to each new message as if it were an emergency that required his immediate intervention, and when he finally called Susan back, he explained he wasn't feeling well.

The weariness seemed to have come upon him almost without warning, settling deep in his bones. On Monday, he rotated all morning between the sofa and his bed with the heating pad tucked snugly beneath him until he was able to make an appointment at the clinic. After a shower and a shave, the short walk to the car parked down the street left him feeling dazed and light-headed. Fighting the urge to return to his bed, he managed the drive downtown with an effort that made him feel as if he might faint at any moment.

His doctor said he didn't think the throbbing ache in Brady's lower back was a pulled muscle and sent him for an MRI to see if he had slipped a disc. Cocooned in a metal tube with bulky headphones cupped over his ears, he was instructed not to move. Despite the metallic clanging, he nearly fell asleep from exhaustion. A specialist was required to interpret the results, and he was told that it would take a few hours. Feeling better after the nurse secured an adhesive pain patch to his back, Brady decided to head over to Susan's to try to figure out why Gracie had run away.

The state of disrepair in the yard as he pulled up to the curb reminded him that it had been some time since his last visit. Tall weeds filled the flowerbeds alongside the fence, and dry blades of overgrown grass covered the walkway to the front door. The porch light flickered in the midday sun, and though it was past noon, the living room curtains were still closed.

When she came to the door in her robe, dark circles under her eyes, Brady could tell that Susan hadn't gotten much sleep.

"I just made coffee," she said dully, jerking her head toward the living room. "Have a seat on the couch and I'll bring it. The kitchen's a disaster."

Brady sat and scanned the room as he waited for her to return with the coffee, noticing the worn sofa, permanently stained by overturned juice boxes, the limp drapes that could benefit from a good cleaning, the old furniture nicked by scuff marks. Silently, he did the math. It had been eight long years since her husband had gone missing, and there was no doubt about it, Susan had let the place get run down.

She brought a tray into the room and set it down on top of a pile of unopened mail on the coffee table. "Thanks for coming, Tony. You're the only one I could think of to call." Her voice was listless and without inflection, but her words were clear, and he could see she was stone cold sober. "I know I'm a lousy mother, but believe me, it hasn't been easy. Raising the kids and putting food on the table, all these years by myself. It's been one thing after another, and I'm not gonna lie, Tony, I've had it."

Brady took the cup Susan had poured for him. Her hair was pulled back with a rubber band, and he realized he'd never seen her without makeup. "Believe me, I know it's been hard," he replied.

"It's just too much," she went on, confessing that at times the relentlessness of it all had overwhelmed her, and that fixing herself a drink to push down the mounting panic had seemed like the only thing to do. "Every now and then, more than anything, I just need to go numb for a while."

He nodded, and slumping on the frayed sofa, deflated, she continued.

"I missed what was happening with Gracie because I was too busy trying to sort out my own problems."

He wished she had taken his advice and gotten her daughter into counseling. "What do you think made her run off?"

She shrugged. "My sister says for sure there's a boy involved. I'm such an idiot. Gracie was always up in her room for hours on her computer. I thought she was working on something for school. The whole time, I bet she was planning something."

"Have you searched her room? Seen any clues as to where she could've gone?"

"I looked around, but I didn't see anything." Absently, Susan picked at her chipped fingernail polish. "Becky says there's got to be something on her computer, but I don't have the foggiest idea how to find it. I asked Andrew to come look, but he can't." She grimaced. "He's too busy."

"You told Andrew?"

"I had to, didn't I? I had no choice!" She threw her hands up. "He's living up at State now, graduating in June. Anyway, Andrew's busy. Doesn't come around much these days."

He shifted his weight to the arm of the sofa and stood up with effort. "Where's Gracie's computer? Let me see what I can find."

Moving slowly, Brady lowered himself cautiously into the wooden desk chair in Gracie's bedroom. An empty Red Vines bag beside the computer explained the stickiness on the space bar. He moved the bag into the trash can at his feet and opening the browser's search window, typed the URL of the website he'd become familiar with. Quickly, he pulled up a new set of alluring photographs of Gracie, and beneath them, a series of messages. The IMs from a grinning young man who called himself Nikko told Brady most of the story.

With exclamation marks and capital letters, the fifteen-year-old girl had told the young man that she'd just learned her whole life was a horrible lie. Brady knew the dramatic declaration was typical of teenage exaggeration, self-absorbed as they tended to be, but her tone sounded ominous. She didn't say what it was she had discovered, but he knew where and how to hunt for the answers, and when he did, it was all there.

Recent announcements from the high school about schedule changes and lunch menus peppered Gracie's e-mail inbox, lying open on the desktop. In vain, Brady looked for messages from anyone who could possibly be a classmate. When he came across an e-mail from a NancyG@hotmail.com, his spirits soared with the idea that the lonely teenager had perhaps made a friend. Clicking on the message hopefully, he was greeted by a rambling paragraph and a photograph of a blonde-haired girl who bore an unmistakable resemblance to Gracie.

Brady read the message, and with one hand massaging his hip, called out to Susan, asking her to come upstairs. His usual composure was shaken by the ease with which NancyG had been able to find Gracie, and he reminded himself that the long reach of social media had made it harder than ever for secrets to remain secrets for long. He shifted his eyes from the flickering computer screen to the girlish décor of Gracie's bedroom. Posters of boy bands adorned the walls, and an issue of *Cosmopolitan* lay open on the nightstand where answers to a personality quiz had been circled in bright purple ink.

He tried to imagine how Gracie would have reacted to finding out that she'd been lied to all her life by the people she'd trusted the most.

That's what made her run away, he muttered. *Why had Susan and Phillip been so intent on keeping the story of their daughter's birth such a secret? Had it really been to protect Gracie? Or was it to protect themselves?*

Susan eyed him hopefully as she stepped into her daughter's bedroom. "Find anything?"

He craned his neck to look up at her. "Remember when I told you about those pictures Gracie posted on the internet years ago? And I advised you to explain to her why it was so dangerous?"

She nodded. "She promised she'd take them down!"

"Well, she didn't. With computers and cell phones everywhere, she probably found it hard to stop posting them. She was still exchanging messages in chat rooms with the kind of men who troll those sites looking for sexy pictures."

A low moan escaped her lips. "Oh my God, Tony. Why would my little girl do a thing like that?"

He saw that Susan honestly didn't know what her daughter had been up to, and he softened a little. "I don't know, maybe she wasn't getting any attention from kids her age. Maybe flirting with older guys made Gracie feel better about herself."

"Poor Gracie." She lowered her face into her hands, a tearful catch in her voice. "The kid must have been so lonely. She never had any girlfriends she could talk to, and God knows she never told me anything. Gracie was never one to open up. Honestly, it was impossible to know what was going on in her head." Susan reached into the pocket of her bathrobe for a tissue and began dabbing her eyes.

He told her about the grinning young man in the photograph who had lent a sympathetic ear to the girl's complaints, showing her the message where Nikko had boasted about a souped-up van and invited Gracie to head to the mountains with him. "An adventure," the man had cajoled with a playful charm. Brady speculated that her daughter would very likely be found in Nikko's company, and that since she was underage, law enforcement and the authorities would need to be involved.

"Oh, God. I can't believe it! This is terrible, Tony. What else did she say? How much personal stuff did she tell him?"

"It gets worse," he replied grimly. "Let me show you." He clicked on Gracie's e-mail.

"What could possibly be worse?" Susan asked plaintively. Standing behind him at the desk, she bent over his shoulder to peer at Gracie's messages.

Brady turned his head. His eyes sought hers directly. "She knew," he whispered.

She frowned, not understanding. "Knew what?"

Brady opened NancyG's e-mail and carefully eased himself out of Gracie's wooden desk chair as Susan leaned over the back of the empty chair to stare at the screen as if hypnotized.

> Hey there!!! I'm Nancy. I'm 18 and I live in San Francisco. I saw a picture of you and I decided to write you cuz we look exactly alike, I'm not even kidding! We could be twins!! Guess what I think we have the same Dad!!! So I have 2 Moms and back in the day they really wanted a kid so they got a sperm donor. Thats how I was born, my Moms told me he was a medical student. I guess he needed money for college and that's why. They said when I turn 18 they wud help me find out about my Dad and guess what, there's a whole bunch of us and we all have the same Dad!! We've been hooking up and it's litrally so cool to have all these sisters and brothers because I always thought I was an only child! What about you. I think you are my sister, I never had a sister before so I'm dying to meet up! You look nice, write back please so we can for real be sisters.

At the bottom, NancyG had attached a link, adding "It's so easy, all you do is spit in a tube!" Brady's hunch that the link would bring up a genetic testing service had been confirmed when clicking on it revealed a list of donors who had provided the gift of life to a host of unsuspecting offspring.

He reached past Susan for the mouse and moved the cursor to Gracie's e-mail trash folder to open a straight-forward message from the service clearly identifying her biological father as *Donor Number 1083*. The donor's profile revealed a nameless medical student who, during a ten-year period, had frequently visited a sperm bank in San Francisco. The e-mail message was all Gracie had needed to know that she, along with a fair number of other progeny of one anonymous sperm donor, had been born during those ten years and carried within her cells this particular medical student's genetic code.

Susan read, folding herself into Gracie's chair as Brady watched her knees give way and the color drain from her face.

"I'm sorry things turned out this way, Susan, I really am."

Wordlessly, Gracie's mother wept as if her heart were broken.

The secret they tried so hard to keep has destroyed what it sought to protect, Brady thought to himself.

"I always wondered if the truth would come out one day. It seems like no matter how carefully we guard our secrets, they always manage to come out," he said.

Susan sat slumped in front of the computer, limp as a ragdoll. "What now, Tony? What do we do now?" she whispered in a broken voice.

He couldn't help noticing she'd said *we*, and he took a deep breath to steel his resolve.

"I think it's time to go to the police." He placed his hands on her sagging shoulders. "Susan, I can't help you find Gracie. It's their job. Let them do it."

She craned her neck to look up at him, a question on her lips. He knew she didn't want to believe him. He'd always been there, and she'd come to depend on him for so much.

"You can't?" she asked, turning in the chair to face him.

"I really can't," he repeated. "I'm sixty-five years old. I just can't do it anymore."

He watched her narrow her eyes at the salt-and-pepper hair receding on his forehead and followed her gaze down to the stoop of his back. He could see she'd never thought of him as someone who might be vulnerable to the aches and pains of growing older, and he tried to explain.

"The thing is, to tell you the truth, lately I haven't been feeling well. I've been having some health problems."

She looked away from him, wiping her nose with a tissue crumpled in her fist. "What kind of health problems? Not anything serious, is it?"

"I'm not sure yet. My doctor referred me to a specialist, and they ran a bunch of tests. I should get the results back soon, but right now, I just feel kind of exhausted." He began inching toward the stairs. "I think I'd better go home now."

She trailed behind him as he clung to the banister, slowly making his way down, one foot at a time. He winced as he took each painful step on his swollen ankles and gave up trying to hide his discomfort.

"Go to the police, Susan. It's time to get a younger guy working on this," he urged. As he reached the front door, he sighed with a quiet resignation held barely at bay. "You can't imagine what it's like to wake up in the morning and even before you step out of bed, everything hurts."

Looking back at her, he could tell from her vacant stare that it would be a long time before she could even begin to understand. Wide-eyed and battle-weary, she looked lost. "I'm not the same guy you started with, not by a long shot. I just don't have that kind of energy anymore," he confessed, his voice so low she could barely hear him. "The thing is, Susan, I don't think I ever will again."

CHAPTER TWENTY-SEVEN

Summer 2013

STEVE

The summer sun beat down, blistering the sidewalk in a pool of heat. The two couples had only strolled a single long Las Vegas block in search of the fancy shoe store on Judy's list before they'd abandoned the notion of shopping, ducking back into the air-conditioned hotel to grab their swimsuits and head for the relief of the Olympic-sized pool.

"It's stifling out there." Rob removed his LA Clippers cap and wiped his brow with the corner of a thick poolside towel. "No wonder Vegas is a night-time town!"

"No kidding," Steve agreed, flagging down the white-vested waiter. "Let's order some of those umbrella drinks I just saw go by."

Rob flung himself into a padded lounge chair. "Hey, look what I got. You interested in a magic show?" Reaching into the pocket of his cargo shorts, he pulled out a handful of tickets a hawker had thrust at him.

"I'm not stepping out of the Venetian again until the sun starts to go down."

"Roger that." Rob tossed the free passes onto the table between them. "You've got until noon on Friday to relax all you want, my friend, but when the tourney kicks off, we're putting you to work," he grinned.

"Yes, sir!" Steve saluted, scanning the pool deck hopefully for a sliver of shade or an umbrella they could commandeer. The getaway to Vegas was the long-awaited vacation the two couples had embarked on together, and he appreciated the support. Squinting through his Maui Jim sunglasses, he noticed that even though his friend had developed a small round gut as he'd crept into his seventies, Rob still bubbled over with youthful enthusiasm. Steve stole a glance at the women, stretched out in luxury on lounge chairs and slathered with suntan lotion that glistened on their pink skin. *This Week in Las Vegas* lay open on the table alongside them, and the women chattered away excitedly, pointing at pictures of stage performers. He lowered his dark glasses to the brim of his nose, and catching Jackie's eye, winked at her, enjoying the way her swimsuit showed off her shapely legs. Music wafted towards them from the row of speakers flanking the crowded pool, a little loud for his taste. As he re-adjusted the angle of his Nike visor, a waiter in a crisp white uniform appeared carrying a silver tray. Steve reached for an icy piña colada and held the glass against his damp cheek before taking a long swig.

"Perfect," he announced, sitting up to scribble their room number on the tab. "Put it on the bill, would you?"

He'd been trying not to think about how grueling the competition was likely to be. The long journey to qualify for the tournament had required more than a little patience as he'd slogged through too many poker nights to keep track of, parlaying the cash he'd withdrawn from the credit union so long ago into a solid bankroll, and he'd been rewarded for his perseverance at last when he'd succeeded in taking first place in a local satellite game. Guaranteed a seat at the table at the WSOP, the gold standard poker tournament, Steve had been gifted plane tickets along with a laundry list of comps. The day they'd arrived, they had settled into a luxurious suite of rooms at a five-star hotel right in the middle of the Strip, and gazing out the window at the neon landscape outside, all four of them had been over the moon. For Rob and Judy, the trip was a long-awaited second honeymoon, and on their first night, they'd celebrated with a ride in the gondola they'd imagined years before. Then they'd all dug hungrily into bowls of Spaghetti alla Carbonara alongside the Venetian-like canal of what might have passed for St. Mark's Square.

Steve examined the condensation on the icy glass and contentedly sipped his drink, savoring the lazy moments that remained before the vice grip tension of the competition began to tie his stomach into knots.

"So what's it going to be, fellas?" Judy asked, breaking into his reverie. "Cirque du Soleil or a Michael Jackson impersonation?"

"If it's tonight, I could swing either one, but you guys can go any night," Steve murmured, shutting his eyes. "This drink is telling me it's my nap time. Why don't you go find the concierge and see if he can scramble up some tickets?"

Rob reached for his cargo shorts. "Come on, girls, let's go check it out."

Steve cracked an eye and watched his friends wander off in search of show tickets. Anticipating the focus that would be required when he sat down to compete with the big guns, he yanked his visor down lower on his forehead and with a yawn, drifted off to sleep under the blazing sun.

On Friday morning, his eyelids fluttered open early, well before the alarm. The Blue Man Group parading on stage at the Luxor in those crazy blue masks last night had made him momentarily forget about the noon kick-off today, but he could sense the beginnings of a headache lingering just behind his eyes. Stirring lazily beside him, Jackie rolled over in the warm bed. Careful not to wake her, Steve peeled the thick duvet cover back carefully and padded as quietly as he could into their ensuite marble bathroom. Under the fancy European rain nozzle that hammered his back and shoulders, he began to prepare for his day, methodically emptying his mind of distractions and counting his breaths, in, then out. His stomach began to growl with the rumblings of a healthy appetite, and he stepped out of the shower to wrap himself in a Turkish robe. He buried his face in a thick towel and wiped the steam from the mirror, deciding with satisfaction that the accumulation of gray in his beard made him look sophisticated. He found a pair of jogging shorts, threw on a tee shirt, and carrying his sneakers, tiptoed toward the door, planning to combat the pre-competition jitters with some exercise.

Sleepily, Jackie squinted up at him, her highlighted blonde curls falling into her eyes. "Going somewhere, handsome?" she murmured.

Steve dropped the sneakers with a shrug and crossed to the king size bed.

"Good morning, beautiful." He bent down to graze her lips. "Sleep well?"

"Mmm. You smell good." She reached up to stroke his curly whiskers. "Been up for a while? Where are you going?"

"I'm heading down to the fitness center. Want to get a little exercise in before breakfast." He tucked the coverlet under her chin and kissed her forehead. "Take your time. We can all go down to breakfast together when I get back."

At the buffet, Steve fixed himself a heaping plate of steak and eggs, the yolks runny just the way he liked them, the steak medium rare. He sprinkled salt and pepper over the eggs and helped himself to a spoonful of potatoes.

Rob reached for a sticky cinnamon bun and placed it alongside his creamy eggs Benedict.

Steve's eyebrows shot up. "You sure that's good for you, man?"

"Hey, we're on vacation!" Rob winked. "I could wait the rest of my life for this kind of breakfast at our house."

In shorts and low-heeled sandals, the women deliberated over a huge display of pineapples, kiwis and persimmons in the middle of the buffet table before they decided on Belgian waffles topped with real whipped cream.

"You guys should enjoy yourselves out there today," Steve urged as they took over a booth. "There's a ton of fun stuff to do in Vegas, way more fun than watching me play cards for hours. Trust me, you guys would be bored to death. Anyway, there won't be much to see today, just lots of tables full of nervous guys trying not to get knocked out. You'll have more fun just about anywhere else."

"But I thought you wanted us there for moral support." Jackie looked up as she licked whipped cream from her spoon.

"Not today, I'm too nervous. Maybe later in the week, if I even last that long."

"There is a lot to do here, that's true. I was thinking we could take a drive out to Hoover Dam," Rob suggested. "Supposed to be pretty amazing."

"Fine, but I still want to do some shopping," Judy countered. "The fancy boutiques inside Caesar's Palace are all air-conditioned." She reached into Rob's plate to break off a section of his cinnamon bun.

Rob shot her a look, feigning annoyance. "What the heck?"

"One little bite!" She poked him with her elbow and wiped a sticky trace of cinnamon from his upper lip.

Steve reached into his wallet for a wad of bills and pressed them into Rob's hand below the table. "Listen, Buddy, if you can take care of the ladies, I'd really appreciate it. Go have some fun today."

By the time they'd finished their breakfast, the sun had mercilessly begun to bathe the concrete sidewalk outside. Approaching the revolving door at the front of the hotel, Steve decided against the stroll around the block he'd been contemplating and instead wandered through the windowless hallways, finally landing on the casino floor to join a long line of hopeful tournament entrants. With over six thousand players, the registration line already snaked around the cashier's cage, and oval-shaped gaming tables filled the banquet rooms from wall to wall. A polished wooden railing separated the viewing area where Steve noticed an array of TV monitors suspended from the ceiling. A television crew wearing satin jackets with ESPN emblazed on the back wheeled heavy tripods into position, and a crane with a camera mounted on it hovered over the crowd. Players of every age milled about, checking the seat assignments printed on their registration tickets. Wearing a vest whose buttons didn't quite meet over his protruding belly, the Tournament Director took the floor at high noon with a handheld microphone and announced the start of the competition, calling out "Ladies and gentlemen, let's shuffle up and deal!"

At crowded tables of nine players each, a palpable nervous energy permeated the room as the action spilled over into a week. To Steve, the days seemed interminable and the air somehow both frigid and stuffy at the same time. More than once, he reminded himself that the tournament was like a marathon and to settle in for the long haul. He witnessed the usual ups and downs in his chip stack, the unpredictable variances both in his favor and against him, occasional lucky wins on the river and a few bad beats as he was dealt a bevy of good cards and bad. He tried to take note of every opponent's *tell*: the seemingly purposeless chatter, the split-second hesitation before a bet, the nearly imperceptible twitch of cheek muscles, the nervous drumming of fingertips on the felt as players peeled back the corners of their hole cards. During breaks that were all too brief, he stuffed himself on power bars and gulped down Gatorade when he wasn't leaning against a wall to soothe the knotted muscles in his back. Listening with half an ear to messages Jackie left for him about the Cirque de Soleil show he had missed, or the jeweled sandals Judy had found in a shop on the Strip, he marveled that so far, he had somehow managed to avoid being knocked out.

When the evenings grew late, tournament play was suspended. "Try to get some rest, ladies and gentlemen," the Tournament Director advised. In the comfort of their suite after a room service dinner, Steve yanked on the heavy curtains to block out the flashing neon lights of the Strip. He developed the habit of brewing a soothing cup of chamomile tea to relieve the effects of the adrenalin coursing through his veins. Lying in bed alone while Jackie was out enjoying the town had been hard at first, but by the third night, he had settled into a comfortable rhythm and found he was able to sleep for five or six blissfully uninterrupted hours and didn't even stir when she crawled into bed beside him.

Competing in the high-stakes tournament was relentless for everyone. *A little like going to war*, Steve thought, as the days began to blur into each other. He had trouble remembering if it was Tuesday or Wednesday and had to ask the cocktail waitress. Action at the tables was so swift and the surrounding chatter so distracting that he'd sprung for a pair of headphones from the gift shop to block out the noise. During breaks, lines for the men's room were so long that twice he'd returned to the table in the middle of a hand. Worn out and completely out of steam, he'd forgotten what it was like to think about anything besides poker, to read a book, watch a movie, enjoy a quiet dinner with friends. At night his dreams were laced with Ace-high Flushes and busted Straight draws, and by the end of the week, he could barely remember what normal life was like.

One by one, exhausted players were eliminated, both men and women, young and old. By that time, although he wasn't even close to being the chip leader—in fact, he was very near the bottom of the heap—Steve had somehow managed to survive dozens of near knockouts. He wasn't sure how.

On the final day of the marathon event, Jackie, Rob and Judy joined the spectators to root for him, standing behind the polished wooden rail with their eyes glued to the screens overhead. "Hang tough, Buddy," he heard Rob shout when he lost a big hand. "You've got this!" Steve nodded appreciatively, and Jackie blew him a kiss. Late in the evening, a noisy cheer went up as the names of those who had made the Final Table were announced on a loudspeaker. The television camera mounted on a crane that he'd noticed on the first day of the tournament swooped down to capture an image of the last remaining group of players displayed on monitors in every corner of the casino floor.

In a daze, along with eight other worn-out competitors, a wild-eyed, unbelieving Steve Phillips found himself among them.

CHAPTER TWENTY-EIGHT

Summer 2013

BRADY

"You comfortable, Dad?" Shane asked. "How about another pillow?"

Brady's eyes were on the dialysis nurse as she bent over him to tape the needles into place. He thought he'd never get used to this new routine. "I'll be okay. You don't have to stay. It takes at least three hours. If it's anything like last time, I'll just doze off."

"No worries. I can hang for a while, then I'll head over to Safeway and stock up on some groceries for you. What do you want for lunch?"

"Can't think of anything." Brady pushed a button, and the chair reclined. "About all I've been able to keep down lately is ginger ale." He closed his eyes. "Maybe I could manage a couple of hotdogs. Some of those ballpark franks, and some potato chips, I guess."

"That stuff's so bad for you, Dad," Shane groaned. "You need to eat some healthy food. How about some fruit? Bananas should be easy to get down. And maybe something from the salad bar?" He pulled a chair up next to his father. "Listen, you got to start taking better care of yourself, Pops. Your body can't handle all that processed crap you put in your stomach."

The orderly tucked a heated blanket around his bony hips. It had taken a while for the diagnosis to come through, but then it had all made sense. The pain in his back, the bruises that wouldn't heal, the fatigue that lasted all day, sending him back to bed soon after he woke up in the morning. Kidney failure had attacked with a vengeance, and advancing age made it hard to fight back.

Brady opened one eye and peered at Shane with the hint of a smile. His son's ruddy complexion shone with good health, and his toned upper body meant he'd been working out. "You sound like a wise old man when you say things like that."

"I am a wise old man! Thirty-eight on my next birthday." Shane leaned back and hooked his thumbs in the belt loops of his jeans. "Ain't getting any younger," he drawled.

"Believe me, from where I sit, thirty-eight is a baby. I'm pushing seventy, and most days, I feel like a hundred and seventy."

"I know, Dad, I know." Shane squeezed his hand, lying limp on the arm of the recliner. The papery skin on his father's wrist was nearly translucent.

At midday, the dialysis center was quiet. Every now and then, the heavyset woman in another chair on the opposite side of the room snored softly. Father and son sat for several minutes, each lost in private reverie. Fluorescent lights flickered overhead, emitting a low buzz they'd become accustomed to hearing in the background. Shane's fingers drummed idly on the green vinyl arm.

"Thirty-eight, huh?" Brady tried to recall exactly how old Brendan would be now, and glancing sideways, he saw that Shane was also doing some mental math. "He'd be thirty-four, if I'm correct," he murmured.

For years Brady had watched Shane's face drop whenever he spoke of Brendan.

"Sounds about right. I still think about him," his son confessed in a low voice, "especially whenever I'm around the old neighborhood."

"Me too, but we have to accept that we may never know what happened." His thin fingers stroked Shane's arm. "But you, Son. I'm so proud of you. I mean it, you've made so much progress."

His son's face flushed. "Thanks, Dad."

He's so handsome when he smiles like that, Brady thought.

"You know, Pops, you're the one who never stopped believing in me. You've been in my corner all along. It's about time things are starting to come together for me."

Brady smiled and closed his eyes again, glad that the choices Shane had made were finally paying off. He knew how hard he'd worked to make it through the Twelve Step program. Then, with a few months of sobriety under his belt, Shane had enrolled in a bartending class, a seemingly adverse course of action that had nonetheless resulted in steady work. Brady had wondered about his ability to stay sober pouring drinks every night, but his son said it had given him a close-up look at the sloppy stupidity of the bar's drunken patrons. He swore it had been just what was needed to turn him away from drugs and alcohol altogether. Now Shane had gone and joined a gym, where pumping and sweating through a spin class, he'd met a girl. Things were definitely looking up for the kid.

Brady opened his eyes and gazed beyond the plastic bags of solution blocking his view. He craned his neck toward the window. "Life goes on out there, doesn't it?" In the distance, a row of billowy sails on the San Francisco Bay beckoned serenely.

"Yeah, I guess it has to."

Lately, Brady had begun to feel ancient. Catching sight of himself in the apartment's cracked bathroom mirror, he saw that a light seemed to have gone out of his eyes and the pallor of his hollow cheeks had faded to a dull gray. Kidney failure had taken its toll, and so had the long days and nights he still tormented himself with the cases he'd never been able to solve. With the stubborn perseverance of a mule, late at night he continued to comb over those old case files every chance he got, relentlessly chasing down leads that anyone else would surely have declared hopeless by this time.

Shane reached around him for the remote. "Listen, Dad, how about I find you something on TV, and then I'll head over to the market. Sound good?"

Brady pulled the warm blanket over his chest. "Sure. Take your time."

His son flipped through the channels in search of a ball game. "Looks like the Giants are off today. No A's games, either."

"I don't care. Just leave it on. Anything's fine."

Shane clicked to ESPN and turned the volume down low, promising he'd be back soon with lunch.

With only the hum of the dialysis machine to keep him company, Brady's breathing slowed, and his eyelids grew heavy as thoughts of Susan drifted through his mind.

He hadn't laid eyes on her in ages, not since she'd gone into the rehab program demanded by the court. She'd reached out a couple of times after she'd lost the house and moved in with her sister in Colorado. The last time, she told him she'd given up hope of ever knowing what had happened. Every now and then Brady persuaded Andrew to meet him downtown for a beer, and that's how he'd heard about Gracie. The police had brought her home soon after she'd run away, but she'd quit school and taken off again several times since then. Andrew said he'd heard she was living on a farm up north in Humboldt County. "She's staying with her half-sister up there. Says they're growing their own vegetables," he'd shrugged. "Poor Gracie. I guess she's still trying to figure things out."

Not for the first time, Brady found himself brooding on the rippling wake Phillip Lynch's disappearance had produced on the lives of those he'd left behind. *The past leaves its scars*, he mused.

Andrew was in grad school now, working part-time at a counseling clinic run by the city and sharing a house with a couple of guys out on Clement Street.

"Everything seems to be going well for you," Brady had told him with genuine affection on their last visit. I'm so glad. I always believed you'd make it."

For years, everyone familiar with the case had maintained that the missing man must have had a reason to take off in the first place, and lately even Brady had begun to believe that maybe where Phillip had gone and why was really none of his business.

A young man clad in baggy jeans hanging loosely below his waist burst into the treatment room, his eyes riveted on the TV mounted on the wall. Brady was jolted from semi-conscious drowsiness when the young man shouted, "Way to go, you've got it on! My ride was so slow I thought I was gonna miss the end of the game! Mind if I turn it up?" Without waiting for an answer, he grabbed the remote from the arm of Brady's recliner and aimed it at the wall, raising the volume so high the heavyset woman across the room opened her eyes in alarm and began calling, "Nurse! Nurse!"

The man's forest green Oakland A's cap landed on the floor as he jerked his body spasmodically from her to Brady and back to the TV set. "You a fan of the WSOP, too? It's *heads-up*, they're down to the last two guys. You know that's crazy, right? I'm telling you, this guy came out of nowhere," he pointed to a hoodied face on the screen. "Look at him. He took out the number four *and* the number three player in a double knock-out, just like that," he snapped his fingers. "Check out the size of his chip stack!" The young man's eyes darted wildly back to Brady, groping for his eyeglasses and squinting at the monitor. "No one knows anything about this guy! This is some crazy stuff! Doncha just love Texas Hold'em? I'm telling you, in this game anything can happen!"

From the corridor, a nurse practically sprinted into the room, and an orderly followed close behind.

"Mr. Mitchell, please calm down!" The nurse placed her hands firmly on the new patient's shoulders and with practiced efficiency, steered him toward the opposite wall. "Come on now, let's get you settled in your chair." The orderly took the man's elbow, easing him into an empty recliner across the room with the promise of a heated blanket.

The sound coming from the TV continued to blare loudly, and Brady followed the young man's gaze to a pair of commentators engaged in a rousing discussion. He thought he heard something about pot odds. Brady pointed to the screen where a bearded man in a dark hooded sweatshirt filled the frame. "That the guy you mean?"

"Yeah, that's him! What the hell's his name? Jeez, I can't remember. He's new on the scene, they said no one knows anything about him. A couple minutes ago, they showed his name. What was it?"

Brady had found his glasses, and he peered closely at the TV but the hoodie and dark glasses obscured the player's features. The man's eyes were well hidden and the lower half of his face completely concealed by the neatly trimmed beard he stroked in thoughtful contemplation as he faced his opponent.

Across the room, the new patient's face suddenly lit up. "Something or other Phillips, I think they said."

Something or other Phillips? Brady struggled to sit upright in his chair, leaning forward so far that the extra blanket slid from his legs to the floor. *What are the odds this guy could be the man I've been looking for all this time?*

"Lie back, Mr. Brady. You too, Mr. Mitchell. Let's all be calm, shall we?" Maintaining her composure, the nurse smoothed the new patient's pillows. With a cheery smile, she crossed the room to the heavyset woman. "You doing okay now, Mrs. Martinez?" She pulled a washcloth from the pocket of her starched white uniform and wiped the woman's damp brow. "Would anyone like some water?"

She made her way toward Brady as the rhythmical hum of the machine that cleaned his blood began to subside. "Just about done for today, now, Mr. Brady." She leaned over to pick up the blanket and began disconnecting the dialysis needles. "I'll just get you unhooked here and you can be on your way."

Bending over him, the nurse blocked his view of the monitor hanging on the wall, and he peeked around her just in time to get a glimpse of the player's name, superimposed on the screen in large block letters.

This fellow doesn't look anything like the face in the poster, he thought to himself.

"Hey, Dad, I hope you're hungry!" Shane stood in the doorway clutching a plastic grocery bag. "I got you a big salad and a roll and guess what, they had sugar-free jelly doughnuts. What a score!"

On the far wall, Steve Phillips tucked a curly lock into his hoodie and pushed the long black sleeves of his sweatshirt clear up to his elbows.

"Dad! Did you hear me?" Shane asked impatiently.

"Uh-huh." Brady's eyes had remained glued to the wall. "What'd you say?"

Brady watched the camera pan down to the fingers of the player's left hand as he peeled back the corners of two cards lying face down in front of him on the green felt. The man's right hand inched forward to curve protectively around stacks of betting chips so high they spilled out in all directions.

"I asked if you were hungry." Shane froze, following his father's gaze.

On the pale underside of the player's right wrist, Brady made out the unmistakable traces of a raised pink scar in the shape of a jagged Z distinctly etched in his hairless flesh.

"Oh boy," shouted Mr. Mitchell, bolting upright and sending the pillow he'd been resting on to the linoleum floor. "Here it comes! He's about to decimate the guy!"

The nurse darted back into the room, wagging her finger in exasperation as she came toward him. "Really, Mr. Mitchell, please! It's very important to stay calm during your dialysis!"

The jagged lines on the man's wrist had told Brady all he needed to know. *Mother of God, it's him,* he muttered under his breath. Phillip's Lynch's childhood scar had given him away. Feeling as if he might faint, Brady fell back in the chair as all the color drained from his face, leaving his skin moist and gray.

The scars we carry reveal us. They give us away, telling everything about who we are, revealing stories we had hoped to forget.

His breath began coming fast, and alarmed, he glanced at Shane from the corner of his eye, which had unexpectedly begun to tear. *And I've got scars, too, scars that never healed.* Blinking away tears, he tenderly lay the palm of his right hand over his chest. The wound was still fresh, and he could feel his heart pounding wildly.

Shane dropped the grocery bag and stared at him. "You okay, Dad? You don't look so good. Why you grabbing your chest like that?"

He looked at his son as if he were seeing him for the first time in years.

Shane has scars, too. We both do. Battle scars buried deep in our hearts, scars that will always remind us.

"Woo-hoo! What a take-down!" Mr. Mitchell yelled from across the room.

Mrs. Martinez groaned loudly and began to retch. "I'm think I'm going to be sick! Nurse! Nurse!" she cried out.

On the flickering screen, spectators had risen to their feet, cheering wildly as a shower of glittery confetti rained down from the ceiling. Brady watched spellbound as two women embraced each other and the beaming man beside them rushed past the rail to clap the player on the back. By that time, the sleeves of the player's hooded sweatshirt had slipped down and covered both wrists, and his dark glasses lay discarded on the felt. His eyes sparkled like diamonds as his arms encircled the waist of the woman clutching a Caesar's Palace shopping bag. Elated, he lifted the pretty blonde off her feet, kissing her with open abandon.

Shane turned down the volume on the TV and searched his father's face with real concern. "What is it, Dad? Somebody you know?"

The orderly sponged traces of vomit from the front of Mrs. Martinez's blouse with a wet towel while the nurse offered everyone a Dixie cup of water. Brady did not respond to the offer, a faraway look in his eyes as a panoply of images tumbled through his memory in rapid succession. Eight-year-old Gracie kneeling tearfully at the coffee table with her small pink diary. Susan sitting all alone in the bleachers at Andrew's ball game. The daunting stack of financial forms the high school student couldn't hope to sort through on his own. A cache of memories that had lingered just below the surface for years cascaded through Brady's mind one after another, bringing him face to face with the enormity of everything the man he'd been looking for had missed.

He left because he wanted to, and he never had any desire to return.

Brady ran his tongue over his teeth, pressing his lips together tightly.

No one else knows, only me. But if I tell them, how's that going to help? Will it make Susan put down the bottle? Will it bring Gracie back?

On the screen, the celebration continued as a huge trophy appeared at the rail and a reporter thrust a microphone into the winner's face.

But if I don't tell, will they ever stop blaming themselves for something that wasn't their fault?

Brady looked into his son's worried eyes. "No, not really. It's nobody I know."

Slowly, he turned his head and surveyed the room, taking in the tubes hanging from the dialysis machines and listening to the rumble of carts in the hallway just outside the treatment room as he recalled that distant day on Mission Street when his colleagues had tried to warn him. *What exactly had Joe objected to? What was it Charlie had argued?*

"Say the guy had his reasons for wanting to take off," they'd suggested. "You can't tell a grown man to go home. Wouldn't that be playing God?"

Now he wondered silently if *not* telling anyone what he'd seen might be playing God. *Which of us has the right to judge the choices another man makes?*

His fists had been clenched so tightly that the knuckles had turned white, and he flexed them to ward off the stiffness.

Even when others suffer because of those choices, none of us has that right.

He saw his son retrieve his cane from the coat rack, the cane he'd brought with him that morning, a morning that seemed to have happened a lifetime ago.

Not me, not anyone. None of us has that right.

Cautiously, he swung one leg to the floor, and then the other, and nodded to Shane.

Maybe it's time for me to let it go.

For ten years, he'd been practically consumed trying to unravel why Phillip had walked away from his life and never come home.

If I can let it go, maybe they can, too.

"All set, Dad?" Shane held out the cane.

Brady reached for it, adjusting his weight as he stood.

Maybe they already have.

The jagged scar that had given Phillip away could easily be seen by anyone who knew where to look for it, but with razor-like clarity, Brady saw that invisible scars may never be noticed, hidden deep inside forever. Searching for eight-year-old Brendan had been the focus of the grieving father's life, but suddenly he understood it was time to stop searching for the child who had never come home.

It's time to rest, he whispered under his breath as he cautiously took a step. *Time to stop looking for someone who's no longer there.*

"What'd you say, Pops? Couldn't hear you."

Puzzled, Shane saw the hint of a weary smile begin to spread across his father's grizzled face. His color had returned, and the corners of his mouth tipped slightly upward.

"Let's go, son. All of a sudden, I'm starving."

He turned to the young patient who had finally settled back in the vinyl recliner as the dialysis machine hummed alongside him.

"Make sure to take in the great view," he suggested, lifting his cane to point at the sailboats drifting peacefully on the bay, and Mr. Mitchell raised his head from the pillow to peer out the window.

Shane led the way, and gratefully, Brady gripped his son's arm. Together, they shuffled down the corridor, the sound of their footsteps punctuated by his labored breathing and the echo of his cane tapping on the linoleum floor.

"Say," Brady turned to ask as the pair reached the exit. "Did I hear you say something about a jelly doughnut?"

A television director with a shelf full of Emmy, Telly and New York and Chicago Film Festival awards, Katherine Russell Becker lives with her husband in the San Francisco Bay Area. She also plays poker and knows from personal experience that sometimes the right decision is to fold your cards and let it go.